An Abaddon Books™ Publication
www.abaddonbooks.com
abaddon@rebellion.co.uk

First published in 2017 by Abaddon Books™,
Rebellion Intellectual Property Limited,
Riverside House, Osney Mead, Oxford, OX2 0ES, UK.

10 9 8 7 6 5 4 3 2 1

By Anne Tibbets,
writing as Addison Gunn

Editor: David Moore
Cover Art: Edouard Groult
Design: Sam Gretton, Oz Osborne and Maz Smith
Marketing and PR: Remy Njambi
Editor-in-Chief: Jonathan Oliver
Head of Books and Comics Publishing: Ben Smith
Creative Director and CEO: Jason Kingsley
Chief Technical Officer: Chris Kingsley

Extinction Biome created by
Malcolm Cross and David Thomas Moore

Copyright © 2017 Rebellion. All rights reserved.

ISBN: 978-1-78108-501-1

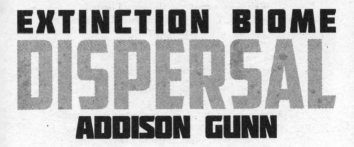

EXTINCTION BIOME
DISPERSAL
ADDISON GUNN

ABADDON
BOOKS

W W W . A B A D D O N B O O K S . C O M

OPERATION REED SNAKE

1

THE SEA HAD enemies.

Alex Miller had nothing against the ocean. On calm days, when the sun burned high and the watery horizon shone like a sheet of polished metal, he looked out over the seascape, listened to the ocean roar, and felt a hint of hope, a contentment that came and went as quickly as the breeze. It would be easy, he thought, to get used to life on the water.

But the sea knew no mercy; one day it soothed the soul and the next it bared its teeth. The waves roiled and drew up from the depths and crashed against the *Tevatnoa*'s bow; a vicious barrage—unrelenting, knowing no compassion.

Whatever Miller thought of the sea, it seemed to *hate* him—and after six months in its unsympathetic coils, his contentment congealed and sickened, eventually matching the sea's loathing.

How could you *not* despise something that persistently strove to kill you?

Perhaps the sea was exacting revenge for centuries of abuse at the hands of selfish and destructive humans, perhaps not. Either way, as Miller stood on the *Tevatnoa*'s bridge and watched the waves thrash the smaller vessels of the Schaeffer-Yeager fleet, he had to wonder.

"The *Dunn Roven* is in distress," said the able seaman manning the com and radar displays. "They've requested emergency assistance."

Miller's eyes swept the starboard horizon, slipping over a fishing trawler, a sailboat and a tug before settling on a thirty-meter pleasure yacht fit to carry a little over a hundred people. Topped to the brim with evacuees from some seaside town Miller couldn't remember, it had teamed up with the *Tevatnoa* after only two months at sea.

It had been the first ship they'd found. More had followed: scattered across the waters, seeking refuge from the chaos on land caused by the Archaean Parasite and the burgeoning new ecosystem that followed it.

They'd hoped, by banding together and pooling resources, to ease the trials and tribulations of life at sea; but the crazed currents, the endless storms, the fungal mats—to say nothing of the carnivorous sea life—tossed the smaller ships about like ping pong balls, and Miller often had to wonder if the *Tevatnoa* wouldn't have been better off if they'd gone it alone.

"Dispatch the *Dawn Rising* and *Robin's Nest* to assist with the evacuation," said Commander Lewis.

He looked up from the chart table and leaned back into his captain's chair.

"If we re-task *Dawn Rising*," L. Gray Matheson said from beside him, "there's a good chance of our missing the fishing quota for the day." He crossed and uncrossed his arms, fidgeting. He seemed out of place on the bridge in his loose three-piece suit, but Miller couldn't fault him for hanging onto the shards of his former CEO life. Miller would gladly chop off his own left foot to have his Armani wool-blend pinstripe back. Now, to his disappointment, his security uniform and gear seemed a part of him.

"You think I care about fish?" Lewis grumbled. "We're talking one hundred and fifteen people, Matheson."

"And how many will die of starvation aboard the *Tevatnoa* if we don't make quota?" Gray shot back. "We've got people eating twice a day as it is."

Lewis's face fell. He scratched his thighs just above each leg prosthetic. "None of the other ships have the maneuverability. They'll drown before either of the cruise liners can alter course."

"Send one of the mega-lifeboats," Miller offered.

"We can't risk losing another one," Lewis snapped. "Or the crew."

"Cobalt can manage it."

"We can't risk losing you, either," Lewis retorted.

"The longer we debate," Miller said, "the more bodies we'll be fishing out of the water."

Gray frowned.

"Fine," Lewis said. Then, to the pilot on his right,

"Full stop." Almost as an afterthought, he said to Miller, "But I want that lifeboat, and all of you, back in one piece."

Miller swallowed his first response. "Yes, sir." Spinning on his heel, he marched from the bridge and hooked a left out the door.

He didn't resent having to oversee a rescue of the *Dunn Roven,* or not much. With the absence of an actual Coast Guard, the five remaining members of his squad were the best qualified and experienced for the task. He only wished it didn't involve going back out onto an angry ocean. He'd grown to hate the feel of salt water.

MILLER FOUND HIS team right where he'd left them, grouped together, away from the rest of the refugees, tucked into a corner of the Crow's Nest bar.

Every last drop of alcohol aboard the ship had been consumed or used as antiseptic months ago, making the bar the driest, saddest spot aboard. But in a ship packed to the railings with hungry, weary, and often seasick civilians, he didn't blame them for seeking out a spot of silence.

Du Trieux, her leg draped over the arm of her chair, looked focused as she sharpened the edge of her new favorite toy—a ten-and-a-half-inch hunting knife she'd traded one of the old compound guards for her smaller, less-ominous-looking one. Her new blade, a black straight-edge, whirred back and forth against the well-worn stone. Beads of sweat collected on her hairline and dripped down to the tip of her nose; she brushed them away with the back of her hand and absently looked up at Miller as he approached.

On her left sat Doyle. At first Miller thought he was asleep, but then his eyes popped open and focused across the room, where a tiny, empty bottle of gin sat propped in the window sill. Then, just as suddenly, his eyes met Miller's.

Focusing exercises. Doyle was attempting to keep his sniper skills sharp despite the mandatory ban on target practice to conserve ammunition.

"What's wrong, boss?" Doyle asked.

Miller pursed his lips. "Why do you assume it's bad news?"

From the far side of the room, Hsiung snorted. Swinging from a makeshift hammock she'd fashioned out of a shredded parachute, she dropped to her feet. "Is there any other kind of news these days?"

From behind the bar, Morland laughed as he sucked down a shot of desalinated water. "Not bloody likely."

Miller shrugged. They weren't wrong. "On your feet. There's a yacht full of people about to capsize."

Du Trieux's blade froze over her whetstone. "It's pretty rough out there for a rescue mission."

Miller didn't disagree. "Gear up. You've got thirty seconds."

THE *TEVATNOA*, BACK in its prime, was a first-class cruise ship. It had over eighteen hundred cabins, and could legally carry thirty-six hundred passengers and thirteen hundred crew. They'd surpassed that number ages ago.

Powered by an on-board fusion reactor, the *Tevatnoa* was close to one hundred fifty tons and larger than many aircraft carriers, so it was no shock to Miller when it took the vast vessel twenty minutes to come to a complete stop. By then, they'd overshot the *Dunn Roven* by a whole nautical mile.

A ship that size, carrying that many people, needed a state-of-the-art evacuation system if needs arose, and the *Tevatnoa* was well-equipped. With fifteen mega-lifeboats, each capable of evacuating three hundred and seventy people, the boats were launched from a davit system that lowered them directly into the water from the second deck landing.

Easily manned by a crew of five, the lifeboats were fitted with two one-hundred-seventy-horsepower diesel engines and twin rudders. As far as they were from the yacht, it wouldn't take them long to reach the *Dunn Roven*.

Once the lifeboat was in the water and quick-released from the cams, Hsiung took the helm, steering it directly into the next oncoming wave. The bow of the lifeboat shot high over the crest and slammed back down into the wave's trough with a slap.

Hsiung swore under her breath, bracing herself against the console. "So much for coming in on the low side of the storm."

Miller, tightening his life vest, smirked. "Not sure

there's such thing as a low side anymore." He'd seen worse, though.

In truth, the waves were moderate—cresting at about five meters and topped with sporadic white caps—but they weren't the main cause for concern. The wind was clocking in at seventeen knots.

As the lifeboat rose and fell, the steering tower creaked and shuddered. The near-gale-force wind shook them like a flag, and although it was the largest lifeboat Miller had ever seen, the fiberglass-reinforced hull was empty; one hard gust, one wave hitting from the side, could send them over.

On their approach to the *Dunn Roven*, Miller surveyed the wreckage. The yacht lay becalmed in the water, tipped on one side, and was surrounded by survivors in life vests. Their Personal Locator Beacons flashed among the waves, not that it mattered: the COSPAS satellite system had been offline since China's collapse into martial law.

"Can you swing her around?" Miller asked, eyeing the corpse of the yacht as it rose and fell in the rush of waves.

"Not enough sea room or steering way to get around," Hsiung said. "The waves are coming from starboard. If we turn here we'll be in the same mess they are."

"Alright, stop here. We'll have to fish them out."

Hsiung slowed their approach until they sat idle, or as idle as any boat could be in the conditions.

Miller looked out the windows to assess the situation and saw the colossal rent in the hull. Given the damage, he was less surprised by the speed of the disaster. Movement caught his eye; squinting through the rain, he could just make out the tip of a scaled dorsal fin as it swam away. His stomach lurched.

"Did you see...?" Hsiung gaped.

He nodded, then clasped the radio receiver clipped to his shoulder. "We've got a live one in the water, Cobalt. Look sharp," he said, releasing the button with a wash of static.

Two life rafts from the yacht floated nearby, but had tipped over in the fuming ocean. Some of the survivors clung to the ropes looped around the sides, beacons flashing, while others floated free, thrashed by the waves and swept off in all directions.

The race was on.

Miller climbed down the ladder to the bottom deck and snatched the Reach and Rescue pole above the door. Opening the hatch, he planted his feet wide, wedging his hip against the hull, and kicked down the cradle, a thick rubberized net used to hoist people aboard. Frigid sea water surged up and over his head, making him cry out. He should have put on a wetsuit, but there was nothing to be done now.

Behind him, du Trieux clung tightly to a strap and opened the hatch opposite his.

"Here we go," Morland said beside her, his rifle hung over his shoulder.

Doyle popped his head out of Miller's hatch, hooking his elbow through the hand railing, and peered through a pair of binoculars. He shouted over the howling wind: "Two at ten o'clock. Three meters."

How Doyle had singled them out, Miller couldn't figure; he could barely focus in the spray. There were too many vests floating in the ocean to choose from— too many arms reaching out, too many men crying for help, too many sobbing women and howling babies heard over the crashing waves. As Miller watched, one woman off to his right was sucked under by some unseen force and never resurfaced.

Swallowing the bile in his throat, Miller extended the arm of the pole at ten o'clock, where a couple had latched arms together. The man, a slight fellow easily in his fifties, grabbed hold of the hook on the end of the pole and held tight as Miller dragged them toward the lifeboat.

They drew closer, the man kicking to drive them, the woman limp and staring blankly. It wasn't until Miller reached down to help her into the cradle did he understand why.

"My wife," the man said, blue-lipped and pale. "My wife... take her first."

She was clearly dead, either drowned or frozen to death, too long exposed to the treacherous and unforgiving sea.

God damn this ocean.

"My wife..." the man repeated again, pushing her body into the looped net.

Given the way her head bobbed in the water, Miller guessed her neck had been broken.

"Come on, now, ma'am," Doyle said, reaching

past Miller and grabbing the net. "Uppsy daisy."

"My wife..."

"We got her, mate," Doyle said, pulling the net.

One hand still gripping the pole, Miller used his other to help Doyle, grasping the net and pulling upward. The woman's limp body rolled up the side of the boat. When she reached the top, Doyle dragged her by the shoulders into the boat's interior and Miller dropped the cradle back into the water.

The man swung around, got into the net feet first and waited. "I'm coming, Lilly! I'm right behind you."

Without a word, Doyle and Miller pulled him up. Doyle held the man's arm until he got inside. The husband dropped to his knees beside his wife and cupped her face. "Lilly? We made it, Lil."

Miller and Doyle shared a grim look.

Turning back to the despicable ocean and the sea of flashing life vests, Miller gripped his pole and flung it far, hooking it around a woman holding a wailing baby over her head.

A wave surged and knocked the pole from the woman's vest, but she never released the screaming baby. It took Miller two more attempts, but he finally roped them in and pulled them to the boat. He went to grab the baby, but Doyle appeared and did it for him, then handed him the yowling infant.

"You'd better hurry up, boss," Doyle said. "Du Trieux's lassoed twice as many as you have."

Miller grimaced, struggling to keep his grip on the squirming infant.

Doyle rolled the woman up the side. When she was on board, Miller handed the baby to her and swung the pole back out into the water.

The next nearest life vest was a teenage boy with lips so blue it looked like lipstick. The kid grabbed the hook and Miller dragged him toward the boat, but had pulled him less than a meter when he felt resistance.

The boy shrieked holy hell, his arms flailing like pinwheels in the wind. "Help me! Help me! I'm stuck!"

Miller leaned into it, tugging harder, and Doyle abandoned his position to help. Like a grotesque tug of war, they pulled the boy. He didn't budge.

With a deafening wail the boy hollered his last. Immediately, the resistance gave way, sending Miller and Doyle reeling backwards into the interior of the lifeboat.

Still holding the rescue pole, Miller scrabbled to his feet and pulled the boy toward the boat.

The boy's face was still, seemingly stuck in an expression of sheer horror and pain.

"Miller," Doyle said, eyeing the survivors watching them. "Don't pull him in."

"What?" Miller dragged the boy closer. After he advanced a few meters more, coming within reaching distance of the cradle, he halted. Something was off. He couldn't place it. "Hey, kid," Miller spoke to him.

The boy didn't answer, or blink.

"What the..." He leaned over the boat to grab the boy by the shoulders of his life vest.

"No!" cried Doyle.

Too late.

Miller was surprised how easily he lifted the boy from the water; it wasn't until he saw the teen was missing the entire bottom half of his body that his grip gave way, dropping the body face first back into the water. Entrails floated out from his gut like the tentacles of a jellyfish.

The nearest survivors shrieked, some of them swimming back to the wreckage.

"Swim!" Doyle shouted at the screeching people in the water. "Swim *here*, you bloody idiots!"

Mass hysteria erupted.

Miller swung the pole out into the water and four people grabbed hold, and others grabbed hold of them. One guy shoved one of the first four off and grabbed hold of the hook himself.

Doyle snatched the net and opened it for the first survivor; two tried to crawl in. "One at a time, or none of you are getting in!"

The two fighting over the net refused to let go. Doyle bent down, punched the more aggressive of the two men in the face, and as he floated backwards, grabbed the other and shoved his feet into the mesh.

It seemed to go better after that.

They hauled one survivor in after another, never stopping. One man cut in front of the line and one woman tried to climb up the cradle like a ladder. It was every man, woman, and child for themselves.

A crowd had accumulated at the hatch, with more fighting the current and the roiling waves to reach them. The ones who'd swum for the wreckage were now gone. For every five that made it aboard the lifeboat, another got pulled under with a terrifying shriek.

After a solid hour of hauling people, Miller's shoulders and arms throbbed and his body shivered. The lifeboat's interior was barely a quarter full.

Then the storm surged, pounding the boat with heavy rain and sending waves up and over the top of the hull. Miller was still hooking people in, but by this point they were pulling in more bodies than survivors.

It was no longer a rescue, but a recovery. Not wanting to leave the dead for whatever it was that was feasting on them, he and Doyle worked, pulling in the corpses until the sun set and the temperatures plummeted.

Eventually, Miller had no choice but to call it.

"Alright, that's it," he said, slapping Doyle's soaked shoulder and retreating into the lifeboat. He snapped the rescue pole back into its bracket. Across the room, a drenched, exhausted-looking du Trieux was doing the same.

A man huddled under a rescue blanket on the first row of benches gawked at Miller with wide eyes. "We can't leave. My brother is still out there."

Without a word, Miller strode past him, clambered up the ladder to the second floor, and went to the steering column.

As the squad closed and lashed the hatches, Miller gave the order to move. Hsiung piloted the lifeboat back toward the *Tevatnoa*, the single spotlight on the forward bow their only means of navigation.

Of the hundred and fifteen aboard the *Dunn Roven*, almost sixty had been saved.

Miller supposed he should have been pleased they'd saved *any*, but all he could do was feel the weight of their failure. He eyed the survivors in the lifeboat, and looked at the hateful sea slapping the hull beneath them.

He spat salt water onto the floor and grimaced.

Fuck. You.

THE WIND CAME up from the east with just a hint of sea breeze, tickling the stalks of alfalfa-barley at the tips. The stems swayed and swirled in unison, as if waltzing to a disjointed tune of dissonant chords.

Samantha Hernandez watched the dance with interest, then turned her gaze to the graying sky. If the weather turned again, the commune ran the risk of losing the entire crop. Ten acres of alfalfa-barley yielded nearly twelve thousand pounds of grain. Properly stored, it could easily feed them through the winter months—or, at least, Samantha hoped.

But if they lost this crop, as they had the artichoke-corn during last week's torrential rain, months of ploughing, planting, irrigation, and careful tending would yet again be washed away, leaving them with nothing but a muddy field and a commune burning with frustration.

Truthfully, this crop had another week—perhaps more—before it was ready to harvest, but another glance toward the swirling sky raised Samantha's anxiety, enough so that it caught the attention of the two Infecteds working a few meters away, weeding.

"Should we start now?" asked Patty, a tall and muscular Regular with a knack for horticulture. She rose from her crouched position in the row and rested her trowel on her hip. The alfalfa-barley wavered in the wind, batting her on the head.

"Not yet," Samantha said, doing her best to feel confident. There was no sense in raising a panic. She fought to control her feelings, pushing her anxiety to the back of her mind with the rest of her repressed emotions. It seemed to work. Patty's concern melted from her pale eyes and she dropped back to the dirt, digging out a weed without another word. The other Infected behind her, an Archaean named Chris, raised an eyebrow, but went back to work as well.

Samantha ground her teeth. There were benefits, without doubt, to the Infected hive-mind—even more so for an Archaean.

Host to the protozoan parasite discovered in sub-glacial Antarctic lakes some five years before, the Archaeans had evolved from the regular Infected after the bio-tech company Schaeffer-Yeager had set off atmospheric air bombs, spreading an anti-parasitic medicine which only resulted in the parasite's mutation, and the birth of a new breed of hosts. These Archaeans, as they called themselves, possessed a greater control over the hive-mind mentality the parasite created. Where Regulars were violent, disorganized and mob-minded, the

Archaeans believed in peace, cooperation and communion, not just with each other but with the new ecology of their planet.

It became obvious to the Archaeans during the invasion that all they had to do was wait for the worst of the Regular Infected to destroy themselves—which they obligingly did, with help from the humans—so the Archaeans could step in and assume command of the masses.

Six months after the blast in the city, the Archaeans were in charge of several thousand Infected, collected from the survivors of NYC and the surrounding areas, and spread out across ten farms in upstate New York, a good distance from the fallout. If all went as planned, Samantha and the council of Archaeans would have re-colonized a sizable area, which had been all but deserted and destroyed.

It was no easy task, but they were progressing well, for the most part. Aside from the weather, the mood of the commune thrived. Samantha only hoped that in the coming winter, when they had fewer duties to distract them, this continued to be true.

"Everything will be fine," Patty said, looking up with a toothy grin, picking up on Samantha's anxiety.

The swell of contentedness flowed from Patty so strongly that Sam momentarily lost herself to the undertow. Her body pulsed with warmth—as if six thousand arms had reached out and swallowed her into a sincere embrace. It took an effort on Samantha's part to identify and disentangle her own mind from the center of the mass.

Samantha seized control of herself and pulled back, literally taking a step backward on the path. When the mist had cleared, she swept a hand over her face and pulled her bandana back over her nose and mouth.

It was hardly necessary, given the scarcity of the burrowing wasps in these parts, but it offered a suggestion of privacy—a falsehood that provided comfort nonetheless.

It would serve no one, Samantha knew, particularly these farms, if the Archaeans succumbed fully to the pull of the hive-mind. It was hard enough on the best days to maintain control. Samantha didn't want to think how difficult it would be on a bad one.

Samantha cast her gaze over the twenty or so souls weeding the field, then toward the expanse of the farm, including Patty and Chris, and lastly to the people coming in and out of the greenhouse, built a few weeks before in a bid to save the melon-berries from the swarms of locust-armadillos plaguing the region and the invasive fungal blooms, which seemed to thrive regardless of moisture. It stuck out like an eye-sore, given the odd mix of windows and glass panels—plastic would just feed the fungus—but so far, it seemed to be getting the job done.

A shadow passed overhead, drawing Samantha's eye. She looked up and was momentarily blinded by the sun as it peeked out from behind a graying cloud. Blinking away the plum-colored splotches, she fought to focus on the shadow hovering above her, wide and bat-like.

A shiver ran up her spine—a rot-glider. Raising her hand above her brow to block the sun, Samantha squinted skyward and caught more shadows. No, *three* rot-gliders.

She opened her mouth to raise the alarm. Patty and Chris looked up, uneasy as panic clenched Samantha's gut. At almost the same time all three of them shouted, "Run!"

"Take cover!" someone else bellowed as fear spread across the field of workers. The Infected workers scattered.

Spinning on her heel, Samantha broke into a run, making for the covered porch of the farmhouse, only ten or so meters from where they stood. Patty, and Chris sprinted close behind her. They pounded down the path, nearly clear to safety when from above, a great force pounced on Samantha's shoulders, crushing her to the ground.

Buried under leathery skin slick with moss, fighting to catch her breath, Samantha writhed to break free, only to feel razor-sharp talons encircle her shoulders and pierce her to the bone.

Someone screamed. The shrill screech sounded inhuman to Samantha's pounding ears.

With a shudder, the creature's grip relaxed. It gurgled in her ear and then collapsed, grinding Samantha's face into the dirt so hard she tasted blood.

"Samantha? Sam!"

The weight lifted and the talons slipped from her skin, leaving gaping, bloody holes. She turned over and blinked away the blackness threatening to consume her.

Patty's pale eyes appeared above hers. "Get up!"

"Hurry!" Chris begged from over Patty's shoulder.

Everything inside Samantha told her to run, flee. Panic swelled in her chest; she couldn't tell if it was her own or that of the Infected she heard shouting and screaming across the farm.

Taking Patty's outstretched hand, Sam pulled herself up—howling at the sharp pain in her shoulders—and looked at the beast on the ground beside her. A gardening trowel protruded from its spine. Fresh blood pooled around the blade and from Patty's fist.

"Go!" Chris snapped, taking off down the path with Patty.

Willing one foot in front of the other, Sam followed. Behind her, the blanket of terror from the farm shifted, evolving into a call to action. Gripping at her bleeding shoulder with one hand, she trudged forward, fighting to keep up with the others.

The unmistakable whir of bows and arrows filled the air, bringing about brief pangs of satisfaction and frustration as the archers struggled to hit the swooping rot-gliders, and then Samantha felt an odd lifting sensation, as if her feet had left the ground.

Nausea clutched her stomach, stopping her in her tracks. She doubled over. The hunger clenched her abdomen in a vice of acid and pain.

Sam was on her knees, her vision blurred. All she felt was the desperation of her pack as they hunted, the terror from their prey on the ground, and a frustration at the air currents that looped and swirled recklessly, making it difficult to glide for more than a few strokes.

Samantha pounded her skull with angry fists, fighting off the connection. Communion with the rot-gliders was not welcome or pleasant. Their need to feed was pungent in her mouth, sour and rancid. Their blood must have mixed—it shouldn't last long, but for now she clung to humanity with a slipping grasp.

Beside her, Patty had stopped. "Sam?"

"Go!" Samantha managed to say. "Don't wait for me!"

Before her eyes, a rot-glider cascaded from the air, folded its leathery wings inward and crashed straight into Patty like a wrecking ball.

Talons the size of backhoe blades pierced Patty's shoulders and bashed her head against the ground. From just a meter away, Samantha heard the audible crack of the woman's neck.

With a pang of delight and excitement, the rot-glider opened its wings wide, flapped them a few times and pushed off the ground, carrying the entirety of Patty away, her pale eyes open and blank.

Samantha's mouth watered in anticipation.

She shook the hunger from her head and ambled up, swaying in the wind and covering the last few meters to the farmhouse porch on unstable feet. Chris and a few others also cowered there, watching the carnage. Once under the patio awning, Sam allowed herself to collapse—welcoming unconsciousness—but it never came.

She lay on the porch, listening to the shouts and shrieks from the farm below, pushing away her pain and mounting terror. Eventually, the voices began cheering and whooping with celebration; the rush of excitement and relief told Samantha the rot-gliders had left. She pulled together a plea for help to the forefront of her mind and cast it out like a fisherman's net. Within seconds, Samantha was surrounded by Infected.

As squares of fabric were placed on her wounds, and tied around her shoulders, Samantha bit back her pain and took stock of the faces of the survivors. She felt an emptiness where Patty had once been, and two other absent minds which had once worked the fields. But there was more: presences that had been there, which had not disappeared, but gone away.

"Who else is gone?" Samantha asked.

"Bernard and Rose, I think," Chris said.

"Where are the others?"

"They're hiding in the greenhouse and the barn."

"What of the alfalfa-barley?"

"It's partially trampled," someone answered.

"...but sections are salvageable," another completed the sentence.

Samantha swallowed and licked her scabbed lips. "We should harvest..."

"...before the rains come."

"Yes."

"Who else is wounded?"

"Just two others."

"But there's more missing than that," Samantha said.

"We should send for the apothecary."

Words bled into one another, voices sounded as one: *...missing... wounded... the crops... won't be back*. For a moment, she released her resistance and was swept into the hive-mind. The pain in her shoulder was shared—spread wide, dulling as it extended across the others—and her fear, absorbed by the sense of control and calm as plans of recovery were discussed, evaporated into the throng.

It lasted only a moment. Just as Sam's eyes darkened, and her mind eased, the sky opened a downpour like no other, cracking the sky wide with lightning and pounding the roof of the awning so forcefully, specks of paint chipped off and floated down onto the heads of those below like snow. The onslaught was torrential, catastrophic.

"The crops," Samantha managed to say before unconsciousness mercifully took hold.

The crops...

She just managed to acknowledge the sad realizations from the commune before slipping into the void; she knew, then, the salvageable crops were being washed away by the rain.

3

THE SURVIVORS OF the *Dunn Roven* gathered on the second floor landing and huddled together, their rescue blankets wrapped tightly around them against the bitter, cold sea wind that drove up and over the railing.

Miller pushed through the crowd of survivors and made his way down the corridor in search of the deck officer—it was only after a few meters that he realized the lot of them were following him.

Raising his hands, he eyed the wet, sunken faces of the survivors and bit the inside of his cheek hard enough to taste blood. "Wait here," he mumbled, then took off as quickly as the swaying ship would allow.

Past the hollowed-out gift shop that now served as a barter station, and a lounge area stacked high with storage crates, Miller found who he was looking for: Jennifer Barrett, formerly the head of IT at Schaeffer-Yeager. She'd found herself without a job after the compound's collapse. The *Tevatnoa* had their own crew for that sort of thing. These days, she was reduced to coordinating living space for the survivors: it was beneath her skill set, but she'd taken well to the demotion and immediately let the power go to her head.

Standing in the center of a crowd of enraged people, she watched with gritted teeth and an insincere smile as Miller approached. "Miller! Such a pleasure, what can I do for you?"

"The *Dunn Roven* capsized. I have survivors who need to be placed."

Her smile immediately fell. Gripping her clipboard tighter to her chest, she squared her shoulders. "How many?"

Before Miller could answer, a man in a woolly red cap shouted in her face. "Hey! What about my toilet?"

Jennifer blinked at Miller, then faced the man with a stony expression.

"It's been two weeks since our linens have been cleaned," hollered a woman on her other side. She waved a gray towel in the air. "And we're all sick. What are we supposed to do? Wash them in our sink?"

Jennifer barely batted an eye. If Miller didn't know any better, he'd think she was enjoying this.

"That would be a very good idea," Jennifer suggested. "If you want to use your fresh water rations for laundry—by all means..."

"We have three new people in our room and one

of them keeps taking showers!" bellowed another woman. She had a squalling baby on her hip. "Can we get more water?"

"What about my toilet?" shouted the man in the cap again.

Thrusting an arm into the air, Jennifer raised her voice above the hubbub. "If you would please submit your requisition slips to the Rationing Office and repair requests to Maintenance, I will be sure they get to them just as soon as they can. There is nothing I can do for you today. Please stop blocking the walkways and return to your living quarters."

"But *what about my toilet?*" the man shouted again from right beside her.

"I submitted a requisition slip for more water a week ago," said the woman with the baby, "and I never heard back."

Jennifer rolled her eyes and ignored her, turning her gaze once again to Miller. "How many?" she asked again.

The man with the cap grabbed Jennifer's arm, yanking her to face him. "What about my toilet?"

Just as Miller took a step forward to intervene, Jennifer ripped her elbow out of the man's hand and cracked it against his nose with a wet *thunk*. "Don't you touch me!"

The man's face burst with blood. Squealing, he faltered backwards into the crowd, which had instantly quieted—as did Miller.

Smoothing her rumpled Oxford with an open palm, Jennifer raised her chin. "We will get to the slips as soon as we are able. Now please, stop blocking the walkways and return to your living quarters." When nobody moved she added, "*Now*."

The grumbling crowd dispersed, including the man now gripping his bloody nose. Miller felt a mixture of contempt and sympathy for them as they slunk away like scolded children. They were right to complain: conditions were poor and worsening by the day. But it wasn't Jennifer's fault, no matter how much she put them off.

Meanwhile, Jennifer, red-faced, turned on Miller like a pit bull. "I asked how many, Miller. I don't have all day."

"You okay?"

She squinted at him. "I'm fine."

"I think you broke his nose."

"Serves him right. You have to be firm with them. They're fucking savages."

"These are savage conditions."

Her eyes widened. "That's no excuse. You don't see me accosting people in the halls. My linens haven't been cleaned in weeks either—you don't see me bitching and complaining. My God, they act like they're on *vacation*, not floating on a godforsaken death trap in the middle of the ocean."

Miller had no response to this. He waited as Jennifer shook her head and looked down at her clipboard. When she looked back up, she'd collected herself.

She opened her mouth to speak, but before she could ask again, he said, "Sixty."

A flash of panic crossed her face, but she masked it quickly. "I see."

"There could have been more, but that was all we could save. Try not to look disappointed."

Her face hardened at that and she clenched her jaw. "I'm not..." She stopped short and didn't complete the thought aloud. "Have they been to the infirmary yet?"

"No."

"Take them there." She sighed and spread her palms against the back of her clipboard. "They'll need to be inoculated against the influenza that's going around. And it'll give me some time to figure out where to put them."

"Sorry to be such an inconvenience."

"That's not it, and you know it," she snapped.

Miller shifted his weight; his boots squished with salt water. "Can't you take them below? I've got to report to Lewis and Matheson. And I'm drenched."

Jennifer tucked her clipboard under her arm and walked away. "Get yourself checked out while you're down there." And then she was gone.

Miller pursed his lips and watched her disappear into the bowels of the ship. *Now* who was acting like a savage?

AFTER DISMISSING THE shivering members of Cobalt, Miller gathered the *Dunn Roven* survivors and took them through the bowels of the ship toward the infirmary.

Wordlessly, he led them to the stairwell and down one flight to the lower deck, the able-bodied helping the wounded. It was slow-going: the elevators had been out of action for a week. He wanted it over with, but the people had begun to ask questions, and eventually—as they waited for the stragglers of the group to catch up—Miller found himself an unwilling tour guide.

"Can we get something to eat?" asked one man.

"Tomorrow morning," he said, reluctantly slowing his pace. "I suggest you wake up at dawn and get in line at the Food Rations Distribution Center, here"— he pointed to a ballroom down the hall—"or on the third floor. There's enough to go around, but you don't want to be at the tail end of the first line and maybe miss your chance to get in line for the second meal. That's been known to happen."

"What about clothes?" asked a young man over the grim mumblings of the others. The man's sea-sodden pants stopped at his shins. "Can we get new clothes?"

"We ran out of fabric a few months into the voyage," Miller confessed. "There's a patch-and-repair place over by the galley—a lady named Donna runs it. But unless you find somebody to trade with, no, there aren't any clothes to buy. And besides, what good is money now anyways?"

They walked by a door labelled *Writing Room*; the line of people waiting outside pressed themselves against the wall to allow them to pass. Miller gestured at it. "If you need anything, you submit your request slips there. Those are the offices. Be nice to the staff. Everybody's doing the best they can and you catch more flies with honey."

"What about a room?" asked a woman with droopy eyes from the middle of the horde. "When can we get our cabins?"

"Each living quarter has about six people in it, which is pretty tight," Miller explained. "You'll be lucky to get a bed, quite honestly. We save those for the sick, elderly, and pregnant women. Everybody else is sleeping on the floor. We get, I don't know, about twenty gallons of desalinated water for each room a day—so we all keep bathing down to a minimum, and the toilets use salt water now. Someone will assign you rooms once you get inoculated for the flu that's going around."

"Jesus," gasped a woman on Miller's left.

"There are three pools aboard," he continued, "which are now hydroponic farms. Crew and personnel train and study in the old library, and a teacher's set up a schoolroom for the younger kids in one of the bars, but space is limited and there's a waiting list to get in. There's also a dentist in the old hairdresser's salon; no cleanings, just fillings and extractions these days. And the cinema is now the infirmary. That's where we're headed now."

A rumble from outside the ship shook the air around them, and the lights overhead flickered and went out. Plunged into darkness, the survivors cried out and froze. After a few seconds, another crack of thunder boomed outside.

Miller snatched his flashlight from his utility belt and snapped it on. It blinked once or twice but came on when he pounded it. "Looks like there's a storm. Generator must be down again. Move over to the right. Don't clog the hallway. Come on, the infirmary is just this way."

"Does this happen a lot?" asked a voice beside him.

Miller recognized the man with the short pants and nodded, although he realized he'd never see it in the darkened passage. "More than I'd like," he said.

The guy wrapped his arm around an older shivering woman beside him, pulling her along.

"Maybe we should have stayed on the *Dunn Roven*," he heard the woman whisper.

Miller came to the infirmary and pushed the door open. Inside was a flurry of activity. Flashlights flickered across the room as voices rose in volume, becoming louder as panic set in.

In the far left hand corner, just under the stage, a woman in labour heaved and puffed, accompanied by a midwife up to her elbows in birthing fluid and holding a flashlight in her mouth. Up on the stage, several doctors and nurses bustled around a crowd of people, all coughing and hacking.

As the *Dunn Roven* survivors stared in horror at the chaos, a doctor with a flashlight approached and scanned them with a critical eye. "Any of you have medical training?" When no-one immediately replied, he asked again. "Anyone?"

The woman huddled with the young man in short

pants nodded. "I'm trained as a medical assistant," she said sheepishly.

The doctor's face brightened. "You're hired. Come with me."

"But..." She held tightly to the young man, obviously reluctant to leave his side. "My son."

"You can meet up with him later, he'll be fine. Come here. I need you to compress the bag valve mask on this patient. He's arresting."

"Go, Mom," the man said. "Go."

She handed her rescue blanket to her son and followed the doctor into the crowd. He led her to the right, where a nurse was performing CPR on an elderly man stretched out on a mat on the floor.

Miller saw his chance. "The rest of you stay here. Someone will be around shortly to check you out and assign you rooms."

"That's it?" asked a man, eyes wide. "You're just leaving us here?"

Miller's throat clenched and he nodded. "Yep."

BACK OUT IN the hall, Miller hooked a right and made his way back toward the stairwell. He hated the infirmary. Maybe the whole first deck. No, in truth, he hated everything aboard this ship. Feeling more helpless with each step, he quickened his pace. He had to check on Cobalt, and he had to report to Gray and Lewis on what had happened to the *Dunn Roven*.

The memory of that huge, scaly dorsal fin when

the lifeboat had first arrived—the survivors they'd lost—could only mean one thing. The yacht hadn't been sunk by the weather; the sea life was on the hunt, and if his fears were correct, every vessel in the S-Y fleet smaller than thirty meters was in danger of the same fate.

SAMANTHA'S DREAMS WERE scattered and fierce, a cross between an unyielding urge to run and hide, quickly overtaken by a starved, airborne search for fresh meat.

She awoke after the rot-glider attack, stitched, bandaged, and propped up in bed with pillows. The pain in her shoulders—a low throb which pulsed through her body with every heart beat—dulled only when she allowed her mind to wander inside the hive-mind and pull contentment from the masses, but she dared not linger there for long.

Finally able to take to her feet, Samantha dressed, braided her hair, and exited the communal bedroom in search of food. She found the farmhouse kitchen bustling with activity.

The space was crammed wall-to-wall with people. Dirt, sweat, and an acrid stench of rot flooded Samantha's senses. She gripped the wall for balance, her fingers brushing against peeling wallpaper, and strained to listen.

"They were spotted to the west," someone said from beside the oven.

A voice from near the deep sink chimed in: "... living in some sort of camping ground in the forest."

"But they wouldn't come," said a voice near the table and chairs. "Kept running off before we could re-commune."

"...I don't understand their hesitation."

Samantha cleared her throat, taking in the confusion from the group and zeroing in on the source. A man, Aaron, stood by the kitchen door. He was covered in mud from head to toe, and his frizzy hair, normally pulled back into a hasty pony-tail, splayed far and wild around his head, haloing him in a wreath of curls.

"We should send more," someone said, before the horde took over the conversation.

"...bring them back by force..."

"...not safe for them..."

"...we have no choice."

"Wait," Samantha said, broadcasting a sense of ease to the multitude in the kitchen. "How many fled the farm?"

"Three today. Five yesterday," Aaron said, running his palm over his arm. An orangey patch of lichen had accumulated in the crook of his elbow and he scratched at it, drawing blood.

Sam saw three others scratch the insides of their elbows.

How long had she been in bed for? Long enough for the hygiene regiment to become lax, allowing the Regulars to sprout fungal skin growths again. "Where are Chris and Joseph?" she asked.

"Joseph is at the yucca-flax farm," someone said.

"Why did he leave?" Sam asked.

"Some emergency," someone answered.

"Chris is in the greenhouse, trying to save the melon-berries."

"Bring my husk-mutt around," Sam said. "I'm going to see Joseph."

"But what about the deserters?" Aaron asked, still digging into his arm.

"Leave them," Samantha said, sounding as resolute as she could muster. "Help Chris with the melon-berries and care for the livestock. Plough and re-seed the field. We still have time to harvest a crop of alfalfa-barley before the season turns."

A HUSK-MUTT WAS a four-legged predator, smaller and faster than a thug behemoth, tamer and less volatile than a terror-jaw, and *fast*. Riding it made Samantha feel especially strange, as if she were holding the reins of a giant bristled iguana. The beast swung side to side in slither fashion, rather than up and down like a horse, and although the Archaeans had tamed a handful of the beasts as a faster alternative to the behemoths, the motion made Samantha feel as if she weren't getting anywhere.

Holding onto the ridge of soft bristles lining the mutt's spine, she gripped the leathery torso tightly with her thighs and turned the beast eastward with a flick of the reins. Passing the forest to the west, and bypassing a string of communal farms all connected via dirt roads and footpaths, she urged the beast on, trying to maintain mental control as her shoulders throbbed.

Communing with these particular animals was an acquired skill. Half a dozen Regulars had been killed in the initial stages of domestication of the husk-mutts, until the Archaeans recognized that it was a task best done by them. This had proven to be true of all the new animals, for whatever reason; it wasn't unheard of for a Regular to be able to do it, but it was rare.

This helped solidify the Archaean's ruling position. Each commune farm had three to five Archaeans living amongst the Regulars to maintain control and order.

Reaching her destination, Samantha pulled up the reins and slowed the husk-mutt to a stop. The farm, raising the yucca-flax they hoped to turn to the production of cloth and fabric, sat at the northern tip of the commune at the edge of a forest, beyond which lay the remains of Connecticut.

Flinging her leg over the beast, she slid off its back and pulled up her bandana.

The farm was thick with insects. Locust-armadillos clouded the air, heavy and unruly. She swatted them away as she walked, her feet crunching beneath her. The ground swarmed with fallen and burrowing bugs. Airborne, the insects moved in a massive flock, like birds trying to hide their numbers.

They were silly-looking things, she thought, sort of cartoonish and twee—as if an armadillo had shrunk and grown wings. And they weren't particularly aggressive, but they were armored—she assumed to help keep them from being a meal for everything else. Swatting didn't do more than bend their wings and knock them aside, but it was the better than walking straight through the onslaught.

In front of her, down a gentle slope and past the decimated yucca-flax field, a ring of Regulars and several Archaeans walked around the farm's greenhouse. They wore face masks and pushed motorized smokers; Joseph had built a fleet of them a few months before from old lawnmowers.

Catswort extract and lemon oil was pumped through a quarter-inch copper pipe, wrapped around the mower's extended muffler to heat it up. When the mower was turned on, the foggy exhaust served as a natural insect repellent, causing little to no harm to the crops. The method had been effective at keeping down the locust-armadillos at first, but now, near to the end of autumn, the situation seemed to have worsened.

Normally—if there appeared to be an increase in the insects' activity—Joseph would enlist three Regulars to fog the area around the greenhouse in a constant loop. As far as Sam could tell, there were now at least ten on a constant rotation, jumping in and out to refuel and refill liquids as necessary.

The whole field stank of citrus and herbs. The cloud of repellent extended far beyond the greenhouse, and several feet into the field itself. Surrounding that haze—hovering the misty circumference—was a barrage of locusts, barely kept at bay, waiting for a break in the fog.

Samantha spotted Joseph standing by the barn at a makeshift ethanol refueling station. With how low supplies were, she was surprised he'd authorized the fuel. Making her way through the field of destroyed yucca-flax and wading through the bugs, she stopped wondering. If they'd lost this crop, as well as what was in the greenhouse, there would be nothing for the hundred-plus Infected living here to do; there would be no fabric to weave during the long winter months.

"It's fine," Joseph reassured her as she planted herself in front of them. "The fuel reserves are enough to see us through to the end of the season."

"If we last until nightfall," an Archaean woman added. "They should dissipate in the dark."

"And if they don't?" Sam asked. "We'd have used all our fuel and lost the crop anyway."

"Seemed a risk worth taking," Joseph said, looking up from his work. He snapped the cap back onto his canister and gave the go-ahead for the Archaean to rejoin the smoker parade.

The Archaean, Susie—an especially busy blonde with an exceptionally loud voice—reached up from her mower's handle bar and touched her shoulder. "You should be resting."

"They'll heal." Samantha felt undeniable annoyance from Joseph at the remark, and wondered if it had originated from him or Susie, but she supposed it didn't matter.

Just then a Regular approached to refuel, and Susie moved off to give him room. As Joseph refilled the fog solution for the Regular, Samantha brushed a locust from her sleeve and watched Susie push her smoker back into the revolving line. The ground was littered with fallen and burrowing locusts and the wheels of Susie's mower crunched and popped over the tiny corpses as if rolling over a path of gravel.

Looking down, Samantha spotted, among the tiny bug corpses, a smattering of holes. The earth was littered with them—tiny burrows all leading directly toward the greenhouse.

The moment the realization hit Samantha, Joseph's head popped up.

"What is it?" he asked, urgently.

"They're burrowing toward the greenhouse."

Dropping the can of repellent fluid, Joseph pushed through the rotation of mowers toward the greenhouse door.

On his heels, Samantha called, "Wait! Don't open—"

Throwing back the doors, Joseph stepped into the greenhouse—and into a swarm of locust-armadillos. Every square inch of air in the shed teemed with them. Like an avalanche, the bugs gushed from the pen—brushing right over the top of Joseph and Samantha—and filled the air around the smokers, thousands of them dropping to the ground as soon as they hit the repellent. Overwhelmed, the circle of smokers broke and scattered, spreading the bugs farther and wider.

Inside the greenhouse, Joseph inspected the crop—a batch of sunflower-grapes, now eaten down to their stumps. He gripped the sides of his head, scowling. "Son of a bitch!" With a primal cry he swatted the air and smacked a locust down, then another—as if he could bat the teeming millions away with his bare hands. "Fuck!"

"Joseph!" Samantha cried, feeling the rage permeate him with growing intensity.

"*Goddamnit!*" he continued, ignoring her. He kept smacking the air, punched the locusts, repeating, "Fuck! Fuck! Fuck!"

The full scope of his anger hit Samantha in the chest, filling her so quickly, her skin slicked with an icy sweat. Her fists clenched, her teeth ground together with an audible crack. She wanted to kill everything. She wanted to set fire to the whole farm and watch it burn. She dug her nails into her palms and tightened her grasp, using the pain and the throbbing in her shoulders to pull herself out of the anger.

She didn't want to burn *anything*, she reminded herself. She didn't want to destroy the Earth.

"Joseph," she called, stepping through the swirling throng and grasping his shoulders. "Joe!"

His tense body slackened in her grasp almost instantly, and he fell to his knees beside a sunflower-grape stump. Reaching up, he clasped her fingers in his and heaved, panting as he fought to control himself. "Oh, Sam. Every crop is lost. Everything." He choked back tears.

She held him there, on his knees in the dirt, pulling his anger out and calming his aching fury. After a moment, he got to his feet and turned to face her. The handkerchief covering his nose and mouth was soaked. He rubbed his eyes with the heels of his hands and sighed. The relief radiating off him was palpable.

Once she felt comfortable, she released his shoulders, then dropped her hands to her sides, but before she could speak, a surge of panicked energy struck her from behind.

Sensing it too, Joseph jogged passed Samantha, coming to a skidding stop at the greenhouse doorway.

Outside, every man, woman, and Infected child, Regular and Archaean alike, had scattered across the farm. Every soul ran in unbridled chaos, smacking locust-armadillos out of the air with their bare hands and sobbing into their face coverings.

In a unified chorus their voices chanted, "Fuck! Fuck! Fuck! Fuck!..."

"WHAT THE HELL was it?" Lewis demanded.

Miller shook his head and took a sip from his mug. Seaweed tea was bitter and grassy, but it was all there was available these days. It was no substitute for coffee and lacked any caffeine at all, but it was hot. He still hadn't had the chance to change out of his wet uniform and could feel the early stages of hypothermia setting in.

Gray's makeshift office was cool now that the sun had set. Initially the games room, Gray had commandeered the space early on in their voyage because of its ample size with the full intent on moving 'once things settled down.' They never had.

Miller shifted with a wet squish in the folding chair, where he sat across from Gray's desk—ping-pong table—and eyed Lewis, leaning against the wall by the dart board. "Your guess is as good as mine," Miller said, cracking his aching neck with a sharp twist. "A shark, maybe?"

Gray slid off his suit jacket and tossed it onto the back of his chair. "With scales?"

"What else has a dorsal fin?" Lewis asked.

"Who knows anymore?" Gray grumbled.

"The ship's manifest had a hundred and fifteen people and we only brought back seventy-eight," Miller explained. "Sixty of them alive. That's thirty-eight unaccounted for. Some may have been swept out to sea—but it's also possible they were dragged under by whatever was under that dorsal fin. I know of at least one for sure."

"We've had our ships attacked before, this is nothing new," said Gray.

"Sure, by tusk-fiends and goliath brutes"— Miller examined his blue-tinged fingernails as they gripped his mug—"mammal-like predators, but the marine creatures have pretty much left us alone. The occasional whale now and then pops up, even a shark, but they don't do much more than bump a ship a few times and move on when they realize boats aren't edible. There's never been a hull breach."

"Are we near a coral reef? An uncharted sand bed, or something?" Gray asked.

Lewis shook his head. "No. We're in deep."

"None of the other small ships reported problems," Gray said. "Right?"

"It was a deliberate attack," Miller said. "Something poked a hole in the *Dunn Roven* on purpose."

"You're saying a sea animal figured out that if it stabs a hole in a boat, edible things fall out?"

Miller raised his eyebrows. "I guess I am."

Gray puffed out his cheeks. "And what are we supposed to do about that?"

"Bring the others on board. Us, or the other cruise liner. The two sailboats especially. Anything less than thirty meters, or with a wooden hull."

"And put them where?" Gray asked. "We're packed to the hilt as it is. It's worse on the *Princess Penelope*; even with the new hydroponics farm, they're down to feeding people once a day."

"It's only forty or so more people," Lewis interjected. "I think the *Rose Bud* has twenty. *Minerva's Wand*, maybe fifteen. *Robin's Nest* has ten."

"But when does it stop?" Gray asked. "Every time we see a small boat we can't just absorb the crew."

Lewis frowned. "How can we not?"

"Do you know how many people die on board every day?" Gray asked.

Miller didn't know and didn't care to guess, but he had the sense Gray was going to tell them anyway.

"We've got a flu going around, and it's rough," his boss continued. "The labs can't produce the meds fast enough to keep up with demand, and food supplies are wearing thin. I know, initially, I said there was safety in numbers, but now I'm rethinking that. We can't bring any more people on board. The next ship that goes down will have to be absorbed someplace else."

"You're leaving three ships exposed," Miller said. "That's forty people. The least we can do is warn them."

"And have them *demand* to be brought on board? No." Miller frowned and went to speak, but Gray cut him off. "Don't tell me you hadn't thought the same thing. Conditions here are deteriorating by the day. Let's not add to it."

Miller had to confess, he *had* thought the same thing—not too long ago, in fact. But the reality of leaving forty people out in the water like sitting ducks was a lot different than thinking it. He'd seen what this creature could do. "I don't like it."

Gray nodded. "Me either. Let's hope we come across another wayward cruise liner and we can dump them there. In the meantime, we head toward Iceland as planned."

EVERY JOINT ACHED. With heavy footsteps Miller left Gray's office, passing the hydroponics pool on the sun deck. Sweeping past the empty observation area—normally packed with people desperate for fresh air—Miller didn't bother to seek shelter from the drizzle, but plodded through the wind and rain, his mind racing with images of scaly fins, entrails, and the drowned victims of the *Dunn Roven*.

What he would have given for a chance to walk on solid earth! Gripping the railing for balance as the ship swayed, Miller felt his fingers throb with every grasp.

He needed sleep. He needed a hot meal. A lukewarm shower in his cabin and a semi-clean set of sheets seemed like a luxury he didn't deserve.

They were failing. Maybe they were doing their best, but Schaeffer-Yeager had done a fuck-shit job of maintaining control of their compound in Astoria—much thanks to that crazed lunatic Bob Harris, now ash under a nuke of his own making—and somehow, floating on the high seas on a cruise liner, S-Y was doing it again.

They weren't even fighting Infected anymore, aside from random boats here and there, and they were still somehow fucking it up.

Yes, they were self-sustaining, self-policing, and surviving on the high seas, but Miller would hardly call it *living*.

It was purgatory, he realized. Passing the stadium on his way to the Crow's Nest Bar and the rest of Cobalt, the thought crossed his mind. They're trapped in a hellish limbo.

Somewhere between Heaven and Hell lay the oceans of this new Earth—changed by the awoken Archaean parasite and evolved from whatever the hell this new ecosystem had become. Neither free nor slaves, the survivors of New York City merely existed.

Miller knew he should look for solutions, that there must be answers to all this. Somewhere in the depth of all the images floating around his mind, the key to the future lay.

Maybe it didn't. Maybe that was just fatigue talking.

His mind wandered to thoughts of Samantha and the Archaeans, left behind in the fallout of Harris's nuclear bomb. Then voices raised in anger caught his attention, dragging him back to the ship.

"I don't have time for this!" Doyle was yelling.

Miller entered the bar and surveyed the scene.

Standing from his stool in the corner, Doyle swiped his hands in the air at Hsiung's fist. "Give it to me."

Stepping back, Hsiung swung her fist high and away, extending her free hand in front of her to fend the sniper off. "No."

"This is none of your business," Doyle spat, red-faced.

"It is if you're on this shit while on duty," Hsiung shot back.

"Never bothered you before. Besides, what I do in my downtime is not your concern."

"There's no such thing as downtime anymore," du Trieux drawled.

"Bugger off," Doyle snapped at her.

"What the hell is going on here?" Miller asked, stepping into the middle of the room and positioning himself between Doyle and Hsiung.

No one spoke a word. No one moved.

From his perch behind the bar, Morland merely shook his head, then looked to the floor. Du Trieux, standing beside the door, stared back at Miller with a blank expression.

"Does someone want to explain to me what's happened?" Miller pressed.

More silence.

Finally, Hsiung lowered her arms and held out a plastic baggie toward Miller. He knew immediately what it was.

Doyle stepped forward to retrieve it, but Miller

beat him to it, snatching it from Hsiung's hand. He looked inside the baggie at the thin piece of paper. There was hardly any left—a square barely three by three inches.

He hadn't known Doyle was still on the stuff. Miller wasn't sure where or how Doyle had managed to get more, if he had. He'd assumed, given how rough Doyle had behaved at the beginning of their sea voyage, that he had come off his addiction—hell, Miller had taken some himself, during the worst of the Charismatics battles—but to know that Doyle was still taking it was unwelcome news. He thought this was over with.

How had he missed this?

"Where'd you get this?" he asked Doyle.

"You fucking hypocrite," he said.

"Where did you get this?" Miller repeated.

Doyle clenched his jaw and spoke through tight teeth. "That's old."

"You don't have someone cooking this aboard, do you?"

"No," Doyle said.

"He's high as a kite," Hsiung said. "Look at him. His pupils are black holes."

"Have I ever missed a shot?" Doyle spat at her. "Have I ever *not* done my job?"

"That's not the point and you know it," Hsiung argued. "We could get called up at any moment. Haven't you noticed? It's twenty-four-seven on this stupid boat."

"I know," Doyle said, reaching his hand out to

Miller for the baggie. "Don't you think I *know* that?"

Miller tightened his fingers around the plastic. He knew Doyle had been acting tense lately—hell, he could hardly blame him—but he'd always believed Doyle had a handle on his drug use.

Doyle was right about one thing: he'd never missed a shot. He'd never been off his game, at least, not that Miller had noticed.

Had Miller been so distracted with his own shit he'd failed to see Doyle struggling? He didn't think so, but it was a real possibility. He wasn't perfect.

"Okay," Miller said, handing the baggie to Doyle.

Doyle took it and stuffed it in his pocket.

Hsiung cursed and kicked a barstool.

"But if I find out you've got a supplier on board, then you and I have a problem. You understand?"

Doyle had good enough sense to look sheepish. "You got it, boss."

"Last thing we need on this ship is a bunch of strung-out refugees."

"I said, I got it," Doyle said, sinking back onto his stool.

"This is bullshit," Hsiung said, walking out the door.

Miller had no reply to that. He looked to du Trieux and Morland, then back to Doyle. "Get some sleep. That's an order."

Wordlessly, Doyle hopped off his bar stool and exited. Morland followed behind them, mumbling his good-bye.

Du Trieux lingered at the Crow's Nest door, her arms across her chest.

"You got something you want to say, Trix?"

She pursed her lips, then shook her head. "No." Then she left, leaving Miller alone in the bar.

Standing there with his thoughts and in the wake of his deteriorating team, he'd have given his whole left leg for a shot of whiskey.

ANGER AND FRUSTRATION pulled Samantha down, threatening to drag her into darkness.

Before her, the farm swirled in disarray as people slapped locust-armadillos out of the air, cursing in loud, chanting voices with every swipe.

At the mouth of the greenhouse, she watched the turmoil, equally disgusted at the display and intoxicated by its power.

"Fuck!" shrieked Joseph beside her, slapping at the locusts.

Samantha reached out and gripped his forearm, concentrating on filling his mind with a controlled, steady energy. "We must stop them," she said to him as he raged.

They stood together, their feelings mingling. Joseph's frustration pulsed as her cognizance soothed. Back and forth, ebbing and flowing, Samantha gradually prevailed, bringing Joseph into the light and using him to amplify her sedate message.

A ripple of calm floated from them, cascading across the field of enraged Infected until their arms fell, their cursing subsided, and finally they stood among the smokers and the locust-armadillos, staring about themselves in confusion.

"Cut the smokers," Joseph shouted across the field.

The rattling din of the motors stopped. The roar of the insects was almost quiet in the aftermath.

Confident the crisis had been averted, Samantha dropped her hand from Joseph's arm.

He looked at her with an expression of bewildered awe. "How is it possible for one person to wield so much power?"

Samantha shrugged off the suspicion coming off him and stepped into the field. Ignoring the puzzled expressions and moods radiating from the crowd, she walked down to a small crowd gathered beside the farmhouse.

A rising sense of perplexity radiated from the group, as they parted to reveal Susie—the Archaean—lying on the ground, bloodied and bruised beside her trashed smoker.

"What happened?" Samantha cried, dropping to her knees beside her and pulling off her own overshirt to cushion the woman's head against the ground. "Who did this? How?"

Semi-conscious, Susie blinked at Samantha. "The Regulars."

Hot shame blazed off the crowd and in unison they took a step back and away from Samantha and Susie. Sam's mouth went dry.

It was common knowledge since the spread of the Archaean parasite that once an individual had been accepted into a commune, it was impossible for another member to harm them. It was as if they had beaten *themselves* into the ground.

How was it now that they had turned on their own?

"Take her inside," Samantha said, fighting her dread. It would serve no one to whip them into a panic again. "Tend to her wounds."

As they dispersed, lifting Susie from the ground and carrying her inside the house, Joseph approached and helped Sam back to her feet.

"How—?" he began.

"The guilt. Do you feel it? She must have been struck during the burst of anger, and then a mob formed. I saw it often enough during the invasion." She stopped and took a moment to push reassurance toward Joseph. The remorse emanating from him was strong. "It couldn't have been prevented, Joe. Mobs are a natural consequence of the hive-mind."

"Maybe so," Joseph said, his mouth forming a thin, grim line. "But to turn on one of their own?"

"We're not their own, are we?" Samantha said. "She was an Archaean."

IT WAS SOME days later, and they sat around picnic tables in the barn. Long strips of daylight fell across the floor from the open loft door and windows overhead. There had been no horses for years, but the barn still smelled of oats, hay, and manure.

Around the tables sat Joseph, Susie—still black and blue, her arm in a sling—and the 'Bishops,' the ruling Archaeans, of each of the ten commune farms. Samantha stood and cleared her throat.

"We hold this meeting," Sam began, "to discuss..."

"...the commune is failing," Joseph said.

The talk came in a rush of feelings and words.

"There won't be enough food for winter—"

"—we'll need alternative sources—"

"—what about the archers?"

"There hasn't been any game in weeks—"

"—we'll have to expand the hunting perimeter—"

"—what about the livestock?"

"One thug-behemoth could feed a farm for a week."

"There aren't that many left—"

"—we let most of them go when the grain crops failed."

"Perhaps we should leave, look for alternative land—"

"—the northeast is too cold during the winter, we should head south—"

"—how will we feed the commune during a migration—?"

"—we should have left already—"

"—the trees have begun to turn—"

"—it will snow soon—"

"What about vehicles?"

"There isn't enough fuel—"

"—we could ride the husk-mutts—?"

"—they'll eat the Regulars—"

"—we can't stay, we'll starve—"

"—we can't leave, we'll freeze."

Samantha rapped her knuckles against the table, turning all heads toward her. "The crops have failed. The environment is uncooperative. We have no *choice* but to leave. Staying here will only result in death—the elderly and children are already in imminent danger."

"The elderly and young won't be able to keep up if we migrate."

"We could leave them here—"

"—split the commune—?"

"—not an option—"

"—either solution presents problems—"

"—what about rationing—?"

"—slaughter every beast, salt the meat—"

"—train more archers—"

"—no other alternative."

Joseph, standing from his position to Samantha's right, waved his hand in the air. "It's decided. We fortify for the winter."

"Wait—" Samantha said, absently reaching out to touch his arm.

He jerked his arm out of her grasp and pulled it behind him. "We will not succumb to your will simply because you wish it."

"Joseph..."

"Meeting adjourned," he said as he moved away, heading out the barn and into the sunlight outside.

Samantha felt the resentment and anxiety of the others as they dispersed, heading back to their duties and glancing back at her.

This was not something she had anticipated. The structure of the commune, by design, was meant to give the Archaeans the power to influence the Regulars and maintain order. Since their arrival at the farms, that system had done just that. It seemed only right, and necessary, that there would be a driving force leading the Archaeans as well.

Back during the invasion, it was Samantha's link to Alex and the humans that had saved them from the blast in New York City. Just a few days ago, it had been Samantha's ability to maintain individuality outside the collective mind which had saved the yucca-flax farm from deteriorating into madness. How was it, after all that had transpired, she was now being met with distrust? As if Samantha had ever had a thought in her mind against the commune? As if she hadn't *devoted* herself to the care and cultivation of the Archaean life?

But as the Bishops left the barn and she remained alone, Samantha realized her tenuous position.

How did one rule a group who distrusted any leader with the strength to rule? Harder yet: how did one rule *without being a ruler?* She had seen firsthand how the hive-mind could deteriorate. So had Joseph, now, for that matter. What other choice did he think she'd had but to impose her own calm on the mob?

She shuddered to think what would have become of the Regulars, not to mention Susie.

The possibilities left a sour taste on her tongue. Worse was the look Joseph gave her as she stepped out of the barn and into the muddy field to resume her work at the clean up. They locked eyes for just a moment before he moved off, and her gut lurched.

THERE WAS A change, like the shifting of the wind. Where once it had blown freely, without resistance—always filling her up and moving her forward—now the wind came at Samantha from all directions, pulling, pushing, twisting her around, sapping her energy.

The commune was evolving. The hierarchy the Archaeans had conceived had altered. No longer were the Archaeans controlling the farms directly; instead, on Joseph's urging, they were delving into the hive-mind to find a consensus and then ruling by committee.

A true democracy wasn't a horrible mode of rule, Samantha supposed, but only if the majority were an intelligent, well-rounded lot that weren't partial to forming angry mobs and ignoring personal hygiene—but that wasn't the case.

Several days into their winter fortification plans, Samantha caught the first signs of deterioration. It began with suspicious glances from the workers at the farm she controlled with Joseph and Chris—glaring eyes that jerked away as she walked by. As the days passed, she felt their animosity, their resentfulness pushing at her from all sides.

Muttered imprecations regarding her disloyalty to the commune spread through the farms like cancer, blackening the souls within and turning each away from her. It became so toxic, so quickly, that Samantha took to dividing her days between farms—working in the morning at her own, reseeding the alfalfa-barley, and then moving off in the afternoon to work elsewhere.

She wanted to think it was all in her imagination. Perhaps paranoia had begun to take hold. But the hive-mind provided perfect clarity to the feelings of the others, and from what Samantha could tell, her position in the community—and her safety—were in jeopardy more and more each day.

Finally, while standing in line for her midday meal a month after the incident with Susie at the greenhouse, Sam noticed that not only had the Regulars in line developed patches of fungus, but the two other resident Archaeans—Thomas and Wilma—had begun to grow them as well.

After receiving her plate—a fried grain patty, a half-cup of vegetables and a strip of meat jerky—Samantha sat at the crowded picnic tables inside the barn and ate in silence, feeling besieged, and with the undeniable urge to scratch her skin raw.

When had they stopped enforcing the personal hygiene regiments, she wondered? How was that a good idea?

From the corner of the barn, beside one of the stalls currently used for storage, a woman's laugh pierced the clanging of dishes and the scraping of forks upon plates.

Samantha didn't know what the woman had

found so funny, but like a ripple, the laugh spread across the room. Before long, the entirety of the group, over a hundred people, were all cackling in sheer glee.

Samantha couldn't help herself and joined in—the merriment was too strong to push away—but the moment her soft, hesitant chuckle fused with the multitude, the laughter stopped. With an abrupt yank, the gaiety was gone, replaced instead with glares of disdain and a swell of resentment.

Samantha's face grew hot. She stood from the picnic table, placed her plate and utensils into the bin, and exited the barn.

The weight of over two hundred eyeballs drilled into her back.

She was unsafe; she knew it with a certainty. The tide had turned against her. Just as she was about to break into a run, certain she had put enough distance between her and the barn, she heard footsteps behind her.

She looked over her shoulder. The barn was empty. Every man and woman had followed her out into the field.

Samantha swallowed her panic and tried to remain calm. She couldn't tell what had her more terrified—the sight of the mob, or the hatred washing off them.

How had they turned so quickly against her? What had she *done*, other than try to help them?

They were not running at her, or even carrying weapons, but the malicious intent was undeniable.

Should she run? Would they chase her? Should she

stand and fight? Maybe if she pushed a feeling of love and acceptance at them, it might stop a few... but a hundred?

She stepped backwards, keeping her face to the onslaught as she moved away—one arm thrust behind her, the other held out as if to ward them off. A good twenty meters behind her sat the farm house; to her left—slightly closer—was the corral of tamed husk-mutts.

The muddy field squashed under her feet, sticking her worn boots to the ground and slowing her pace. The sun blazed down onto her head, burning the parting in her hair. Blinking in the stark brightness, she fought to maintain eye contact with the approaching horde, but their eyes had glazed over, as if they didn't see her anymore.

Her instincts told her to crack a joke—maybe lighten the mood with a silly quip or a remark about the weather—but she knew it was hopeless. She could feel their outrage and revulsion. She felt it toward herself as well.

"Hey, what's going on out here?" Susie let the farm house screen door close with a *whap*, then adjusted her arm in the sling with a grunt. "I felt someth—" She didn't finish the sentence.

Sam's stomach roiled as she was surrounded. With the crowd in front of her, and Susie and the farm house staff behind, there was no escaping. She would never reach the corral in time. The forest was an equally bad idea—full of beasts and deserters and heaven knew what else. She would die on that muddy field, torn to shreds by the very people she had helped destroy New York City to save.

She heard footsteps in the mud behind her. Susie approached, her free hand loosely holding a dish towel.

Samantha's mouth went dry as she choked back a sob. Taking what she felt was her last step, she stopped in her tracks, resigned to her fate.

A hand clasped her shoulder. Sam felt a prick of sympathy, a deep and uncomplicated encouragement. Instead of wrapping the towel around her throat and squeezing the air from Sam's lungs, Susie leaned in and whispered into her ear, "Run."

7

ANOTHER DAY AT sea, Miller mused, squinting into the white, soaring sun. Another day tasting salt on his lips. Another day of the sticky film that coated his hair and skin and never seemed to wash off, no matter if he used his entire water ration scrubbing.

Other people had had the same thought. In families and groups of friends, occupants of the *Tevatnoa* crowded the railings around the top deck observation area and stared at the glassy water.

At least the ocean was calm today. For whatever reason, it had exorcized its demons the previous day, and was giving the *Tevatnoa* a reprieve.

It wouldn't last, but Miller would appreciate it while it did. Apparently these other folks around him were as well.

He closed his eyes against the burning sun and listened to the wind in his ears, the hum of the engines, the water splashing and sloshing beneath him, and for just now, he was fine.

Then, like the pounding of a judge's gavel, the sound of heavy boot-steps arose behind him, and the moment shattered like the glassy sea.

Miller twisted to face Morland, who had shaved and combed his hair, looking almost dapper since the previous night's scuffle in the bar—which was more than Miller had done.

"Sir," Morland said. "There's been another distress call."

Miller didn't even bother to register his disappointment. He just turned and strode off, Morland following at his heels.

"Has another boat capsized?"

"No, sir. Looks like some bugger's trying to steal the fishing trawler."

Miller shook his head, barely missing a stride as he made his way back to his living quarters to get dressed and grab his weapons. "Are you kidding me?"

"Wish I were."

"Jesus, does it never end?"

Morland didn't bother to respond.

THE *DAWN RISING* was a stern trawler they'd picked up by Martha's Vineyard, shortly after they'd found the *Dunn Roven*. About forty-six meters in length, the ship could net up to two hundred tons of fish a day, depending on the weather, their location, and the currents.

It was arguably the most important vessel in the

fleet. More vital than the cruise liners, and certainly more useful than the sail boats or the yacht had been.

With only ten crew members, it was also the most vulnerable. This was not the first time Cobalt had been called up to intervene on their behalf, even after Gray assigned three additional security guards to the crew.

Twice before, they'd been attacked by pirates: once from a ship in S-Y's own fleet and once by a random ferry filled with an Infected commune they'd scared off with a few warning shots.

This round, it appeared, was from within their ranks again. *Minerva's Wand* was a ten-meter sailboat, designed for speed. Lightweight, with a hull made of balsa wood and fiberglass, it had a fifteen-horsepower diesel engine with a saildrive transmission—but since it had run out of fuel ages ago, it depended solely on wind power to keep up with the fleet, and had continually struggled to do so.

Manned by seven people, designed to house two, the sailboat wallowed in almost any sea; it wasn't uncommon for *Minerva's Wand* to request the fleet slow down for them to catch up. Miller had heard Gray complain about that more than once.

Honestly, he thought, it wasn't as if the fleet was in any sort of rush—but the cruise liners could certainly go faster if they wanted, and it wasted time and energy to slow down every time the sailboats lost the wind.

Miller understood why Gray was annoyed. It seemed to him, as he rode the dinghy toward the

Dawn Rising, that what *Minerva's Wand* should have done is stock-pile rations so they could leave the fleet and head off on their own, which would have been fine by Gray and Lewis, and for Miller too—given how many times they'd slowed down to accommodate them—instead of blasting their way onto the *Dawn Rising* and demanding extra food, which is apparently what they had done.

When they'd spotted the *Minerva's Wand* some three nautical miles behind, not even attempting to catch up to the fleet, Miller grew even more suspicious. The boat, sails not only down but removed altogether, floated out in the calm waters, eerily still and empty. It hadn't responded to a single request for communication either, which Miller found equally odd.

"I'm getting really tired of playing watch dog," Morland said, from beside him in the dinghy. He wiped sea water from his safety goggles, did it again, then gave up, taking them off and squinting into the sun.

No one replied, not even Miller.

The incident between Hsiung and Doyle the previous day had left things tense. Miller found it equal parts amusing and irritating how Cobalt all looked ahead at the *Dawn Rising* and refused to look at each other; he just hoped they pulled their shit together by the time they reached the trawler.

On reaching the fishing vessel, Hsiung steered the dinghy up the back ramp, driving it straight up the embankment and cutting the engine almost immediately. The trawler nets were out, giving Cobalt clear access. Sprinting onto deck, Miller noted two plastic two-man kayaks, the oars tossed aside as if discarded.

He snapped the safety off his M27 and glared at the kayaks in confusion.

Apparently du Trieux had had the same thought. "How would they carry the fish back in those?"

Miller shook his head as the others prepared their weapons.

Doyle shouldered the strap of his .388 custom rifle and rubbed his sweaty nose on the back of his hand. "So, they're reckless *and* stupid."

Hsiung raised an eyebrow. "Takes one to know—"

"Fuck off," he spat.

"Enough," Miller snapped, feeling more like a referee than a commanding officer. "Watch your sixes."

They fanned out in a three-by-two formation. After a quick sweep of the lower deck, which was empty, they made their way slowly up the ladders on either side to mid-deck, where they merged and rose higher again.

Having met no resistance thus far, Miller suspected the pirates were either grouped inside the wheelhouse, or keeping the crew hostage in the barracks below. First things first, however—they needed to determine who was piloting the ship.

Up two flights to the main deck, they entered the wheelhouse, three on the right, two on the left, guns drawn.

The pirates were waiting inside: three emaciated men, holding spear guns, standing among the trawler's seven-strong crew. The trawler's captain, a bearded man in his forties, stood behind the steering wheel. Raising his hands toward Cobalt he shouted, "Hold your fire!"

"Drop your weapons," Miller ordered the pirates.

At first glance, the crew didn't look wounded, or even worried. In fact, given that there were seven of them, and only three skinny pirates, Miller immediately wondered why there were still pirates aboard at all, when the crew could clearly have overpowered them.

Scanning the wheelhouse, Miller paused to examine the pirates. The emaciated men looked about ready to collapse. One swayed on his feet as his spear gun dipped in his palms, while another had to work to stay awake—his eyes closing and snapping open with regularity.

Miller lowered his M27.

"Put 'em down!" Doyle barked, red-faced and jittery, still pointing his sidearm at the nearest pirate.

"Now!" Morland added.

"Hold your fire!" the trawler captain shouted again. "Please!" Turning his attention back toward the emaciated men, he almost looked apologetic. "See, Greg. See? I told you. Nobody's getting hurt. Nobody. Just put down the spears. Put them down."

The man in the center of the three pirates gawked at the captain with a look Miller couldn't quite place. His clothes were threadbare, his ribs visibly protruded like he hadn't eaten in months. He blinked slowly at the captain, then stumbled once as if he were about to pass out. As the trawler swayed, he buckled to his knees. When he went down, Cobalt surged forward. In a few moments, the three pirates were in custody, not a shot fired.

"Get these three medical attention," the captain said to Miller. "They've been through enough." Then he barked orders to his crew to check the trawlers and the men scurried off to work.

"What happened here?" Miller asked him. "Where's your security squad?"

The captain rubbed the back of his neck. "I sent them below. We're not interested in pressing charges. Just feed those guys, will you? Take care of them."

"Captain, you were just held hostage by *pirates*. There's no 'pressing charges.' They'll be punished, there's no doubt of that," Miller said.

"No, you don't understand. I want you to take them back to their ship, let them go. They won't bother us again."

Miller puffed out his cheeks. "I can't do that."

The captain frowned. "Just ask them why they did it." He swallowed thickly and looked out the wheelhouse window. "You'll agree with me."

He doubted it, but Miller turned and left the wheelhouse without further retort. Outside, he found his team assisting the pirates toward the dinghy.

As Hsiung moved one of the starving men, Miller noticed she didn't even have his hands zip-tied. Mid-deck, he stumbled down the ladder; she slung his arm over her shoulder, helping him walk.

Across the water on the dinghy and back toward the *Tevatnoa*, all three of the pirates lay on the raft floor glancing over their shoulders at their former boat. It was nothing more than a speck on the horizon now. Then, with glassy eyes, they looked to one another, expressions grim.

"Were you not given enough food rations?" du Trieux asked, raising her voice over the wind.

They didn't answer at first, only looked to their bony hands, then out again toward the approaching *Tevatnoa*.

"How did you become so sick?" she continued. "Are you unwell?"

"We're not infectious, if that is what you're worried about," one man said. He had a thick Spanish accent and a patchy beard. "You cannot catch what we have."

"What do you have?" Morland asked flatly.

"Bleeding hearts," one of the other men said.

Hsiung's face contorted.

"Bollocks," Doyle retorted.

The man nearest Hsiung shook his head. "He means our hearts are broken. Two of us died from sea sickness yesterday. We had been giving our rations to them for weeks to save them. But this storm—we ran out, and no one was able to get us more."

"That's no excuse—" Doyle began, his face red.

"Then the children died," one of them said, and

Doyle paled. "We just wanted to get more. Just a few fish more for Lizette, their mother. But they raised the alert when they saw us coming. Then they said they would give us some, but it was too late. You came."

"You're telling me there's a woman alone on your boat, right now?" Doyle asked.

"Why didn't you request medical aid?" Miller asked, aghast. "Why didn't you raise your distress flag?"

"Turn the boat around. We can get her on the way in," Doyle said to Hsiung, who sat at the rear, steering.

The man closest to her placed a skeletal hand on her arm. "It's too late."

"We called for aid," one of the men said. "We raised the flag. For three days. They said to take it down, that help would come as soon as it could. No one came. And then the children died and Lizette used our last bullet on herself."

"We just wanted a couple of fish," said the last man, his head resting against the side of the dinghy, swaying with the motion of the boat. "To tide us over until the rest came."

"Jesus, we were out in the water *yesterday*," Morland said, gaping, then shut his mouth when Miller glared at him.

"It doesn't matter," said the first man. He closed his eyes against the sun and seemed to fall asleep.

Miller closed his lips tight and breathed slowly to calm himself. He wanted to punch the fucking ocean in the jaw, if it had one. He wanted to yell holy hell at whoever had handled this situation, although he knew there wasn't much any of the rationing officers aboard the *Tevatnoa* could have done.

As the dinghy slowed on approach, Miller's face grew hot and his hands closed into fists.

He knew what would happen next. They would bring the pirates aboard. The men would get rudimentary medical attention, and then brought before the tribunal and hanged. Gray would barely bat an eye, and Lewis wouldn't miss a wink of sleep.

By tomorrow, these three men would be dead.

And all for a few measly fish.

THE MOB SWARMED, coming at Samantha and Susie like a freight train. With a shove, Susie pushed Samantha behind her and stood tall before the crowd. "Sam, *run!*"

Spreading her arms out, Susie pushed love and forgiveness through the whole of her being; she managed to reach a good half-dozen people before the horde overtook her. Her screams echoed over the noises that followed.

Samantha watched with rising horror as Susie was stamped to death, then did the only thing she could. She turned and ran.

She waded through the muddy field to the corral in seconds. Behind her, the mob finished their work on Susie, then stampeded toward her.

Sam climbed over the fence and fell to the ground, then scrambled to her feet, backing away from the flimsy barrier and into the center of the pen. The fence—three split rails held together with barbed wire—would hardly keep the horde at bay, but the three beasts within might.

Sensing her terror, the trio of husk-mutts paced about Sam, growling and pawing the ground with razor-sharp claws.

The Regulars pressed up against the circular fence and watched her warily—the two other Archaeans, Thomas and Wilma, among them. Concerned they would turn the animals against her, Sam pushed feelings of attachment and loyalty into the creatures to forestall them, but felt no opposing pulses from the other Archaeans. They seemed to have lost their ability to commune with the difficult animals.

Just then, Samantha had a horrifying idea. Sensing her determination, the beasts slowed their scratching around the corral and turned outward, facing the crowd gathered at the fence.

A warm hide nudged Samantha's hip and she turned to find the largest of the beasts at her side. She swung her leg over, gripped the skin at the animal's nape, and then urged it forward with a kick of her heels.

Kneeling back on their haunches, the other beasts leapt into the air, clearing the fence and scattering half the crowd, knocking them far and wide.

Samantha waited for the count of three and followed, jumping the fence after them. As the first two mutts slashed and clawed their way through the horde of screaming Infected, Samantha rode the third mutt through their wake—coming out the other side of the crowd, tearing over the muddy field, and breaking free of the farm.

Samantha rode down the footpath and onto the adjoining dirt road, tapping the beast to go faster. Fighting self-revulsion and defeat, she shook her head and squinted at the road ahead, trying to keep alert and ready for what might come next. The roads were unusually clear. Normally there would be Infected walking between farms, transporting supplies via thug behemoth-drawn carts, paying social visits, but now there was no one to be seen.

Something was wrong, terribly wrong. Where the hell *was* everyone?

Ahead and to the right, the tomato-squash farm flew by, but the area radiated rage so thickly Sam felt it all the way from the road. Cutting through the trees lining the lane, she turned the husk-mutt toward the farm, determined to either rally them to her defence, or save the resident Archaeans from a fate like Susie's, but once she cleared the trees, she pulled up short.

Below, approximately half a kilometer downslope, the farm was in pandemonium. She was too late. A mob had formed to the right of the field, where two Archaeans—a man and woman—were being hacked to death by a handful of Regulars wielding machetes.

How and why the mob mentality had spread so far and so quickly was baffling, but it was apparent to Sam that any attempt to interfere would only result in her own death. Sickened but determined, she pulled the husk-mutt around and headed back up the embankment, through the trees and onto the road. As she pounded back and forth down the lane, passing farms along the way, she heard the screams and felt the anger rolling off the other properties. Every farm she passed was overrun with chaos. The maddening energy was thick in the air; Samantha had to fight not to join in, even kilometers away on the road.

The only thought that kept her focused was the need to escape. Running off into the forest with nothing but the clothes on her back—especially with the coming winter—would be a recipe for death, so she formulated plans, worked through worst-case scenarios, plotted her getaway.

She had to get back to her farm. She had to somehow sneak in past the horde, gather supplies, and get back out without detection—and without a hint of emotion. If she felt anything—fear, terror, sympathy toward the other Archaeans—she would be detected.

Clearing her mind and concentrating solely on breathing, Sam led the husk-mutt to the outskirts of the main farm and immediately failed at controlling herself.

The outside of the farmhouse was on fire, flames reaching the top of the two-story walls. As far as she could tell, the interior hadn't caught—there was no smoke or fire coming from the windows—but the sight of it filled Sam's belly with dread. She half expected a mob of Infected to come barrelling around the corner to tear her flesh from her bones, but the farm appeared quiet, abandoned but for a handful of Infected gathered around the barn. They seemed distracted by something happening inside; they crowded around the doorway, peering over the tops of each other's heads.

Seizing the opportunity, Samantha hopped off her husk-mutt and ran down the footpath to the farmhouse's back door.

The handle felt hot to the touch, but she risked it anyway, using the tail of her shirt to twist the knob. The door opened, spilling a plume of smoke out and around her. Samantha pulled her bandana up and over her mouth and nose and pushed inside.

The kitchen was empty. Passing through the central room and up the wooden stairs, she reached the bedroom she shared and set to work rummaging through it.

Winter coats were rare. It was due to be a major issue for the commune once the first snowfall came, but she couldn't worry about that. She had vague memories of an Infected woman wearing a down-lined jacket when she had first arrived, and knew she slept in a pile of blankets beside the window, but after digging through the corner for several seconds to no avail, Sam gave up the search and moved on.

Under one bed she found a scarf; another hid a pair of gloves and a knitted cap. Despite her best efforts, the closest she came to a coat was a faded denim jacket with large metal buttons and an embroidered biker emblem on the back. She threw it on and stuffed the gloves and hat in the pockets.

Smoke in the room was turning the air black, and it was becoming increasingly difficult to breathe.

Giving up her search, Sam left the room and rushed down the stairs, the scarf trailing from her hand like a kite.

She turned at a loud, wooden *crack*, to see that the walls of the main room had begun to burn. Flames trailed up and over the tattered wallpaper, spreading across the ceiling like a river of fire.

Holding her breath, Sam raised her arm over her mouth and bolted though the flames and smoke, coming out into the kitchen and smashing into the small table and chairs. She staggered, spinning, to avoid going over, and the knitted scarf in her hands swung wide, passing through the flames. The end caught quickly, scorching up the synthetic yard like the wick of a cartoon bomb. Tossing the scarf, Sam dashed around the table and grabbed the kitchen door knob, searing her skin on the scorching metal and involuntarily screaming.

Pushing her burned hand into the jean jacket pocket, she used the fabric as a buffer and turned the knob, then spilled out into the back yard of the farm house, coughing.

Wet laundry hung abandoned on the line, turning dark in the ash and soot falling from the fire. Samantha managed to find two pairs of thick white socks and a pair of men's long underwear, tossed them over her shoulder, then skirted around the corner and into the adjacent forest.

From the tree line, she felt safe enough to move around the house fire and observe the fields on the other side.

As she feared, the mob had left the barn and were now in the center of the alfalfa-barley field. Joseph and Chris stood in the middle. At first, the crowd did nothing but poke and jab at the two men with fingers and open palms, and Sam momentarily felt a spark of hope. Perhaps the rage had not spread to every farm?

Her hope was quickly dashed, however, when she saw what they had been waiting for.

A Regular, Aaron—his blotchy fungal infection noticeable even from where Samantha hid—walked up from the front of the farm house, carrying a lit torch over his head.

The crowd parted as he approached Joseph and Chris, who still remained unmoving at the middle of the crowd.

Joseph then turned, said something to Chris, and reached out his hand to Aaron. He took the torch— nothing more than a burning plank pried from the house—and lit Chris on fire.

The crowd drew back, giving Samantha a clearer view. She realized Chris was tied to a post, a pile of kindling collected at his feet.

Chris flailed and thrashed against his bindings, his clothing and skin blackening in the flames, his hair going up like a tinderbox, and a cry rose from Sam's throat.

The crowd turned at the sound, searching the treeline, and a handful of them broke off from the mob and walked in her direction. Forgetting all sense, and leaving her husk-mutt behind, Samantha ran into the forest.

OPERATION
BAY
CAT

9

MILLER ENTERED GRAY'S office without knocking.

Gray, sitting at his ping-pong table desk surrounded by slips of paper, looked up and squinted. "That went a lot quicker than expected."

"They were starving," Miller said.

"The *Dawn Rising*? How's that possible? They should be the best fed ship in the fleet."

"No, Gray, *Minerva's Wand*. They've been waiting for rations for *days* and lost three members of their crew—two of them children."

Gray frowned and looked down at the paperwork. "That's unfortunate."

"What happened to their rations?" Miller asked. "You and I both know it wasn't the weather."

Ration packets were delivered to the smaller ships of the S-Y fleet in two ways. On calm days, small drone craft were rigged with nets and flown across the waters, where the payload was dropped on deck.

Unfortunately, that wasn't always viable. If winds weren't an issue, the goliath brutes were: large, blubbery dog-like creatures that plagued the waters. They'd taken to snatching the deliveries from the water if the drone missed the target ship by even a few meters; some even went so far as to board the ships in hopes of catching the net themselves.

Things grew more primitive from there. A delivery squad was equipped with a guard, thrown into a dinghy, and tasked with hand-delivering the rations. But gasoline was in short supply, and the amount spent on ferrying rations to the other ships cut that supply by almost a third in a matter of weeks, especially in the choppy waters.

Then, the goliath brutes seemed to figure out that pattern, and simple food deliveries became running battles. If the brutes weren't bad enough, the tusk-fiends—large pinnipeds with an enormous, and deadly, under-bite—followed suit; and they didn't mind using their colossal teeth to munch the delivery men if the supplies weren't easily obtained.

Entire cargos were lost, crew and all. Out of desperation, Gray then enacted a new edict, both to reduce the risk and to ease the burden on the *Tevatnoa*. From then on, the closest of the two cruise liners would be on the hook for delivering rations, whether by drone, by delivery, or by the zip-lines that were the *Princess Penelope*'s preferred method.

But there was no oversight, no committee or director overseeing rations for the whole fleet, and the *Minerva's Wand*, which had been on the southeast corner of the fleet, should have been cared for by the *Penelope*.

It made some sense that they hadn't any rations during the big three-day storm—those had been difficult conditions—but today had been clear. And there was still no answer as to who had told them to take down their distress flag.

"I'll look into it," Gray said, shuffling his papers.

"Don't bullshit me."

Gray's hands tightened into fists. "Look, Miller, I give you a lot of leeway here. I appreciate you got me and my family out of the compound, I really do—and all those years of service protecting us..."

"I was glad to do it."

"Thank you. We were glad to have you. And I also appreciate that you spear-headed the campaign against the Infected on land, and that you protect this ship and its residents like the soldier you are—"

"I get it, get to the 'but.'"

Gray's face reddened. "...but do not mistake my willingness to listen to your outbursts as a sign that we are somehow equals."

Miller digested this for a moment before answering, "What the fuck, Gray?"

"Let's get one thing straight—*I* am in charge. You have no idea the shit I crawl through every day to keep this boat afloat."

"Now you sound like Harris."

Gray stood from his folding chair, red-faced, and rested his knuckles against the table. "There are life and death decisions made in this room every day."

"You don't think I'm faced with life and death decisions daily? What the hell is the matter with you?"

"There's more to life and death than pulling a trigger."

Miller's mouth went dry. "And there's more to leading this fleet than sitting at that stupid table and playing God. Wake the fuck up. We're *losing*."

"I know that!" Gray snapped, fixing Miller with a glassy stare. "I fucking *know that!* And I don't need some meathead coming in here telling me to do better."

There was a knock at the door.

"Not now!" Miller shouted.

"Come in," Gray said.

The door opened on a doctor from the infirmary. "You'd better come," he said to Gray.

"How bad is it?" Gray asked, dismissing Miller and walking around his desk.

"One hundred and two, at the moment. But the number is rising."

"How long until it's shipwide?" Gray asked as they exited together.

"If we set up quarantine..." the doctor said, and then they were gone.

Miller stood in the center of the office, angry and unfulfilled.

He was wrong. Schaeffer-Yeager wasn't losing the fight for survival.

They'd already lost.

* * *

MILLER RETREATED TOWARD the Crow's Nest, in the hopes of taking a moment to unwind with his team. Tensions had been high since the *Dunn Roven* recovery, and after the oddly anti-climactic situation on the fishing trawler he was certain his team would need loosening.

Perhaps a round of Texas Hold'em was in order, or he could fire up the karaoke machine they'd found stashed behind the bar. Surprisingly, Morland could sing Sinatra like Ol' Blue Eyes himself; on previous occasions, his rendition of 'My Way' had bent Doyle in half with laughter. Whatever they did, relaxation was in order.

The first thing he noticed, as he stepped into the bar, was Doyle, curled into a ball and lying on the floor beside his overturned bar stool. He was slick with sweat and visibly shaking, as if riddled with fever, his tears flowing into the carpet.

Du Trieux stood over him, one arm hovering protectively above Doyle's face, the other warding off Hsiung, who stood in the middle of the room in a white surgical mask.

Morland stood behind the bar, palms pressed against the wood-grained countertop, as if he were about to clamber over it into the middle of the room. As Miller entered, however, he froze.

"He should be in the infirmary!" Hsiung shouted.

"Back off, I said. Just back off," du Trieux hollered.

"He's going to infect us all!"

"He's not contagious," du Trieux said.

"How the hell can you say that? Look at him!" Hsiung shot back.

"What's the matter with him?" Miller asked. He was talking to du Trieux, but Hsiung wheeled on him with a look of stark panic.

"He's got flu!" she shouted. "The one that wiped out the second deck. This whole ship is infected!"

"Trix?"

"He's in withdrawal," she said.

"Search him," Miller said, closing the door behind him. He walked around the bar toward Morland, grabbed a dish towel, wet it from the faucet and tossed it to du Trieux, who caught it one-handed, already rifling Doyle's pockets.

Sure enough, she found the plastic baggie, which still held the last scrap of drug-paper. When Miller approached, she handed the baggie to him, then began removing Doyle's Flex body armor and utility belt. "I didn't realize he'd gone cold turkey," she said, propping Doyle's head up with his vest.

Behind them, a humbled Hsiung pulled down her parachute hammock, then crossed the room and laid it over Doyle's body for warmth.

Du Trieux placed the wet wash cloth on Doyle's soaked face and shushed him once, but he didn't seem to hear. Engrossed in some sort of agitated argument with no one in particular, he thrashed back and forth in a twitchy state, then called himself a 'wanker' and told himself to shut up.

Eventually, when his flailing and mumbling seemed to calm, du Trieux scooted back from him and asked

Morland to toss her an ice bucket. Propping her back against the wall, she set it beside her and sighed; waiting for the nausea to start, Miller guessed.

Pulling up a stool, he sat down and leancd the back of his head against the wall as Morland took up his favorite position behind the bar.

Hsiung slouched on the floor where her hammock once hung, then pulled the surgical mask off her mouth. "I'm sorry. I thought—"

Du Trieux shook her head. "You didn't know."

Morland cleared his throat. "Now what do we do?"

"We wait," Miller said, and the room fell silent. He closed his eyes and concentrated on the noises outside, but it brought him no comfort. All he could hear was the howling sea wind and the rage of an untamed, resentful ocean.

10

SAMANTHA RAN THROUGH the forest at breakneck speed for as long as her legs permitted. She had no idea how long she ran, but when her left knee gave out and she crashed to the forest floor, her throat was raw, her lungs burned, her hands had gone numb, and she had no idea where she was.

Night was falling. Overhead, the stars were peering down through a spider web of naked tree branches. The moon, a shard of a crescent, looked purple amidst the scattered clouds. The chill air prickled the sweat on her brow, her breath rising as a willowy mist. If she didn't find shelter soon, she'd be dead within hours.

She rooted through her pockets for the gloves she'd stolen, only to realize she had dropped one at some point. Sighing, she put the orphan glove onto her right hand, a white sock on the other. Buttoning her jacket closed, she also put on the hat and used the long johns as a wrap.

There was nothing around but trees. Fallen trees, leaning trees, standing trees, slender, broad, short and tall trees—but nothing else. No caves, no convenient hunting sheds or cabins. The ground was littered with branches and dead leaves and the occasional stone or mossy boulder, but nothing of use. The far cries of animals and the buzzing of invisible insects crackled all around her ears, chilling Samantha more than the dropping temperatures.

Setting to work, she combed the surrounding few meters, collecting broken tree trunks and limbs from the ground. Stacking them side by side against a bowed tree, she eventually had a rudimentary lean-to. Scraping the nearby rocks and boulders, she stuffed the seams of her shelter with moss and lined the floor with pine needles. It was damp and smelled of earth and rot, but it was several degrees warmer and would have to suffice until morning. She dared not start a fire.

Exhausted, Samantha lay down, covered herself with the pine needles and closed her eyes. It was a while before sleep came, but when it did, she sank deep and hard into slumber, Chris's dying screams echoing in her dreams.

"THIS CAN'T BE a good sign," a man's voice said.

"We should send a party back to the commune and see what happened," a woman replied.

"Why bother? She'll tell us."

Samantha felt a nudge on her knee, and dragged

her eyelids open. She had thought she'd been dreaming the voices, but it clearly wasn't the case. A man and a woman stood at the opening of her shelter carrying homemade spears and masked in mud, but she recognised them both: deserters from the avocado orchard.

This could go one of two ways: very well, or very badly.

"Binh," Samantha said, sitting up and brushing the needles from her clothes. "Anita. Hello."

"Samantha," Binh said. Smug satisfaction rang in his words. "Rough night?"

"You could say that." Sam stood and knocked the last of her makeshift blanket to the forest floor. She eyed them warily, taking in their appearance and stretching out her feelings to theirs, but hit a wall. She shook her head as if stung.

Anita frowned, but Binh smiled.

Either they had learned to refuse to commune with other Infected—which Samantha hadn't thought was possible—or something else was wrong. Either way it left her feeling naked, exposed. Vulnerable. It had been years since the only feelings in her body were her own. "How's the hunting this morning?" she asked, trying to seem nonchalant.

"Horrible," Anita said, frown deepening. "You scared everything away with your smell and this dumbass shelter of yours. Our camp is a good kilometer from here and even we heard you moaning and groaning half the night."

"You were shouting in your sleep," Binh said.

Samantha blinked. "That's not true."

"Who's Alex, then?" Binh added, raising an eyebrow.

Samantha wanted to smack the smirk off his muddy face, but it wouldn't help her situation. So far they didn't seem hostile, but who knew how they would act if she got snippy? And why wouldn't they commune? It had been a good few minutes.

"An old friend," she said, trying to push her feelings down.

It didn't seem to work however, as Anita smiled. "Interesting."

"The farms have disintegrated into chaos," Samantha blurted, hoping the words would sting them—at least a little—jolt them into some sort of connection.

They nodded, but nothing changed.

"And what part did you play in it?" Anita asked, drumming her fingers on her spear.

"No part. I barely escaped with my life." The words felt foreign on her tongue, and untrue— despite their accuracy. Her jaw clenched and her palms grew moist. She didn't understand why she was so anxious until she listened to what she'd said. It had been years since she had referred to herself in the singular. When an Infected was part of a commune, it was always collective 'we'—a combination of all their wills and all their desires, felt as one. It was an intoxicating and empowering sensation that was now absent in Samantha's mind and it left her vacant, sick to her stomach.

How did humans do this? Be *alone* with their thoughts? No wonder they were so violent and self-defeating. It was horrifying. Samantha reached her hand out and rested it on a branch propped against her shelter, but suddenly felt weak at the knees. She forced herself to kneel to keep from falling over as the trees spun. Far away, yet standing right before her, Anita and Binh spoke in distant, echoing voices.

"She's starting to panic," Binh said.

"How much longer can you hold out?" Anita asked.

"Her will is strong, not much longer."

"Let the others decide."

"What of the hunt?" one of them asked, Samantha wasn't sure whom. A hand griped her under the arm and pulled her to her feet.

The faraway voices echoed in her ears as she moved. She breathed in jagged gasps, clutching her ribs. The forest continued spinning. She wanted to vomit.

"Grab her other side."

"We won't be able to resist if we touch her."

"We're past that now."

It did not happen all at once, but in a long slog, as if waking from anaesthesia: Samantha's mind dragged itself from the pit of panicking isolation, and crystalized, jarring her from a deep hibernation.

She communed with Anita first. In dribs and drabs she felt the woman's impatience, her hunger to please, her fear. Her apprehension was directly related to Samantha, and although she wanted to ask about it, Sam also did not know where they were taking her, or what they planned to do with her once they arrived. It was best, Sam thought, to not poke the bear just yet.

On her other side, Binh's emotions were slower to come and less defined. He was either indifferent toward Samantha, or skilled enough to mask his true emotions. It would serve no purpose, Sam knew, to comment now. Instead, she watched as they first dragged, then helped, then led her to the east, deeper into the forest.

The morning mist, which had kept the air cool and balmy, was now melting away into a wet humidity, making the earth smell dank and drearily of wet, rotten leaves.

Soon they arrived at a camp site. Among the trees sat man-made huts of branches and bark, placed in a circle around a rock-lined fire pit, burning high and hot like a pyre.

Infected, Regular and Archaean alike, milled about the camp grounds performing various chores and duties—raking, skinning, making baskets and cordage—but all came to a stop as Samantha and the others arrived. Soon their emotions came forth, filling Samantha's chest to bursting. The general consensus seemed to be caution.

When she caught sight of Bernard and Rose, two Infected who had fled after the rot-glider attack, she felt their apprehension acutely. Beside them, another couple gawked, feeling downright hostile.

As Samantha sensed a familiar twinge of dread,

Binh released his grip on her arm—she hadn't even realized he was still holding her—and pointed toward an empty area just outside the inner circle of huts.

"You can build your shelter there," he said. "Don't worry. You won't be harmed."

"If you say so," she said, swallowing the thickness in her throat. She set to work gathering branches, but the tension permeated her skin. Over time it gnawed at her, making her joints stiff and sore.

Then again, it could also be because she had slept on the ground the night before. Keeping her paranoia in check, Samantha continued to work—clearing an area, stacking branches, gathering moss and pine needles. She was hungry, but dared not ask for food. Not yet.

Binh could promise her safety until he was blue in the face, but with the Archaean parasite in your blood, there was no such thing as a guarantee. Samantha had seen first-hand what could happen and dared not test the waters so soon.

Once her shelter was built and she had been given a helping of mashed pine nuts and fried frog, the bulk of the occupants of the camp approached and sat before her. Taking the hint, she did the same and, speaking slowly and clearly, told in painstaking detail what had happened at the farms, and all she had seen and felt. The anger, the suspicion, the mobs. The killings. The fire.

After she was done, and the looks on the group's face shifted from horror to contemplation, Binh cleared his throat and spoke to them all. "Let it be a lesson for all of us."

Sam would like to believe it was as simple as that, but knew better. "We must work hard to prevent the same from happening here," she said. "Yes, you are Archaean and Infected as one now. But so were the farms."

"We are not the same as them; that's why we left," Anita said.

"It didn't randomly happen—understand," Sam explained. "It wasn't overnight. A gradual shift toward hate took hold so slowly, no one noticed until it was too late."

"*We* noticed," Anita said.

"We didn't desert because we got bored, Samantha," Rose said. "We knew what was coming. We felt it. The hive-mind was poisoned."

"But it wasn't the whole commune," Samantha continued. "Joseph poisoned them against authority, he whipped them into a frenzy. All it took was one angry man—and the entire dynamic twisted. How do you know someone won't attempt the same here? The hostility is already apparent."

"The only hostility is what you brought with you," Bernard said. "Are you poisoning the pond, Samantha?"

"No!" she snapped. "Everything I did was for the good of the commune. *Everything.*"

"How can you say that? You helped the humans blow up New York City," Rose said.

Samantha felt her face flush with heat. "That was

different. The Exiles and the super-wasps needed eradicating."

"Is that what you're calling it?" Rose blurted. "'Eradicating'? It was *extermination*."

"You weren't there!" Samantha said, her chin rising in the air. "You didn't see them. They weren't people anymore. They couldn't commune, or speak—their minds were nothing but wasp's nests— literally. We did them a favour."

"You say 'we' as if the commune had any say in what you did," Anita said. "We've heard the stories. *You* made the plan with your human friends and the commune suffered catastrophic losses. Just like at the farm."

Samantha clenched her teeth. "Of course the commune had a say—to help the humans was a unanimous decision. We voted."

"Voted?" Binh gaped. "Any commune with you at the helm is at your disposal. You are not a true Archaean, Samantha. Your will is too strong. Your temperament is too harsh. You twist our emotions to suit you. You are no better than Joseph."

Anita, sitting beside him, looked aghast. "Binh!"

"You are not *part* of a commune," he insisted, standing. "You *command* a commune. That is why we fled the farm. That is why Joseph rallied the rest of them against you."

"You cannot possibly defend what he did," Samantha said.

"We do not defend it, we understand it," Binh explained. "Know this, Samantha, because we won't tell you again: if you try to command *this* commune, if you push your will on us, if you attempt to take control at any time—we will turn on you as Joseph did. We will not only excommunicate you from the hive-mind, we will extinguish your life."

Samantha's mouth dropped open. "Threats are unnecessary. I am not here to stage a revolution."

"This commune is one. Do not jeopardize it or you will suffer the same fate as Chris." With that, Binh moved off.

Over the next few seconds the rest left, back to their camp duties and assigned chores. Samantha sat in the mouth of her shelter, unsure if she was hurt or angry. She was both. Angry that they had threatened her life, when all she had ever tried to do was build a strong and peaceful community. Hurt because perhaps, in the depths of her mind, she knew they were right.

She was not Archaean. She could never submit to the will of the hive-mind, not fully. She knew what it could do. She knew the evil of which it was capable. She did not trust it. How could she relinquish her free will to a mob that was so easily corrupted? And in refusing to do so, she was not truly one of them.

She eyed the fire at the center of the camp, the others milling about, and then she knew.

She knew exactly what she had to do.

THE *TEVATNOA* RAN out of surgical masks within a few days. By the end of the week, half the ship had fallen ill with an influenza so contagious, two entire decks had been quarantined.

When Cobalt, including Doyle, finally emerged from the Crow's Nest after three days, Miller was alarmed to note the ship's rapid deterioration.

Crowds remained wrapped around the railings of the vessel—that had not changed—but now they were suspicious and paranoid, with masks, towels, or strips of fabric covering their faces and noses. Fear had taken hold. For every cough, sneeze, or sniff out of place, one more person was dragged to the quarantine area kicking and screaming. Rumour had it the death rate, once infected, was as high as seventy per cent.

Miller could hardly believe it. Just when he'd thought conditions aboard couldn't get any worse, they had.

Doyle squinted into the obscured faces outside the Crow's Nest, then pulled his bandana up over his mouth. "What do we do, boss?"

Miller stopped himself from shrugging. "I'm certain the labs are working on a cure."

Morland raised an eyebrow, then pulled his gas mask from his pack. "I'm not taking any chances."

Hsiung put on her surgical mask. "I'm starved. Anyone want to brave the rations line with me?"

Du Trieux covered her mouth and nose with a handkerchief. "*Oui.*"

"Meet back here in an hour," Miller said, securing his own bandana. "I have a sneaking suspicion we're about to get busy."

MILLER FOUND GRAY'S office empty, then braved the stairwells and made his way to the captain's quarters on the second floor.

Miller hadn't seen Gray's ex-wife, Barbara, or his kids James and Helen, in quite some time. He just hadn't found time to visit. In truth, they meant a great deal to him, but standing in front of their cabin, he suddenly felt guilty. He'd been so wrapped up in his job and his team, he hadn't considered them or how they'd fared until just that moment.

When he knocked, Barbara answered. She wore a surgical mask and glared at Miller for a moment as if she couldn't comprehend why he would be there. Then, nodding to herself, she stepped aside and allowed him to enter.

"It's good to see you, Alex," she said, sounding defeated. "Are you well? Don't touch anything if you can help it; James has influenza."

Miller swallowed the lump developing in the back of his throat. "Shouldn't he be in quarantine?"

Barbara shook her head, her hand lingering an inch above his arm as if she had wanted to pat it. "Gray won't hear of it."

"Jesus, Miller, where the hell have you been?" Gray stood by the kitchenette—really just a countertop with a small sink and range—his surgical mask propped on his forehead. He looked old and tired, and was holding a mug of seaweed tea, going by the smell. Bags under his eyes sagged like cinema drapes.

"Doyle was ill," Miller explained.

Gray expression flooded with concern. "The influenza?"

"No," Miller answered quickly. "Something else."

"You sure?"

"Quite."

Satisfied, Gray turned his droopy eyes to the back of the cabin, toward the beds. "We weren't so lucky."

Across the sitting area, and standing beside the farthest bed, stood a doctor from the infirmary. He spoke in hushed tones to Barbara as she approached, then turned back toward the frail form of James, Gray's sixteen-year-old son. The boy looked stretched and motionless, a whisper of a man.

"Where's Helen?" Miller asked.

"Staying with friends up on third deck," Gray said. "We couldn't risk having her exposed."

Not sure what else he could say, Miller replied, "I'm sorry."

Gray tilted his head as if a snide comment was about to escape his lips, but stopped himself and frowned. "Me too. I need you to do something for me." He set his tea on the counter and replaced his mask. "Lewis has himself quarantined up in the bridge. Don't look so concerned, it's a precaution. The last thing we need is the commander taking ill. But I can't bother him with this, and besides, I need it off the books."

Miller felt his mouth turn sour. "Yeah?" He wasn't sure what Gray meant. As in, behind Lewis's back? Gray was supposedly the head of this vessel, even if he wasn't the commanding officer—but Miller hadn't realized anything happened aboard the *Tevatnoa* that was *on* the books. What books? Who kept them?

"The influenza is dangerous, don't get me wrong," Gray said. "But it's the secondary infections that are killing people. Some sort of bacteria—some sort of streptococcus, a pneumonia or something—is getting into the lungs and causing pneumonia, and the infection is resistant to the antibiotics we have aboard."

The hairs on the back of Miller's neck prickled. "I see."

"I've been in contact with the lab," Gray went on to explain. "And they're making some progress in developing a stronger antibiotic. Some sort of two-prong approach: one chemical kills the bacteria's immunity and then some sort of penicillin derivative kills the bacteria. But progress is slow." He glanced over his shoulder toward the beds. "Too slow."

"I'm not sure how I can help the labs..."

"No," Gray snapped, catching himself. He ran his hands through his thinning hair and took a long, slow breath. "I'm not finished. The labs tell me they're also working on a solution over on the *Princess Penelope*."

"That's good. Have they made any progress?"

"Would you just shut up and listen?" Gray barked. "I've been trying to reach them, the *Princess*, but they aren't responding."

"I'm sure their lab will be in contact once they have a viable solution."

"No," snapped Gray, drawing Barbara and the doctor's attention. His eyes went wild and watery behind his surgical mask as he glared at Miller. "The *whole ship* isn't responding. Not the captain, not the security squad, not the lab. *Nobody*."

"Maybe the storm knocked their communications offline? Have we sent a team over yet?"

"Lewis won't let me," Gray hissed. "He doesn't want to risk spreading the influenza aboard the *Penelope*. He says we could all be carriers and not even know it."

Miller opened his mouth to reply, but let the words shrivel on his tongue.

"You have to go," Gray said. Tears welled in the corners of his eyes, and he wiped them away absently. "You have to get over there and bring back their research, or a sample—and you have to *hurry*."

"We don't know they have anything, Gray. If we're carriers, like Lewis fears, going over there could kill thousands. And for what? The chance they might have something useful?"

"Miller," Gray heaved, his exterior cracking. "Please, for James..."

"Sir, I—"

"You orchestrated and launched a full-scale frontal assault on the Astoria Compound with a god-damned *nuclear bomb* strapped to your back to get to me and my family out. Alex," Gray pleaded, "I need another one of your miracles."

"We don't know it's a miracle," Miller said, trying to get Gray to see reason. "I could bring back nothing."

Gray inhaled sharply and swallowed. "I know," he said, his voice catching. "But you're the only chance he's got."

SAMANTHA LAY ON a mat of pine needles in her shelter, the wind and the noises of the forest keeping her awake. Her first full day at the camp had been odd, but also comforting. It was soothing to feel the flow of a well-working commune about her, even if it was flawed. It had been so long since the farm had functioned properly, she had forgotten.

Her mind kept turning over the events of the day.

What most troubled her was the division of labor around the camp. One group of men and women had been designated as the 'hunters,' while another was deemed the 'gatherers.' As the two groups left camp to perform their duties, a third group were tasked with remaining around the outskirts of the shelters to gather firewood and tend the central fire. The fourth, smallest group prepared food and maintained the shelters. At first, this system seemed perfectly logical and functional to Samantha, but as the day progressed she began to see ways in which it could improve.

For one, it made no sense to have a group of five responsible for preparing the food and repairing the shelters; the two jobs were unrelated.

Food preparation was relatively simple in the forest. You boiled the drinking water, you butchered the meat, you cooked it over the fire, cut the portions, and then cleaned and disposed of any remnants. When all that was done, that same five people would gather supplies and repair any damage or wear and tear to the shelters in preparation for the cold night.

By the time they got to it, there was hardly enough daylight left to *see* the small huts, much less repair them. It seemed to Sam that three people could easily take care of food preparation for a group this size, while the other two repaired shelters in the light of day; it was much easier to spot holes in roofs with sunlight coming through them.

But she had been warned upon her arrival not to 'lead' the commune, so she kept her mouth shut. It proved painful to watch.

Thoughts like this, and that the hunters were over-dependent on spears—traps would be much more effective in this environment—kept her awake the first night, which was why she heard the attack coming.

Footsteps from behind her shelter crunched and swept across the forest floor like a swarm, spreading far and wide. She heard the unmistakeable *click-*

click-click of metal upon metal and knew someone was starting a fire.

Sitting up inside her shelter, Sam immediately thought to scream, sound an alert, to pulse a warning through her body to signal the rest of the deserters, but she hesitated—stuck between self-doubt and self-loathing.

She *could* cry out and raise the alarm, but it would also lead the marauders straight to her—and not just that, hadn't she been told not to take command? Would sounding the alarm be considered an act of leadership? Who knew anymore what her people would deem unworthy?

Immediately on the heels of these thoughts she felt a surge of self-hatred, especially after she realized she had already decided to remain silent and let events unfold. If she kept quiet, she reasoned, perhaps the attackers would center their attack on the inner-circle shelters, giving her the opportunity to escape.

She paused only a moment, but it was enough. In a burst of shouting and broken glass, the attack began. Smoke filled the air first, then the twang of bows and arrows. Sam crawled out of her shelter and into pandemonium. The camp was on fire, people running back and forth in total disarray. It was hard to tell who was the enemy and who wasn't.

A bottle of burning fluid flung past Sam's face and smashed into the structure beside her. An arrow shot by her head and she ducked, dropping low and moving fast.

With no weapon, she had no choice but to run,

zigzagging between trees and blindly searching for cover. The fire from the burning camp, and a sliver of moonlight from above the canopy, provided limited visibility. She stumbled, tripped, fell into holes, and crashed her way through the forest—marvelling at how she wasn't spotted and shot down.

As she ran, she saw two Infected, a pair of brothers she knew from the potato-arrowroot farm: skilled archers. They were hunkered behind a boulder, taking aim at the camp and cutting down anyone trying to escape the inferno. Once their eyes met, the pair took aim directly at Samantha and let arrows fly.

She ducked behind a tree and increased her speed. An arrow shaft whizzed by her shoulder as she moved, and a second pierced the tree beside her.

"Over here!" someone shouted.

"I see her!"

Running in the dark, Samantha toppled, fell, then picked herself back up again and kept going. Her knees stung, the palms of her hands burned. She sprinted blindly, stumbling into the night. Behind her, she heard the crashing and snapping of twigs and branches as her pursuers bulldozed closer. Someone—or many someones—were in pursuit.

"Samantha!" a voice called. "Sam, stop!"

Joseph's voice.

With a sudden burst of speed she changed direction, and ran headlong into a trench.

Smashing down in the dirt, her face driving into the ground, her eyes blurred. She tasted mud and blood, but managed to get back on her feet. Shaking out her arms, she was relieved no limbs appeared broken—but the footsteps behind her kept coming. She dragged her body out of the hole and kept running.

Cries and hollers from the camp echoed off the trees and through the forest, pushing her farther away.

"We need you back at the farms!" Joseph shouted.

From what she could tell, he was approaching from the right. At least, she thought so; her sense of direction was off. She had no idea if she was facing east or south. She couldn't even tell if she was running toward the farm or the camp. She saw nothing but moonlit trees and crumbling earth below her feet; the glow from the burning camp was too far away to provide a bearing.

"Please, Sam! I can't control them alone!" Joseph shouted. He sounded closer still. She was losing ground.

Switching directions again, she crawled over a fallen tree and stalked to her left. In the silent forest, every move she made rang out, so she froze in position behind a tall, wide tree. As Joseph's voice neared, she held her breath.

"We need your strength," Joseph continued, closer still. "We need you to guide us through the winter."

She sensed his lie. He was reaching out to her with his feelings, pleading. His passions tickled her skin, and the hairs on her arms and the back of her neck rose.

His oncoming movement had ceased. All was quiet now. Only the bugs and the nocturnal predators moved. Just as she wondered if he had gone away, a hand reached out and grabbed her by the side of her hair. A thin blade came from around the tree and touched the base of her throat.

She grabbed the hand in her hair with one fist, and the wrist holding the knife with the other. Twisting with all her might, she dropped to her knees and wrenched her body down and around, turning to face him. He looked momentarily confused, and Sam balled her fists and punched, nailing the inside of Joseph's elbow with an audible crack, knocking him forward at the waist as he reached for his broken arm. Sam then stood and sank her knee with as much force as she could muster into Joseph's groin.

He folded like a chair, dropped the knife and howled, falling to his knees. Snatching up the blade, Sam slashed the air in front of her in hopes of sending him jumping back and away, but—distracted by the pain—he merely squatted, his eyes wide. In the low glow of the moonlight, a dark slash bloomed across his belly.

She'd gutted him.

She felt like she'd stabbed herself, his pain consuming her. Dropping the knife, she could only stare as Joseph fell sideways onto the forest floor, his insides spilling from the wound.

THE *PRINCESS PENELOPE* cut through the waves at ten knots. It was a slow and steady pace for the cruise liner, but it would take the dinghy time and full throttle to catch up from the *Tevatnoa*, on the far side of the S-Y fleet.

Under the cover of night, Doyle steered the dinghy at low speed past the *Dawn Rising* and the tugboat, *Robin's Nest,* until they were in the *Penelope*'s thirty-meter-wide wake, where Doyle hit the accelerator, pushing their tiny boat to catch up.

Once abeam the ship and keeping pace, Miller, du Trieux, Morland and Hsiung tugged their adhesive elastomer gloves and kneepads over their uniforms and hopped directly onto the hull of the cruise liner.

Climbing up sheer sheet metal—especially with the wind and ocean spray—took care, and time. The adhesive interwoven with the stiff material held their weight, but had to be carefully peeled away and placed with every movement, slowing their pace to a crawl.

Since the pilot's door could only be opened from the inside, they proceeded up the cruise liner some twenty meters above sea level. Twice they had to wait for Morland to catch up, his vertigo slowing him down, but they reached the lowest deck without incident and seemingly without witness. They gathered behind a mega-lifeboat and Miller surveyed the situation on board, a cold sweat icing the back of his neck.

The noise was unreal. The *Tevatnoa* was generally quiet at night, the residents—for the most part—asleep in their cabins. Sure, there were midnight crews performing maintenance, small security patrols, a straggling insomniac every now and then, but for the most part, the voluntary curfew was respected.

Aboard the *Penelope*? Not so much.

Shouting could be heard from all areas, rivaling the roar of the ocean. What they were shouting, Miller couldn't say. Then he recognized the undeniable pop of automatic gunfire, and the squad crouched as one and drew their weapons.

"How long has the ship been without communications?" du Trieux asked in a taut whisper. She slapped the safety off her Gilboa Viper II.

"Three days, at least," Miller said. He'd told her that once before, but didn't push it. He chambered a round in his .45 Gallican and re-holstered it.

"And the labs are where again?" she asked.

In the dark, Miller squinted at her. They'd covered this. "Mid-deck, near the bow."

She nodded, as if hearing it for the first time. "*D'accord.*"

Morland popped his knuckles. "I'll take point."

"Go," Miller said, and they were off.

The team took the corridor from the lifeboat's dock, then climbed a ladder onto a promenade of sorts, running down the center of the ship. Further toward the bow, they happened upon a recreational pool and waterslide, now converted into a hydroponics pool.

Another ladder took them back down, still heading toward the laboratory, when Morland stopped cold in his tracks and threw himself against the wall, holding up his fist.

Following suit, du Trieux, Hsiung, and Miller waited for the go-ahead—which didn't come.

"What's the hold up?" Miller asked Hsiung.

Shrugging, she nodded to du Trieux, who shrugged back.

They waited a few minutes, until Morland inched forward as if to move, and then abruptly twisted around to face Miller. "Incoming!" he said.

"Incoming *what*?" Miller gaped.

Like a tsunami, Cobalt was surrounded by passengers. Dressed in civilian clothes with a variety of make-shift masks and coverings, the mob took one look at the four of them and swarmed like a pack of hyenas.

"Who are you?"

"Where did you come from?"

"Who sent you?"

"Take them to Taylor!"

"Grab their weapons!"

Unwilling to open fire on non-combatants, but also uncertain of their intentions, Miller watched mournfully as a hand reached out and removed his blessed M27 rifle from his hands.

"My name is Alex Miller and I've been sent from the *Tevatnoa* to—"

The woman holding his rifle shouted over her shoulder. "He says they're from the *Tevatnoa*!"

"Do they know?" someone asked.

"Shit!" somebody else shouted.

"We've been sent to speak to your chief science officer?" Miller volunteered.

"Ha!" said the woman beside Miller, through the handkerchief around her face. "You, me, and every soul on this boat wants to talk with *her*."

"Betsy, shut up," a man beside her said.

The woman glowered back at him. "Sod off, Perkins."

"Miller?" Hsiung grimaced as she was stripped of her sidearm and rifle.

"Just play along for now," he said.

Miller felt a hand shove him from behind, and the four of them, surrounded and separated by the crowd, were escorted forward toward the hydroponic pool at the bow.

Miller was reminded of the time he and du Trieux

were captured by the Archaeans. His thoughts flashed to Samantha, but quickly came back to the present. He tried to remind himself these people were not Infected. They were human; there was no hive-mind, none of that weird group violence.

At least, he hoped they weren't.

Once at the pool, the crowd wheeled to the left and into another group, which parted to reveal a tall gray-haired man in medical scrubs and a surgical mask.

Squinting at them, he asked, "Who the hell are you?"

"They're from the *Tevatnoa*. They asked to speak to the science officer," said the woman beside Miller.

The gray-haired man raised a bushy eyebrow. "Well, that's rich."

"We're not here to cause trouble—" Miller began.

The tall man put a hand on his hip. "Sneaking aboard a ship in the middle of the night, fully armed and wearing tactical gear? Shouldn't you open with 'This isn't what it looks like'?"

Miller ran his tongue across his teeth. "No, sir. We're here on unofficial business."

"Unofficial business with the very same science officer we've been trying to contact for the last seventy-two hours?" the man asked. Obvious disdain dripped from his words. "I suppose that's a coincidence?"

Miller blinked. "You can't get inside the lab?"

The tall man rubbed his eye wearily. "You're not here to evacuate the science crew, are you?"

Morland's mouth gaped open. "Why would we—?"

Miller raised a hand and cut him off. "The *Tevatnoa* has been trying to communicate with the *Penelope* for more than three days, sir. We've been tasked to locate and negotiate with the chief science officer for the release of medical research aboard."

"What the what?" The woman holding Miller's rifle gaped.

The tall man seemed to understand, however. He nodded slowly, then waved his hands at the crowd surrounding Miller and his team. "Give them their weapons back," he said. "They're after the same thing we are."

The crowd grudgingly complied.

Miller snapped his sidearm back into place as the tall man approached.

"I'm Taylor," he said.

"Miller," he replied.

Neither offered to shake hands.

"Why are communications down?" Miller asked.

"Come with me. You should speak with the captain."

Taylor led the team upstairs and toward the bridge. They passed a crowd of passengers guarding the crew, who'd been bound and gagged with duct tape, bed sheets and towels. Slumped against the walls like prisoners of war, they saw Miller and the team and started thrashing and straining, shouting into their gags. Their efforts were met with slaps and kicks from the passengers, which instantly silenced them.

Miller grimaced. Nothing came easily, did it?

A simple snatch-and-grab, and now he was up to his eyeballs in a mutiny. What had come first, the communications blackout or the mutiny? He supposed it didn't matter.

Past a sundeck and two perfectly fine-looking communications arrays, they entered the bridge unhindered. The captain sat in his chair, arms bound behind his back, ankles duct-taped together. There was a bloody bump by his temple. Seeing Miller and the rest of Cobalt, the grizzled man's face reddened, then paled.

"Thank God," he sighed. "Are you from S-Y?"

"We are," Miller said. "What happened here?"

The captain set his jaw, then swallowed thickly. "Outbreak," he started. "First in the lower levels, then all over. We tried to quarantine, but it was too late. There wasn't enough medicine, people started dying. The rest got scared. A group of them stormed the lab and killed one of the techs. We fought to get them out, but then Dr. Dalton shut us out and barred the door, and now nobody can get in."

"And the mutiny?"

"Right after that."

"What about communications?"

"They won't let me answer," the captain said, nodding toward Taylor and the other passengers with him.

Miller turned on them. "Two passengers aboard the *Minerva's Wand* starved to death because *this ship* didn't send them their rations. Do you understand what's happening? You can't shut down this ship's operations. Who's manning the engine room? Who's in charge of deck security, or keeping the storm petrels at bay? They'll nest in the exhaust and invite predators; did you know *any* of this?"

"I'm sorry to hear about the *Minerva*," Taylor said, without a hint of sincerity. "But we got problems of our own here. He didn't tell you half of it."

The captain's face flushed again.

"Tell him how you locked down the bottom two floors."

"That was to prevent the spread of the..."

"Bullshit!" Taylor seethed, pointing his finger at the captain and spitting in his face. "You locked us down there, then stopped sending rations. Not everyone down there *had* the disease. You condemned us all to death, and when that didn't work you tried to starve us."

"The rations staff got sick," the captain said. "Production slowed when the hydroponics pool on the top deck was contaminated by salt water during the storm and the filtration system broke down. We weren't trying to starve anyone!"

"Why didn't you contact the *Tevatnoa* for assistance?" Miller asked him.

"I tried!" the captain shouted, straining against his restraints. "I had the laboratory staff contact the *Tevatnoa* to see how their research was coming, but these guys launched a fucking mutiny and we've been sailing wild ever since. Thank God you figured it out. Who knows what would have happened to me if—"

Taylor laughed, silencing him. It was a soft chuckle

at first, growing into a deep, nasty chortle. "You think they came to save *you?*" he said.

The captain's eyes drilled into him, and Miller found himself resting his palm on his side holster, as if the tied, bound captain could somehow come up out of his chair and tackle him.

"You mean you're not?" the captain snapped.

"Not exactly," Miller said, dropping his hand and stepping past Taylor toward the com.

"What are you doing?" Taylor asked, looking mildly concerned.

"You can't operate like this," Miller said, picking up the microphone and pressing the button. "You'll all die." Then, into the comm, he said, "*Tevatnoa*, this is Miller aboard the *Penelope*. Do you copy, over?"

After a sharp burst of static, Commander Lewis's taut voice could be heard. "*Miller? What in the blue blazes are you doing over there?*"

"If you don't mind, sir, I'll explain that later. For now, I'd like to request a tactical team from the *Tevatnoa* be brought aboard the *Penelope* to assume command. There's been a mutiny."

"*Where's Captain Duran?*"

"Here on the bridge with me, sir. But he's not in command."

"*I can't risk sending a team over with the outbreak aboard, Miller. By all respects, you shouldn't be there either,*" Lewis said.

"It's already here, sir. It's why the mutiny happened in the first place."

Lewis's voice trailed off into faint cussing before the

communications line was cut. After a few seconds, the line opened again. Miller could hear the strain in Lewis's voice. He'd have bet a thousand dollars the old commander was scratching a hole the size of Texas into his thighs. "*Fine. Stay put until they arrive, but when you get back, you're going into voluntary quarantine until your team is cleared, and you'd better have a grade-A excuse for being there in the first place, son. You hear me?*"

"Loud and clear, sir. Miller out." After the line went dead, Miller put the mic down. Taylor's and Captain Duran's expressions suggested it would be a challenge brokering a peaceful solution to the mutiny, but Miller couldn't concentrate on that. He'd leave it to the approaching team, which by his calculations would arrive in less than half an hour, giving him little time to secure the research from the lab.

"Hsiung," he said.

She snapped to attention. "Yes, sir?"

"You've got the helm until the team arrives. Morland, du Trieux, you're with me."

"What about me?" Captain Duran bellowed, struggling against his restraints until the chair groaned in protest.

Hsiung looked to Miller for guidance.

He shrugged. "Up to you," he told her, and then left with Morland and du Trieux trailing.

He could just make out the captain's wails of protest as they passed the communications arrays on their way back toward the hydroponics pool.

It was time to perform another miracle.

*   *   *

THE LABORATORY WAS still surrounded when they arrived, if the crowd seemed less of a mob without Taylor in the center. Despite eyeing Miller and his team with deep suspicion, the crowd parted, allowing them access to the door.

Miller yanked on the handle, confirming it was locked; a glance through the tiny window suggested it was also barred. Scratches and jagged scrapes tracked the edge of the door—perhaps from a crowbar—along with what appeared to be bullet holes. It couldn't be more than hollow aluminium, yet somehow it had held.

Miller knocked. He wasn't expecting a response, and there wasn't one. After pounding a few times, he raised his voice and shouted into one of the bullet holes. "My name's Miller. I run security on the *Tevatnoa*." He waited a minute. When still no response came, he pounded again. "I'd rather not blast my way through this door—especially since there's a mob of angry passengers behind me."

"What do you want?" a woman's voice shouted back, from some distance away.

"A squad is coming over from our ship to broker an end to the mutiny."

"Great!" the woman shouted back. "Let me know when it's over."

"We will, ma'am. But I'm under additional orders that pertain to you. Would you let me in?"

"Do your orders involve destroying my lab, or

killing me and my technicians?"

"If it did, do you think I'd tell you? But no. That's not why I'm here."

"That's what that other guy said, and they killed Benji."

Miller gritted his teeth. "I heard about that. But I'm here to ensure your safety and that of your team and research. *Tevatnoa* wants an end to this situation, including the epidemic."

The voice remained silent after that. Miller thought he heard rustling and the distinct sound of furniture being dragged across a floor, but it was hard to tell for certain with the sloshing of the ocean and the murmur of the mutineers.

Finally, the door opened an inch and a sliver of a face appeared. "Just you, no weapons."

Miller wanted to move fast, lest the crowd behind him figure out what was happening. Grabbing hold of his rifle strap, he handed his M27 to du Trieux, his Gallican to Morland, and his hunting knife back to du Trieux, then slid through the door and slammed it behind him.

Inside, the overhead lights were dimmed and buzzing. The room—previously some sort of towel dispensary and snack bar—smelled of sweat and peanuts. A wooden counter followed the wall three-quarters of the way around the room, piled high with scientific equipment. There was evidence of a struggle: chairs were broken, desks overturned, and shattered glass crunched under Miller's boots.

Beside him stood a woman with dark hair, round

glasses and a white lab coat. Behind her, two technicians stood behind overturned desks, wide-eyed.

"How many of you are there?" the woman in front asked.

"Are you Dr. Dalton?"

"Yes. How many of you are there? Enough to get all three of us out of here safely?"

Miller pursed his lips. "That wasn't the plan."

Dr. Dalton bit her lip. "What *is* the plan, then?"

"I think it's best if you hold up here until the rest of the security forces arrive. Shouldn't be more than an hour. Let them organize the passengers and set up some sort of chain of command. *Then* you let them in. That is, if you've got enough provisions to sustain you for another day or two?"

"A *day* or two?" shrieked one of the techs.

Dr. Dalton looked to Miller with a tinge of apology. "We've been living off condiment packets."

"I'm sick of mayo!" the other tech griped.

"If you're not here for evacuation, then what are you doing here?" the doctor asked.

"I understand you've been experimenting on a new line of antibiotics."

She wrung her hands. "Yes. But as I've said before, it's not tested extensively on humans, and it's a little"—she looked back at her technicians, shifting on her feet, her thick-soled nursing shoes squeaking—"controversial?"

The techs nodded.

"I don't care about that," Miller said, "as long as it's effective. There's an influenza epidemic here and also on the *Tevatnoa* and a secondary infection of pneumonia on top of that. The death rates are climbing."

"I'm well aware of all that," Dr. Dalton said, stepping back and moving to a refrigeration unit under the counter. "But once people here found out what I'd made, well... I'm assuming you heard what happened?"

Miller nodded.

"If their reaction was that bad, I can't imagine anyone on your ship will want to try it." She opened the refrigerator door and pulled out a rack of test tubes. Each tube contained a brown fluid.

"They will if it will save their life."

"Really?" Dr. Dalton challenged him, taking a sample and holding it toward him. "Would *you* drink cockroach tea?"

Miller reached out for the tube, then hesitated.

Dr. Dalton nodded glumly, then moved to put the test tube back with the others.

"Wait," he said. "Explain to me how it works."

Dr. Dalton raised an eyebrow. "There are nine molecules with antibiotic properties in the brain and nerve tissue of a cockroach, did you know that?"

Miller shook his head.

"It's why people joke that after the apocalypse, the only thing left will be plastic bags, disposable diapers, and cockroaches. Well, they're not wrong. Anyway, protein molecules from the roaches can eliminate ninety per cent of the MRSA superbug without any harm to human cells. They were working on it in England a few years ago, but it never really caught on. I figured, what have we got to lose? This *is* the apocalypse, isn't it?"

"But you haven't tested it on real people yet? Just cells?"

Dr. Dalton motioned to the tech on her left, a skinny girl who couldn't be more than twenty with stringy long hair and an overbite. "Well, we tested it on one subject. Becky."

The girl nodded and Miller. "The secret," she said, "is to drink the tea at the first onset of infection."

"What about people who already have resistant infections?" Miller asked.

Dr. Dalton shrugged. "We don't know. But it won't hurt them to try."

"How much of this can you give me?"

She motioned to the other refrigeration unit tucked under the counter on the other side. "We have almost a thousand units, but the refrigerators are full, so we've held off making more the last few days. My fear was that the people would come in and trash the lab and destroy all the tea, or take it themselves rather than get it to those who need it. Or worse, destroy the research."

"Or us," Becky added. "Like they did with Benji when he tried to stop them."

Dr. Dalton's eyes teared, and she flattened her lips. "I can give you a sample and the formula, to take back to the *Tevatnoa*. The tea takes twenty-four hours to produce, assuming you can find enough cockroaches."

"Which doesn't seem to be a problem, at least on this ship," the other tech said.

Miller took the samples from her outstretched hand and pocketed them. He waited a moment for the doctor to copy the formula, then folded and secured that as well.

"Can you stay until the other security team arrives?" Becky asked.

Miller shook his head. "Bar the door as I leave, and do it quickly." He tried to ignore their cries as he reached for the handle. Their panic cut him to the quick, but he had no other option. He yanked back the handle enough to slip out.

Back outside, du Trieux and Morland handed back his weapons. He listened for the dragging sounds as the door was jammed from the inside again. The crowd gathered around, pestering him as to what had happened, and what he had learned. Miller flat-out ignored them.

They were scared. The captain had screwed up, and quite probably made the situation aboard intolerable, effectively creating the mutiny that overthrew him. But just then, Miller was having a hard time telling the difference between a mob of ruthless humans, and the mobs of Infected he'd gunned down in New York. If he thought too hard about it, it might keep him up at night. So he ploughed through the crowd unyielding, and headed back to the bridge to retrieve Hsiung.

In the distance, the unmistakeable sound of dinghy motors floated up and over the deck in the sea breeze. The other security forces were on their way.

Good.

They could contain this mess.

Miller was done.

14

SAMANTHA AND THE other survivors trickled back to the ruined camp the morning after the raid, shaken and scared. Out of thirty or so deserters, half remained.

The camp itself was destroyed, and the fire had spread from the huts and into the surrounding forest. A scorched path cut through the trees; no-one knew where the burnt path led, or if it continued to burn, and no one dared check.

The bodies of the dead were missing. It was unclear how many had died, and how many had been taken back to the farming commune to work, if any. Regardless, they searched the embers for signs of life, to no avail.

Of those that Samantha knew, Binh and Anita returned, as did Bernard. Bernard's wife Rose, however, was nowhere to be found. They'd run off in different directions at the start of the attack, and Bernard wasn't sure where she'd gone. His guilt became his utter ruin.

After they'd scoured the ashes, Samantha found Bernard sitting in the remains of his scorched shelter, rocking and sobbing.

Beside him, a woman going through her own shelter turned to watch Bernard, then joined him in tears. She dropped to her knees in the ash, and black dust rose in a cloud around her.

From there it spread until the entire group were racked with sorrow. All around Samantha voices wailed, tears streamed, and hope was lost. Before long, she was in tears with them.

So much life wasted. So much hate and fear. The deserters had done nothing against the farming commune but take her in, yet the mob's violence had persisted and they'd attacked. It was pointless. Samantha herself had become all she despised when she'd murdered Joseph.

It seemed to her, that evolved or not, Infected or not, humans were a violent species. No amount of communing, no amount of cooperation or empathy— nothing could prevent human nature from revealing its ugliness. Humans consumed and destroyed. It was what they were meant to do, and they did it well. Humans were the parasite of the planet, and it was they who would destroy the Earth, not the parasite. Desolate and overcome, Samantha sank to the burnt forest floor where her hut had once sat and wept bitterly.

After a few moments, Binh appeared at her side. "We are gathering what we can and moving south. If we find warmer land, we might yet survive the winter."

Wiping tears from her cheeks with ashen fingers, Sam nodded, then stood. Joining the group, she abandoned the remains of the camp and slowly trudged away.

THEY TRAVELED FOR days, eating what they could find—scraps and mouthfuls, gobbled in haste—and drinking from dwindling supplies until streams or creeks were found to refill containers. Samantha could tell she had lost weight by the fifth day, and cinched her belt tighter.

Luck was on their side, at least for now. The weather was holding. It was uncomfortably cool at night, but they had taken to sleeping in one large, hastily-constructed shelter, huddled together for warmth and comfort, and that had helped some. For now, the torrential rain was not a factor.

There were twelve of them—a handful of survivors had opted not to come—but soon smaller groups formed within the larger, and Samantha found herself working with Anita and Binh day after day in their hunt for game.

After many failed attempts, Sam discovered spear-throwing and archery were not her strengths. She did have a knack for the sling, however. Often, she was able to find and catch enough of the smaller game—rat-things, the rabbit-like burrow-tail, occasional smaller terror-jaws, which she could at least stun long enough to dispatch with a knife—to feed the whole group. This became especially helpful when the archers, who concentrated on larger targets—wild husk-mutt, thug-behemoths, and even rot-gliders—came back empty-handed.

Her usefulness was not lost to the group. As the week progressed, their fear of her dissipated, and Samantha almost felt a sense of acceptance. She was part of a commune now, fully. Not leading, not following. She had lost herself to the will of the group, and she had to confess, it felt nice, solid, smart—even if the living conditions of her first true commune were less than comfortable.

It was the beginning of their second week traveling, in the middle of a freezing downpour, that they finally found a semblance of civilization. At the abandoned town of Old Forge, near the center of upstate New York's forest, they discovered an operational dairy farm, complete with a herd of docile thug-behemoths, a milking barn, a field of some sort of wheat-derivative, and a large farmhouse with several adjoining sheds. The farm sat in the middle of a large clearing a few kilometers from a desolate highway.

They didn't see anybody, Infected or human, but it was obviously occupied. A spinning wheel sat on the porch of the farmhouse, a basket of wool at its feet; candle light could be seen in the draped windows of the farmhouse; smoke rose from the house's tall stone chimney.

"Do you smell that?" Anita asked, her mouth gaping.

The twelve of them crouched at the edge of the clearing, watching.

Binh, whose view was obstructed by the rear end of a gently ruminating behemoth, scrunched his nose. "Smell what?"

Anita opened her eyes and sniffed the air. "They're cooking meat. Can't you smell it?"

A few others from the group nodded. Samantha wasn't sure if they could actually smell anything, or just wanted to. Bernard went so far as to lick his lips.

Samantha, on the other hand, couldn't smell anything. "We should wait until nightfall," she said. "Take what we can."

"You mean raid their farm?" Binh stared.

"Not raid—just commandeer a few things. We don't want contact. Not until we know who or what they are. We can't risk communing."

"There's three of them over there," someone said down the row, but a clap of thunder muffled what followed. All Samantha caught was, "...those sheds."

Binh rose to peer around the behemoth in front of him. "Where? What are they doing?"

"Looks like they're smoking cigarettes," the woman said, squinting through the rain. "Or something."

"Come on," Anita said, a tinge of impatience in her voice. "We're getting soaked."

Retreating back into the treeline, they huddled closely, keeping low and a few meters back from the clearing.

"We can't camp here, they'll see the fires," Bernard said.

"Good luck with fires tonight anyway," Binh said. "Everything is drenched."

"We should move away and send in a search party tonight, just to feel them out," Anita suggested.

"No," Samantha said, a little sharper than she intended. "We're not splitting up."

"What if a couple of us approach them—find out what they are?" a woman suggested.

"Not splitting up," Samantha repeated.

"What do you suppose is in those sheds? Do you think it's food?"

"Or maybe clothes?"

"I could really use a jacket."

"Not. Splitting. Up."

A sharp crack made them all go silent. To their right, the three smoking farmers appeared, cautious, unarmed, and calm. The smell of cloves surrounded them like an aura.

Samantha's hand unconsciously went to the tails of her sling, tucked into her belt.

"Don't run," one of them said. He had a thick beard and wore a knitted cap. One of his boots had a hole in the toe. "We're not looking to hurt nobody."

"If you could just *not* shoot us, that'd be swell," said the one with the thick glasses. His palms were held in front of him.

Samantha half-rose, ready to run, but something stopped her. She felt it almost immediately: their energy.

Suddenly, and overwhelmingly, she felt the desire to sit. The three men before her were so open, so gracious, so full of love and understanding, the sensation startled her. The men's calm, soothing quality hit her hard enough that she lost her balance. She drove her knees forward into the dirt to keep from tipping over. Like dominos, her fellows did the same.

The three men came forward and stood in the center of their group.

"We accept and love you individually and as a whole," said the one with the cap.

"Please come with us, so we may clothe and feed you."

"Come where it is warm and pleasant. No harm will come to you."

All of Samantha's group—Binh, Anita, Bernard, even Samantha—couldn't seem to keep a thought in their heads. Before Sam could stop herself, she was standing alongside the others; helping one another, leaning into each other for balance. They linked hands and followed the three men out of the trees, over the hedge of ferns, and onto the field of thug-behemoths toward the barn—not a word of complaint or resistance uttered.

"Come on now, folks," one of the men said. "Everything will be fine."

"That's right," said one of the others. "We offer peace and tranquillity."

With no worry or care, they entered the milking barn, where a dozen or so people worked at milking stations. Three-legged stools sat beside moaning behemoths who straddled buckets filled with purplish, milky fluid. All—people and behemoths alike—turned and looked at the new arrivals.

Samantha knew she should feel uneasy—in fact, she was sure of it—but was overpowered by pacifying, comforting love. She couldn't help it. She felt... happy?

"More recruits," said the man with the glasses to the others inside the barn.

"Praise the Lord!" one of the milkers answered.

"Sister Emma," said the man with the knitted cap. "Could you be so kind as to run up to the main house and gather up warm blankets and clothes, and a couple loaves of bread for our new friends? Brother Jim," he added, turning to the tall man on the other side, "why don't you help her?"

"Of course, Brother Ed."

The two milkers rushed off into the storm.

"My new friends," the first man then said, turning toward the dripping group. "Sit. Rest, please. You must be tuckered out."

In unison they sat on the barn floor. It was warm inside; it stank of dung and buzzed with black flies, but was still tremendously more comfortable than Samantha had felt since before her own farmhouse had burned to the ground. Or maybe ever in her life. She couldn't figure how. They were in a smelly, gross barn, she was soaked through to the skin, hungry and exhausted—and she couldn't have been gladder of it.

On either side of her, Binh and Anita sidled up close, resting their legs beside hers for warmth.

They watched Brother Ed attentively as he cleaned the raindrops off his glasses on his undershirt, then tucked the white tee back into the top of his corduroy pants and planted the large lenses onto the bridge of his pocked, bulbous nose.

"Welcome to the Brotherhood!" His words reverberated off the barn rafters.

Immediately the hairs on the back of Samantha's neck rose and her good feelings drained away.

"To the Brotherhood of the Archaean," he added, making Binh and Anita relax on either side of her. "Our mission," he continued, "is to spread the Archaean parasite like the word of God. It is our job, my brothers and sisters, our reason for existence, to reach far and wide and ensure that every man, woman, and child of this Earth shall be brought into the communion of the Archaean."

"Amen," said the man with the knit cap.

Jaw set, Samantha turned around and checked for exits. As far as she could tell, they had entered through the only door, which was now lined, shoulder to shoulder, with the milkers who had occupied the barn before their arrival. Behind Brother Ed and the two others was a ladder leading to a hay loft, but there was no visible back door.

Samantha's stomach roiled with anxiety and hunger.

"Tomorrow," Brother Ed said, "we shall find you jobs in the fellowship. For everyone has a God-given gift on this earth, and it is our calling to find yours. First, however, you must sleep. You must rest. Eat.

Enlightenment shall wait for the light of morning. Ah—here we are..."

From the entry the other two men reappeared, carrying a heaping armload of blankets, jackets, and an overflowing basket of bread.

At the sight of the food, the newcomers rose to their feet. Brother Ed raised his hands to stall them, as the two followers walked in amongst the crowd, their arms loaded with goodies.

The refugees were instructed to sit down and pass the blankets and jackets to one another. Then, like priests, Brother Ed and the two other men walked through them and handed them each a chunk of bread, ripped from the loaf.

"This is a symbol," the one with the knitted cap said to Samantha as he handed her a chunk of bread.

Greedily, she stuffed it in her mouth and chewed.

"This is the bonds of humanity, broken by the Archaean parasite for you." With that, the man moved off, handing bread to Anita and then to Binh.

Samantha listened to him repeat the line, then swallowed the lump of bread in her throat. "Oh, Jesus."

AFTER A SURPRISINGLY restful sleep huddled together— carefully guarded—on the floor of the milking barn, Samantha and her group awoke at first light.

They were each given a tin cup filled halfway with mashed oats and raisins, then escorted to the farmhouse and lined up single file. One at a time, they were marched onto the porch and sat before an elderly woman, who embroidered a starched white linen as she talked.

After brief conversations with the woman, Bernard, Binh, Anita, and the others were escorted to various parts of the farm. When it was Samantha's turn, the woman tucked her needle into the fabric, rested the embroidery hoop on her lap and blinked at her with white eyes.

"What do you feel are your best skills, my child?" the woman asked.

Samantha shifted in the straight-backed chair, causing the wood to creak. "How do you mean?"

"Do you feel emotionally connected to children?"

"No," Samantha snapped, without meaning to. "And I'm not looking to change that, if that's where you're going with this."

The woman looked taken aback for a moment, but covered it quickly with a yellowed saccharin smile. "Of course. Do you knit or crochet?"

Samantha almost laughed. "No."

"Sew?"

"No."

"Have any proclivities toward gardening?"

"Some."

The woman's wrinkled face brightened. "Excellent. How about cooking?"

"No."

"Housekeeping?"

"What century do you think this is, lady?"

The old woman's smile fell. "I beg your pardon?"

Samantha gritted her teeth. "My proclivities involve domesticating, riding, and caring for wildlife, hunting, and farm management."

"I see. Well, come time to harvest the wheat and next season's planting period we will always need more hands in the fields, so that's helpful. In the meantime, I will assign you to the care of the behemoths. Report to Brother Paul in the barn and he will instruct you on your duties."

Samantha opened her mouth to ask a question, then thought better of it. Instead, she followed the escort—a man who introduced himself as Brother Daniel—to the barn, where Brother Paul instructed her, and another woman named Sister Ethel, to muck out the behemoth stalls and fill them with fresh hay.

Sister Ethel worked in complete silence, ignoring any questions Samantha put to her concerning the settlement, going so far as to move to the far side of the stalls when Sam persisted. The subsequent solitary labor was uncomfortable, but provided Samantha enough silence for her to better think through the situation.

Her circumstances weren't at their worst, she knew. She had a roof over her head, she had food, fresh clothes. There did not seem to be a speck of hostility in a living soul within a kilometer radius, which Samantha—given all her commune had gone through—found comforting.

But things could turn on a dime. The religious tone of the commune was more than a bit concerning to her, especially since she had no true idea what their church's doctrines were—if any—and what plans they had for their new arrivals, including her.

And it was very clear that the longer they stayed with the group, the harder it would be, if ever, to leave.

Samantha felt connected to the group's positive energy, and wanted to pitch in and help out any way she could—which was truly how a commune was supposed to work. But she couldn't shake her underlying distrust. How could this peace be maintained in long term? How was this commune any different from the others she had encountered?

Before she was able to come to any sort of conclusion, she and Sister Ethel finished their chores, and were tasked by the old woman with re-stabling the thug behemoths from the field, then setting up wooden benches in rows across the center of the barn.

It was long, back-breaking work, and by the end, as the sun began its descent, Samantha's muscles wailed with strain and her hands ached with new blisters. Where, she wondered, would all these new followers sleep, and when would she be able to? If the barn was full of benches, were they all to pile into the farm house?

Samantha didn't find the idea of a wooden farmhouse floor too appealing—but then, she wasn't looking forward to sleeping on the floor of the barn again either. Either way, she hoped the meeting wouldn't take long. Exhaustion dragged at her eyelids like anvils.

Some time after the benches were laid, the whole of the dairy farm sat in the pews, waiting. Those who arrived too late for a seat stood in rows at the back and along the sides.

Finally, just as the sun disappeared over the horizon, Brother Ed walked to the front of the crowd and adjusted his knitted cap as if it were a crown of thorns. "Like the word of God," he said, raising his voice and arms, "the Archaean parasite demands to be spread."

The crowd around Sam in the back row nodded in agreement. She couldn't argue with it, but she couldn't quite explain the sickly feeling in her stomach.

"Through the use of our 'outreach' program," Brother Ed continued, "it is our sacred duty to reach out into this world and spread The Word."

To Samantha's utter astonishment, Anita, who had taken a place on the bench beside her, nodded and muttered, "Amen," under her breath.

Binh, on Sam's other side, nodded as well.

"Then I call upon you," Brother Ed shouted suddenly, "my brothers and sisters of the Archaean, to volunteer! Rise up!" Raising his hands, Brother Ed spread his fingers wide, then brought them together with a booming clap. "Fulfil your destiny and come with me! And we will unite this world under one parasite!"

"Spread the word!" chanted the congregation, all rising to their feet as one and clapping their hands together once over their head.

"Brother Binh, Sister Anita, come with me!" Brother Ed shouted. "Brother Donald, Brother Bob. Sister Pam, Sister Samantha. You have been chosen!"

Anita raised her arms over her head and cheered at the top of her lungs. "We are chosen!"

Samantha, rooted to her pew, the only one sitting in a barn full of cheering people, felt a sudden desire to please.

This was wrong. This was insane. They were going where? To do what?

She wanted to run. She wanted to get as far away from this madness as possible. But she also wanted to rise up and clap her hands over her head. The energy was powerful, intoxicating. Conflicted, she merely sat there, awe-stricken.

Anita reached down, grabbed her by the shoulder, and yanked her up. "Come on, Sam!"

Pulled along, Sam followed the others to the front of the barn, where Brother Ed raised a fist in the air and marched the newly chosen to the exit.

As they left, the crowd chanted. "Spread—the—word! Spread—the—word! Spread—the—word!"

Despite herself, Samantha's heart beat faster and her mind went foggy with exhilaration. What was she doing? Why was she following Anita?

Anita pulled Sam's hand as they marched across the empty pasture and into the forest. "Isn't this exciting?"

Samantha was surprised to hear herself cry, "Yes! Yes, it is!"

15

Du Trieux GLARED at Miller from across the Crow's
Nest bar with such venom he couldn't help but ask
if there was something she wanted to say. After only
a few seconds, he wished he hadn't.

"How you can kowtow to that man's hypocrisy is
beyond comprehension," she ranted, mumbling in
French before continuing. "There is no way in hell
we should have been taking *anything* off that ship;
they're in worse condition than we are."

"It's a good thing we did go there, though, Trix,"
Doyle said, frowning when she turned her glare on
him. "Who knows how long that mutiny would
have lasted?"

"Thank God they mutinied!" Hsiung blurted out,
her mouth contorting. She flung the tattered ends of
her parachute hammock up and over a ceiling beam,
then hastily tied the ends together. "I honestly don't
know what the captain was thinking. You should
have heard the excuses he was making. He's lucky I

didn't stuff a grenade down his throat."

"And to take medical research *away* from people in the middle of an epidemic, Miller?" du Trieux added. "It's not justified. I don't care what Matheson says. We're just as bad as the pirates."

"They hanged those men from the *Minerva* for *attempting* to steal food," Hsiung said, flopping down into her hammock with a grunt, "and look at the shit we just pulled."

"I don't disagree," Miller said. That surprised them, especially du Trieux, whose eyebrows shot high. "We didn't know the situation going in. That's my fault. We went in blind. But I didn't take all their meds, and I didn't take their research. I took a copy of a formula and a sample, and that's it. I'm not a complete tyrant."

"We shouldn't have been there at all," du Trieux said, apparently not done.

Miller rubbed his face then eyed his team. Their anger and disgust sent him to his feet and out the door.

There was at least one good thing that came out of this, he realized. They were united against a common enemy again, instead of attacking one another.

Unfortunately, the common enemy was *him*.

GRAY'S QUARTERS SMELLED of sick and antiseptic. The dim orange haze of the sunset blazed through the clouded windows, painting the cabin.

Even in the twenty-four hours since Miller's last

visit, James had declined. His breathing, previously labored and chunky, was now weak and shallow. Once flush and feverish, he was now pale and gray.

Barbara sat beside his bed, looking small and feeble as she held James's limp, bony hand in hers. On the teen's other side, the doctor took the boy's pulse.

Miller watched the doctor's expression, trying to gauge the result. Eventually, he wrenched himself away and focused on Gray, who sat across from him, looking beaten. "Ten men isn't going to cut it," Miller said. "They need at least twenty to calm the mutineers, and that captain is a moron."

"He was a captain of a luxury cruise liner, and now he's managing the lives of almost four thousand people, long term, with no land support," Gray said. He picked at a cuticle until it bled, then dabbed scarlet droplets on his opposite sleeve. "He's out of his depth."

"Obviously." Miller kept his thoughts regarding Gray's own depths to himself.

"Did the lab say how long it would take to reproduce the formula?"

"Twenty-four hours, but before you give in to panic I brought you something." Miller reached into his belt pouch and handed Gray two vials of brown fluid.

His eyes opened wide. "Is this from the *Penelope*?"

"Yes, but you didn't get it from me."

"What is this?"

"It's like a tea. Don't ask too many questions;

the lab and I have decided to keep the specifics classified."

"Even from me?"

"Yes."

"And this will work?"

"I can't promise anything, but the science officer on the *Penelope* said it won't cause any harm to humans, so it's worth a shot."

Gray stood, legs shaking as he hastily rounded the sofa and went to the sleeping area. After a brief exchange with the doctor, Barbara and Gray propped the limp boy up. The doctor uncorked the tubes and gingerly poured the solution into the kid's mouth.

He immediately began to choke. Like a geyser, the tea spewed from James's mouth and ran down his chin, soaking his nightshirt and spreading across the sheets.

"Swallow it!" Gray ordered.

He either couldn't hear or couldn't comply. The doctor dropped the vials onto the bed and reached over to close the boy's mouth and massage his throat, trying to force him to swallow. The boy coughed again, shooting splatters of tea through the doctor's fingers, covering him and his parents. The doctor released his grasp and James vomited all over the bed.

"Swallow it, James! Swallow!" Gray barked at his son.

"He can't; stop shouting at him!" Barbara let go of her son and burst into tears.

The doctor went to wash his hands in the basin,

and Gray cradled James in his arms, rocking the vomit-soaked teenager as if he were an infant.

Gray's eyes met Miller's, standing frozen in the middle of the room.

"Is there more?" Gray sobbed. "Did you bring more?"

Miller shook his head helplessly.

"Is there a shot we can give him? Can we inject the tea into his stomach?"

"I wouldn't advise it," the doctor said in a wavering voice. "If we puncture the stomach at this stage of the infection we risk sepsis."

"What do we do, Miller?" Gray sobbed, clasping his son in a pool of tea and bile. "What am I supposed to do?"

Miller's throat closed like a vice. He shook his head and stormed from the room, barely making it back to his quarters before his gut twisted and he rushed to his bathroom to puke.

"I'VE SPOKEN TO the lab," Miller said, staring down at Commander Lewis. He swallowed the acid collecting in the back of his throat and shifted his legs, feeling off-balance.

Lewis pursed his lips and raised an eyebrow. He barked an order to the able seaman manning the com, then rotated in his captain's chair. "And?"

"Before the invasion, I'm told that Winston and Winston in Jacksonville, Florida had created a cure for the superbug."

Lewis opened his mouth to speak, but Miller pressed on.

"That's the MRSA, sir."

"I know what it is, son."

"To stand a chance of survival," Miller kept on, "we need to combat these infections. I've seen what they can do. It's not pretty. And after what's happened on the *Penelope,* we need to do something. Fast."

"What exactly are you proposing?"

"We make for land, sir. Send Cobalt into Jacksonville. We'll infiltrate the facility and bring back the cure."

"Assuming it still exists."

"We have to try, sir."

Lewis's eyes narrowed. "You really think five of you are going to stand a chance against an entire city of Infected? Stealth or not, that's a hell of a trek. Last I heard, Jacksonville was overrun."

"Then send me with a squad."

"I don't have squads just lying around, Miller."

"Sir," he said, regretting the sharpness in his tone. "Have you been to the infirmary? Have you seen the effects of the pneumonia? We aren't going to make it, sir."

Lewis clenched his jaw, then scratched his thigh with his thumbnail. "I've seen it. Is this what Matheson wants?"

"Matheson is compromised, sir. This comes from me."

"Are you certain *you're* not compromised? You're pretty close to Matheson's family."

Miller licked his lips and shook his head. Truthfully, he wasn't sure, but the way he figured, if he didn't do something—*anything*—he would be stuck on that rotting ship, on that angry ocean, watching thousands of people slowly die a gruesome death. At least this way, he was working toward a solution, on land, with his team, performing the one task he knew he could do, and do well—fight Infected.

Six months ago, he couldn't wait to get away from the hive-mind crazies—now, he was running right back into the shitstorm. How was it he felt comforted?

Lewis seemed to be thinking the same thing, or something close to it. He looked dubious, and dug at his left thigh with all five of his fingers with a vengeance.

"All right, Miller. Ready a squad." He turned in his captain's chair, then barked at the able seamen manning the bridge stations. "Look alive!" he boomed. "Set course for Jacksonville."

16

THREE RVs SAT still and silent, facing southwest on Highway 28, not two kilometers from the dairy farm.

On the eastern side of the road, Samantha and five others, including Binh and Anita, sat crouched in the tree line, biding their time.

The moon cast a purple sheen across the road, streaking the RVs' shadows like smeared paint. The very air was thick with mist and the smells of forest and fear.

From what Sam could see, the caravan had stopped due to some sort of mechanical difficulty. An older man and a middle-aged woman had popped the hood on one of the Winnebagos and stood in front of it, inspecting the motor and discussing it quietly in the light of two tiny torches.

In the meantime, men, women, and children—about two dozen or so—moved in and out of the vans, making preparations for a meal. Propane-powered grills were folded down from the sides of the RVs, chimneas were hauled out with stacks of firewood, awnings were opened, lawn chairs and picnic tables set out.

There was something odd about the gathering that Samantha couldn't quite place, and it wasn't until one of the children fell and scraped his knee that she understood why.

The boy sobbed and wailed until a young woman—his mother, Sam supposed—approached him calmly, seemingly unaffected by his cries.

"Done scraped yourself up good, didn't you?" the mother said.

The boy continued to sob, gripping his scraped knee as if it had been forcibly amputated.

"What did I tell you about running in the street, eh?"

The boy snorted, snot running down his nose and over his mouth.

"Maybe you'll remember that next time, eh?"

With that the woman reached down, picked up the boy and brushed him off, then let him loose. Like a shot he took off, running after the ball he'd dropped.

The mother shook her head and went back to the middle RV, where they were spreading table cloths and setting out plates.

"They're human," Binh said, startling Samantha.

"How have they kept going in those RVs?" Anita asked. "They can't be finding gasoline. Those things use a ton."

"Look at the roof," Binh answered her. "Solar panels."

"Must be why they've stopped for the night," someone else said.

From the other end of the line, obscured by the forest, Brother Ed whispered orders to the others, then approached the end where Binh, Anita and Sam waited. "We attack the front first," he said, crouched low. "Then work our way back."

Samantha's mouth went dry. "Attack?"

"Incapacitate the men," he added. "Kill them if they resist. We need the women and children alive."

Binh and Anita chimed, "Yes, Brother Ed."

As he moved back toward the other end of the line, Anita and Binh nocked arrows to their bows and adjusted their stance, eyes bright and unblinking in the moonlight.

"You're not going to do it, are you?" Sam stared them down. "We're Archaeans. We don't *kill* humans. We don't kill *anybody*." She tasted the lie the moment it left her mouth.

Anita squinted at Sam and pursed her lips. "We've been chosen."

"We must spread the word," Binh said, giving Sam a quizzical look.

On the road, the humans sat at the tables to eat. There were a few women who didn't seem to sit for very long, continually standing to serve and re-serve food and drink. Just when Samantha had hoped Brother Ed had changed his mind about the attack, he gave the go-ahead, and like a swarm, the five Infected raised their weapons and descended on the RVs like the plague of Egypt.

"No!" Samantha shouted, giving them away. "Stop!"

The humans, at hearing Samantha's cry, got to their feet just in time for the Archaeans to spring on them.

The human men, pulling guns and blades from tool belts and holsters, made a valiant effort to fend them off, as the women, grabbing up the children, ran for cover. But their efforts, despite their superior numbers, were futile—lost with the element of surprise. Soon, the men were incapacitated or dead where they stood, having fired perhaps half a dozen shots to no effect.

The Archaeans sought out the women and children, who had scattered into the night. Some were inside the RVs, some had taken off into the woods on the opposite side of the road. Samantha heard their screams and cries as they were captured and caught, then dragged back to the road.

One woman started up an RV and tried to drive away, but was soon stopped when the Archaeans pierced her tires and jammed their spears into the driver side window, breaking it open and pulling her out by her hair.

A second woman, overcome with horror, broke down into hysterics, screaming and shrieking in Brother Ed's grip. Finally, rolling his eyes in exasperation, he sliced her throat with a sharpened gardening trowel and dropped her gurgling body to the asphalt.

When the chaos subsided, they had captured four

men, six women, and ten children. Six men had been murdered in the attack. One Archaean, Sister Pam, had been killed, her neck broken in the fray. In retaliation, Brother Ed slashed her killer's throat open as well and left his body in the road to rot.

The humans were bound by zip-ties and lined up. Brother Ed, beaming, congratulated the Archaeans. "I am so proud of you all!" he cheered, walking down the line of prisoners as Anita secured their restraints. "You are the finest disciples anyone could ask for! Come, my brothers and sisters, let us lead our new followers home."

The humans were marched on, led by Brother Ed, Binh and Anita herding them from the rear. Samantha lingered at the side of the road, unsure and conflicted. She felt a great draw to follow them: after all, she was Archaean. But if there was ever a time for her to break free, this was it. She knew, deep within, the commune was trouble—it was doomed to suffer the same fate as the others, she had no doubt. Chaos and death would take over, just as they had before. The Infected would turn on each other and the community would implode. She would be powerless to stop it; even the ruling brothers would be helpless.

Yet, as Samantha watched them lead the humans into the forest, she could not help but want to follow. The Archaeans were her people. The Infected were linked to her soul. How could she, after all this time—after everything she had done in the service of the Archaean parasite—turn her back on them now?

It was impossible. She couldn't fathom the notion of being alone, much less without a commune. Standing from behind the bushes, she joined the others and walked alongside the humans, feeling defeated and beaten—yet complete.

For the most part, the humans were subdued, whimpering and sobbing softly—save for one, a stocky, bald man near the end of the line, who seethed with anger and cursed with every step. When Anita poked him with her spear and told him to be quiet, he spat at the ground at her feet and cursed at her.

"You don't know who you're dealing with," he said. "When they find out we're missing, they'll come for us. You're done for, all of you. Fuck the lot of you."

"Who's coming? When *who* finds out?" Samantha asked him.

"You'll see," he sneered. "Just you wait."

"Don't listen to him," Brother Bob said, coming up beside Samantha. "We know better than to listen to serpents. He's yet to be enlightened."

The straggling line reached the dairy farm sometime in the middle of the night. Upon their arrival, several members of the commune emerged from the farmhouse and helped sort the new arrivals into groups of five. They were taken to the sheds and locked inside with a bucket of water and a bowl of mash.

"Things will be different in the morning," Brother Ed said. "Until then, rest. You've all earned a good night's sleep." Then he assigned a few of his trusted brothers and sisters to keep watch through the night and meandered off alone, toward the barn.

Unsure where she was supposed to go, Samantha followed Anita and Binh back to the farmhouse.

The old woman who had interviewed Samantha stood at the door, instructing men and women up the stairs to different-colored rooms.

"To the red room," she told Anita. "The green room," she then said to Binh. She squinted at Samantha, then said, "The red room."

Samantha followed Anita up the only flight of stairs inside. The interior was surprisingly lush and clean, more suggestive of a manor house than living quarters for dairy farmers. Up the carpeted stairs were several bedrooms, all crammed wall-to-wall with bunk beds, with little more than a foot between them.

The women entered the red room, slid down the narrow aisles and filled the bunks, leaving their shoes in baskets at the foot of each bed.

Samantha, for all her conflicting emotions, was thankful to be back on a mattress, even if it was stuffed with hay and duck feathers and covered in burlap. She fell asleep quickly, slept soundly, and awoke at first light, refreshed.

After collecting her shoes and walking outside, the sounds of shouting brought her across the field.

A few of the humans who had been brought in kneeled outside the shed doors, surrounded by Brother Ed and a handful of armed Archaeans.

Brother Ed took notice of Samantha, but continued to pace back and forth in front of the prisoners, pointing to an empty pail, and an overturned bowl of uneaten mash. As he spoke, a pair of brothers dragged a barrel of sloshing water from the barn toward the group of them.

"Stubbornness," Brother Ed said, his voice growing louder, "is the path to Hell. Salvation lies within." He closed his eyes and turned toward the sunrise, raising his palms to the sky. "Let us take water together, to commemorate your indoctrination into the faith."

"Don't drink it," said the bald man who had cursed at Anita the night before. "It's poisoned."

Brother Ed sighed and dropped his hands to his sides. "It's not poisoned, I promise you."

Dropping the barrel in front of the captives, the two Archaeans popped off the lid and dipped in several tin cups, handing one to Brother Ed. He took it wordlessly.

"It's laced with parasites," the old man said. "You'll become one of *them*."

A teen girl—no more than fifteen, by Samantha's estimation—stared down the row at the older man and sucked back a sob. Licking her cracked lips, she blinked and stared to the ground. Beside her, a woman nodded. Two of the children cried.

"Mommy," one of them whimpered. It was the boy who had scraped his knee. "I'm thirsty."

"Don't drink the water," the mother said, voice hard.

Brother Ed nodded to the crying boy, a soft smile on his lips. "No harm will come to you, I promise."

"He's lying, Jeffrey," the mother said.

"You'll die," the older man said. "It's poison."

Stress and strain battled on the little boy's face. Caught between following his elder's commands, his fear of Brother Ed, and his thirst, the boy visibly wavered.

"Do we look dead to you?" Brother Ed argued, waving at the other Archaeans surrounding the prisoners. "Are we not alive? Our hearts beat in our chests. Our minds and hearts are filled with the holy Archaean. You too can become one of us. You too can live here on the farm in peace and tranquillity, surrounded by the love of the Archaean."

"It's a trick," said the mother. "Don't listen to him."

Brother Ed took a sip from the cup in his hand. "You would rather watch your children die of thirst than allow them to drink?"

"The others will come for us," said the old man at the end of the row. "We will be saved."

Brother Ed poured the remainder of the water from the cup in his hand and into the dirt at his feet, and shook his head slowly. "Why must everything be so difficult?" Handing the cup to a nearby Archaean, he turned away. He said simply, "Baptise them," then walked toward the barn, brow creased with sad resignation.

At the barn waited the two other leaders, the one in the knitted cap and the one who had greeted

Samantha's group in the forest. Brother Ed nodded to them, and all three entered the barn, closing the door behind them.

Back at the shed, one at a time, the old man and the young boy's mother were dunked face first into the barrel of parasitic water, over and over, in and out, until they inhaled, choked, and then swallowed.

Soaked, coughing, sobbing, they were tossed back into the shed to recuperate while the teenaged girl and the two youngsters greedily drank cup after cup of tainted water. All the while, a member of the fellowship stood by, reciting scripture and passages of welcome.

It took every ounce of mental strength Samantha had not to intervene.

OPERATION FRILLED SHARK

THEY SURROUNDED THE research facility on three sides.

As Lewis had predicted, a week earlier, what was left of Jacksonville, Florida was overrun with Infected. It was also five meters under water.

It had taken Cobalt and a squad of ten security staff the better part of three hours—coming up the St. John's River in patched dinghies, rowing around the flooded city to conserve fuel—before they were able to moor atop an abandoned rail station north of the Jacksonville Landing. It took another hour after that to make their way across rooftops and through new jungle growth before they were able to position themselves three points around the Winston and Winston medical research facility. By then, it was late afternoon.

The sun burned hot and the air was thick. The neighbourhood, drowned and covered in vines and greenery, was more like a swamp than the ruins of a metropolis. Herds of watery wildlife crowded

Jacksonville. Once-proud skyscrapers had become crumbling, algae-eaten piles of streaked glass and cracked cement. Schools of goliath-brutes and packs of tusk-fiends lurked around every watery bend, while terror-jaws moved in herds atop buildings, and rot-gliders nested high on sunken towers ready to swoop on prey below.

Miller, who'd fantasized of falling to his knees and kissing the dirt, soon realized there was no solid ground to smooch. From the angry sea to a flooded wasteland: one was no better than the other.

Mold, algae, and mildew grew on all surfaces. Infected communes popped out of every other building, starved, malicious, peppering them with spit darts and makeshift spears, hoping for one of their rafts to drift closer so they could rip them to ribbons.

Home sweet home.

It was a relief when they finally positioned themselves around the office building where Winston and Winston had once had their MRSA research laboratory, for all that the first two floors were underwater, and there was a commune of Infected living on the third floor. From what Miller could tell through his binoculars, there were about two dozen of them.

"*This doesn't bode well,*" Hsiung breathed over the com.

"I can see fifteen on the third floor—south side," Morland said from beside Miller. "At least."

"*Five more here on the west side,*" du Trieux confirmed. "*Doyle?*"

"*Three visible in the north,*" he answered, "*but it's dark inside. Infra-red isn't reliable in this humidity. What's the play, boss?*"

"Hold on," Miller said. "I'm thinking."

Tempting as it was to open fire on the third floor, the uncertainty as to numbers worried him. A smoke bomb might force some out, thin the herd, leaving the possibility of picking them off one at a time as they swam away. But they'd still have to wade through an indeterminate number of them once they got inside, and it was a twenty-story skyscraper, with plenty of space to hide.

If they climbed the building's exterior to the tenth floor—where the laboratory was—they'd be spotted. The building was glass, top to bottom, and a great many panels above and below sea level were shattered and broken. Not only did Cobalt risk being seen, they'd run the risk of being dragged inside and mauled—or worse, falling and being eaten by a school of tusk-fiends. Rappelling from the roof would leave them trapped below.

"A chopper would sure come in handy about now," Morland said.

"*Oui,*" du Trieux said.

"*Where's the stairwell?*" Doyle asked.

"*Your guess is as good as mine,*" Hsiung said.

"Cripes, I miss the internet," Morland spat.

"All right," Miller finally snapped. "We'll push them toward the north."

"*Toward me?*" Doyle chuckled. "*Awww, how sweet. You shouldn't have...*"

"*Can they get out that way?*" du Trieux asked.

"*Affirmative,*" Doyle answered. "*There's a grouping of broken windows and a crumbled wall. I suppose you could call it a grotto? There's a handful of Infected trying to hunt in the shallows of the second floor. They suck at it, by the way.*"

"Remind the others to pick off the Charismatics first," Miller said. "Du Trieux and Hsiung's squad will cover from the west and flank the rest as they scatter. If they swim off, let them go. Kill any who stick around. Morland and I will wade across with our squad and head up the stairs to the tenth floor. Swim in and meet us there once you've got the lower levels swept. Watch out for wildlife."

"*And if there are more upstairs, boss?*" Doyle asked.

"If we're overrun, then abort mission and get back to the ship, understood?" Miller waited until each of his team answered in the affirmative, then switched his com to mute and unpacked the rucksack he'd brought from the ship. His MGL Mk 1 grenade launcher was a welcome sight.

Along the south side of the office building, Morland, Miller, and three of the grunts were crouched atop a two-story train station. Several stairwells rose out of the water to the raised tracks, which rotted like blown arteries above the waves. Hunkered behind the overgrowth on top of one of the arched roofs, Miller raised the launcher and eyed the south side of the tower through the scope.

He pulled the lever and rotated the load. The Mk 1 had a conventional trigger and a recoil reduction system, making it ideal for launching standard-to-medium-velocity munitions as far as twelve hundred meters. Miller had brought it along in case they needed a last ditch effort for exiting the building. He hadn't considered they'd need it to get in.

Miller sought his target through the scope. He was using Hellhound rounds, armor-piercing explosive shells with an effective radius of about ten meters; they should easily clear an entry point into the building, and hopefully push anyone near the explosion clear out the far side.

He squeezed the trigger, and the shell punched the glass wall of the third floor like a needle. The resultant blast filled the air with fire, glass and smoke.

"*Here we go,*" Doyle said on the com.

People spilled out in two different directions, not quite what Miller had hoped. From his vantage point he spotted a small pack of Infected, covered in moss and lichen—near-skeletal forms of splotchy, gray and green skin—spilling out the eastern side into the murky water like rats from a fire. Then, trickling forth into an adjoining parking lot, they clamoured upwards, climbing atop one another to reach cement pylons in front of a dilapidated office building.

"*I count twelve,*" Doyle breathed over the com. A shot rang out, echoing across downtown Jacksonville. "*Eleven.*"

"*Same on my side,*" grunted du Trieux.

"Take out the Charismatics," Miller reminded them, slinging the Mk 1 strap over his shoulder.

Then he, Morland and the others jumped down into the green sludge and swam across the street toward the office building.

As careful as Miller tried to be, it was impossible not to get the water on his face; breast stroke wasn't his strongest. Spitting the sweet tasting murk from his lips, he pushed forward, Morland on his right, the other three a stroke behind.

Luck was on their side: no wildlife got in their way. At the mouth of the building, the skeleton of a half-moon glass enclosure, shattered and bent, extended from the second floor like a ruptured tumour. Miller helped Morland and their team climb on top of it, then they hoisted themselves over a cement railing, which led to an exterior walkway on the third floor.

Glass crunched under his sodden boots as Miller crossed the hall into the building. His grenade blast had taken out four to five Infected upon impact, their charred, jagged bodies smoldering beside what had once been a reception desk.

"Two o'clock," Morland said, turning to aim at two more Infected, who were wounded but still mobile. Two brief pops and he turned back around.

As the rest of the group swept the area, Miller got the lay of the land. Elevators stood open on their left. Behind the reception desk was another door, leading to a conference room—also deserted. Another door lead to be a foul-smelling bathroom, past which was a long hallway of cubicles and offices.

Beside the elevator foyer was a fire stair, the red

sign over the door partially obscured by fungal blooms. Miller pointed and led the way.

Pushing down the metal bar, he jammed his shoulder into the door, which opened a fraction of an inch, then stuck.

"Jammed," Miller said.

"*They've found us,*" Doyle said over the com. "*We've locked the door, but it won't be long. Du Trieux? Hsiung? A little help?*"

"*Almost...*" Hsiung gasped over the com, "*there.*"

"Get behind the desk," Miller said to his team, pointing. He chambered another grenade, blasted the stairwell door and ducked down to wait for the dust to settle. When he rose again, the door had been disintegrated. Someone had stacked furniture behind it—a bookcase, a metal desk, several file cabinets—which were also blown to bits. Scattered papers fluttered around the reception area and stairwell like confetti.

Once over the desk they sprinted up the stairs.

"*There's three of them,*" Doyle said over the com, "*to the east.*"

"*I see them,*" du Trieux replied.

"*I'm here. Where are you? Did you move positions?*" Hsiung huffed.

"*Had to,*" Doyle said, shots ringing out over the com. "*Got overrun. We're two buildings west. Busted my knee pretty good jumping, though.*"

Hsiung cussed under her breath and the com quieted for a moment.

Morland, Miller, and their squad were at the

sixth floor and still climbing, when the door burst open and a handful of Infected spilled out. They looked at them quizzically for a moment, then began pursuit.

The squad turned around and fired, mowing down the front line in a bloody heap.

"We're boxed in," Miller said into the com, taking two steps at a time up the flight. "Gonna need extraction."

Morland unholstered his sidearm and risked slowing for a heartbeat to snap off three shots behind him. One round ricocheted off the rusted railing; two snagged the front-most Infected in the chest. Two of the three grunts behind him were swarmed by the horde, unable to keep up. Their screams echoed through the stairwell as they fell.

At the tenth floor landing, Miller grabbed for the handle and pulled.

Locked.

"Move!" Morland shouted.

Miller stepped back, taking out his .45 calibre Gallican and turning to shoot into the approaching throng. He took out one in the head and another up the nose. The soldier beside him emptied his assault rifle into the crowd, then fumbled to reload. Miller watched as the mob overcame him when he bent to pick up his magazine.

Morland had emptied a mag into the locked door handle and wrenched it open. Miller dispatched another from the mob, dropped an empty mag on the floor and reloaded, and he and Morland threw themselves through the door and barred it from the inside.

"*I've got Doyle,*" Hsiung said. "*Du Trieux?*"

"*We're cleaning up down here in the water,*" she answered. She grunted once, something messy making it over the airwaves. "*Find cover back at the dinghy, we'll rendezvous there. I'm going for Miller and Morland.*"

"*Copy that.*"

"*You're a peach, Trix,*" Doyle said. "*Go get 'em, tiger.*"

"*Never mind him,*" Hsiung said, as du Trieux snickered. "*I gave him morphine. His knee is mush.*"

"*Be careful, you two,*" du Trieux added before cutting the line.

Inside the tenth floor, Morland and Miller barricaded the broken door, piling up as much broken furniture and trash as they could find, then lit up their barrel-mounted flashlights and scrambled down the dark, claustrophobic hallway.

Decay claimed every square inch of surface. Black and green mold, intertwined and swirling like a vast Jackson Pollock, covered the walls and floor. The smell of must and mildew hung thick and heavy in the air.

At the end of the hall stood double glass doors covered in fungal blooms. Miller and Morland stopped short, aware of the racket from the barricaded doors behind them, and scraped away the thick growth before prising the door open. It gave way with a creak, revealing a large circular room.

White glass countertops ringed the room. Other than the ubiquitous mold, they were seemingly bare and empty.

Miller, feeling his panic rise, yanked open drawers and cabinets, only to find rotted—unreadable—papers, broken and crumbling hard drives, and the glassy shards of a laboratory long ago destroyed. "Fuck."

"I found a thumb drive," Morland said, stepping out of what had once been a supply closet.

"*That'll be some secretary's holiday photos, then,*" Doyle said over the com, laughing and then apologizing under his breath.

"This has been empty a while," Miller said, kicking a cracked floor tile with the edge of his boot. "A long while."

"*A wild goose chase?*" du Trieux asked.

"Afraid so."

Morland sighed and pocketed the thumb drive. Bending over, he opened the bent door of an overturned specimen refrigerator with the tip of his rifle, finding nothing but darkness and mold.

"Take a sample," Miller said. "Just in case."

"You hoping we're standing in a heap of super penicillin?" Morland frowned.

"You ever see this much mold?"

Morland shook his head. "No."

"*Third floor is clear,*" du Trieux said. "*But I hear movement above and I don't think it's you.*"

"We left a crowd outside the tenth floor stairwell," Miller said.

In the distance, a great boom sounded. Three distinct pops resonated off the buildings with a reverberation and an echo.

"What the hell was that?" Morland asked.

"*Uh, sir?*" Hsiung said.

"Anybody have eyes on that?" Miller asked.

Hsiung cleared her throat. "*Do we have a battleship in the S-Y fleet I don't know about?*"

"A *what?*"

"*I'm looking south across that parking structure and over the performing arts center, sir. There's a battleship on the river, not three clicks from the* Tevatnoa. *It's just blown the Fuller Warren Bridge to pieces and it's headed straight at it.*"

Doyle gushed. "*It's fucking huge.*"

"Use the long-range radio, Hsiung; see if you can't establish contact with the *Tevatnoa*. Make sure Lewis knows what's coming."

"*It's hard to miss,*" Hsiung said.

"Just do it. We're on our way." Miller turned toward Morland. "Find anything else?"

He shook his head. "I don't think anybody's been in here since before the invasion."

Miller's frown deepened. "Alright. Let's go."

As Miller and Morland reloaded and braced themselves for the Infected back on the stairs, du Trieux's voice crackled over the com. "*I just hope there's a ship left by the time we get there.*"

DAIRY FARMING WAS an excuse, Samantha soon realized; a cover. The true purpose of the farm, the true 'calling'—as Brother Ed, Brother Jim, and Brother Dan called it—was to spread the Archaean parasite to every living creature on the planet, willing or not.

Samantha understood the logic. Humans were unsympathetic killing machines, born and bred to consume the planet's resources and destroy everything—including each other—in the process. Looking for a way to rein in that behaviour was understandable.

But unlike the rest of the Archaeans, Samantha didn't believe the Infected were immune to those failings. They weren't enlightened. They weren't exempt from ambition, or ego, or arrogance, or any other destructive human trait. In fact, Samantha increasingly believed, the Archaeans were worse.

If you had one ambitious, egocentric and arrogant

human, you had a fighting chance against them, one on one. An Archaean with the same outlook, with their ability to project their emotions across the Infected, was a potential mob, a horde—*hundreds* of ambitious, egocentric, arrogant monsters, all acting in unison.

These were not winning odds. Anyone acting against the majority was doomed.

You didn't need to be a rocket scientist to figure it out. One trip with the farm's 'outreach' program and Sam understood perfectly well that she, and everyone who had come with her, were under the control of an angry cult. There was no point in resisting the majority rule; in fact, thanks to the parasite, it was impossible to do so.

Days of toil turned into weeks. Samantha spent her time herding thug-behemoths back and forth to and from the fields, shovelling waste and occasional snow, laying fresh hay in the stalls. Evenings she sat on a hard wooden pew and watched as a raiding party was 'chosen,' watched as they returned— hours or days later—with humans to convert, or with blood on their hands.

The fellowship had numbered maybe a hundred or more on Samantha's arrival. Now, the farm house— the only true living space—was full to the brim, too full.

Sheds formerly used for storage or prisoners had to be converted to living spaces. Stone chimneys were built against the walls to add heat during the harsh snowstorms; fungus-covered trees were felled, planked, and hammered into bunk beds. Mattresses of pine needles and goose feathers became precious commodities. All the while, the behemoths were milked, butter was churned, cheese was made, and the sun rose and set, day after day.

Samantha felt neither joy, contentedness, nor comfort in her life. From what she could tell, no one else on the farm did either. The only ones who showed any positivity were the three 'Brothers' who preached each night, but the moment the message was finished, and the workers sent back to their duties, the good vibrations faded and ultimately disappeared, amidst the cold, the wet, and the daily grind.

Was this her life now? Was Samantha to feel discontented and alone, living in a crowd of people *just* like her?

These thoughts came and went from Sam's mind, until one afternoon—as she smacked the broad rumps of the thug-behemoths, urging them back into the barn for the night—she barely registered the sound of a gunshot.

A gunshot?

Looking up, Samantha dropped her stick and turned toward the noise. A string of pops and snaps, like firecrackers, echoed through the air and spooked the livestock.

The beasts moaned and shifted, shuffling toward the southern side of the pen, away from the barn door.

Samantha felt irritated, if less than she should. She *knew* it wasn't firecrackers, but somehow, she couldn't convince herself the sound had any significance. Her mind was hazy and tired, sluggish and filled with fog. She worried briefly that the disturbance would affect the behemoths' milk production, and then picked up her stick, almost forgetting what she'd just heard.

Across the field, the farmhouse sat, beautiful and yellow, the black shutters tacked back for the day to let in the cool winter breeze. Beside it, a large transport truck had appeared, a camouflage canvas top raised over the bed.

Samantha squinted at the vehicle, listened to the firecrackers pop—and thought to herself, *What's for supper?*

Just then, a band of people, armed with rifles, shotguns, and various handguns, burst through the ferns, jumped the property line and ran west, scooping up and capturing members of the fellowship along the way. They shot anyone who resisted and dragged survivors behind them like captured pigs.

It took several seconds before Samantha's mind understood what was happening. Dropping her stick, she ran, jumping over the split-rail fence and scratching the length of her calf as she skimmed the barbed wire.

Inside the barn, Sister Ethel screamed, "What's *happening?*"

"Run, Ethel!" Sam barked.

The six milkers working at the stations on the north side of the barn looked up from their pails, then scattered.

Behind her, the barn doors swung wide, crashing against the wooden pews stacked against the wall. Samantha ran straight down the center of the barn, aiming for the stage. Sister Ethel's screams reverberated off the rafters.

"Somebody shut that one up," a man said.

"What's *happening*? What's—"

A gun shot rang out and Ethel fell silent.

At the end of the barn, Samantha hopped onto the platform and sprinted upstage toward the ladder, the shrieks of the milkers sounding behind her. Sam scrambled recklessly up the ladder.

"Where's that one goin'?" someone asked.

"Hay loft, I reckon."

At the top of the ladder, Sam threw herself into the hayloft and picked her way through the bales stacked haphazardly to the only other door: the loft door. It offered no ladder or stairwell, but it was a way out, and hopefully one the raiders hadn't accounted for yet.

Sam yanked open the door and was relieved to find the rope and hooks still hanging from the pulley. Grabbing the hook, she kicked off the edge of the barn and held on. She dropped to the ground and took off running.

Behind the barn stretched miles of dense forest; she ran headlong into the brush, weaving between trees, jumping fallen limbs and tree trunks. She heard movement behind her, the sound of pursuit, and increased her pace.

She wasn't sure how far she'd run. The late morning

sun climbed the sky, extending fingers of light through the dense canopy. She felt her legs tiring, and knew there was no way she could outrun the pursuit. She scanned ahead, looking for a hiding place.

She sprinted to the left and cut across a creek, stopping to fill her pockets with rocks and stones from the bed. Ahead was a particularly tall pine tree; Sam jumped onto its lowest branch and climbed. A few branches up, her foot slipped, spilling a tuft of needles to the forest floor.

"Over there!" someone shouted.

Once above head-height, she wedged her body between the trunk and a thick branch, pulled her sling from her waist band and a rock from her pocket, leaned out and fitted the first stone.

She spotted three in pursuit, spread out. The closest, a blonde woman in camouflage gear with a rifle in her hands, was just arriving at the creek.

Samantha adjusted her body, swung the sling over her head, and released.

The woman took the stone straight between the eyes, spun mid-step and pitched face-first down the bank and into the water.

Sam grabbed another rock from her pocket and reloaded the sling.

The next pursuer, a man all in black with a pistol in hand and a rifle over his shoulder, approached on her left. Whoever these people were, they were well equipped.

Sam leaned back from the tree, gripping the trunk with her thighs, and swung the sling once more.

The movement caught the man's eye, and he dropped to one knee and squeezed off a shot. Twisting, Sam swung down from the branch, hanging by her knees, and the bullet went wide. Sam had barely lost her momentum. She released.

The rock sliced through the air like a blade, hitting the man on the side of the head beside his ear. Cushioned by his knitted cap, the stone didn't knock him out, but he went down, clutching his head and howling. Sam was pulling herself up and reached into her pocket to grab another stone when a searing hot pain sliced through her.

The bullet punched straight through her body and into the tree behind her, splintering bark, pine needles, and sending blood in all directions. Sam cried out, nearly slipping. Her sling dropped from her nerveless fingers; she watched it helplessly as it fell to the leaves below.

She grabbed hold of the trunk and struggled to maintain consciousness, but the pain was blinding. Her arms spasmed and she fell, crashing into tree branches and smacking onto the ground straight on her right shoulder.

She just managed to make out the angry face of a man in a bloody black cap when the butt of a handgun filled her world.

All went black.

SAMANTHA AWOKE WITH a splitting headache and a throbbing in her shoulder. Her clothes were stuck to her skin with blood and sweat. Her mouth tasted metallic and dry. It was pitch dark. She heard the muffled voices of people around her and felt the terror and fear of nearby Infected. It wasn't until she blinked a few times that she realized she was blindfolded.

The world shook, like a massive earthquake; she bounced into the air and slammed back down onto her shoulder, sending pain through every nerve in her body.

No. She was in a vehicle. Probably the transport she'd spotted back on the farm. Something nudged her in the stomach. Gentle at first, then like a kick to the gut.

"This one's awake," a man said.

"Keep an eye on that one. It killed Lisa."

Her hands were bound behind her back, and the pain in her shoulder was so bad she was having a hard time staying conscious.

After a long while, the transport stopped and Sam was yanked to her feet by two sets of hands, under each arm.

She was dragged a few meters, and her blindfold was ripped off. Afternoon, by the looks of the sun. She stood at the mouth of the trailer, bloody-stocking-cap guy holding one arm, another man in full camouflage gripping the other. With a shove they pushed her off the edge of the bed, face-first into the dirt.

Spitting earth from bloody lips, Samantha looked up at the entrance to a wooden fort. A log wall, at least six meters high, extended around the fort, topped with a walkway and manned by guards in camo. Within the walls stood several huge log cabins and a fenced enclosure, also guarded. There were at least three dozen humans in sight, armed with weapons of all types—and who knew how many more inside the cabins.

In front of her, a line of Infected marched by, manacled and chained together.

Samantha swallowed the lump in her throat and wrenched her shoulder off the ground, flipping herself onto her back. The two men yanked her roughly to her feet.

"Where are we?" she asked, as they pulled her toward a fenced walkway.

"Hell," one of them said, laughing.

19

THE SOUTHERN SKY bled orange. A thick wall of red dust—originating about eight thousand kilometers away in the crusted deserts of the Sahara—moved high, wide, and fast across the waters of the Atlantic, over the St. John's River and through the ruins of the Fuller Warren Bridge, rushing at them like a six-hundred-meter-high door closing on a tomb.

Just west of the dust cloud, Miller and Cobalt raced their rubber dinghy through choppy waters, losing ground against the oncoming haze. The surviving members of their security squad zoomed ahead of them.

Before them was the Acosta Bridge, blown apart not long after the Fuller Warren by the battleship still approaching from the southeast.

The battleship, which flew no colours, looked like it could have been American or British at one point, but there was no way of telling who was in control now. The name of the ship had been covered over with thick black paint.

"Everybody got a gas mask?" Hsiung asked, steering the motor at the stern of the dinghy, watching the approaching dust storm with wide eyes.

"Got mine right here, Tea Blosshom," Doyle said, swinging his gas mask in the air.

"She's not your fucking Tea Blossom," du Trieux snapped at him, snatching his mask from his fingers. "How much morphine did you give him?"

Hsiung frowned. "Half a syrette."

"You should shee my knee," Doyle slurred, pointing to his left leg. "It looks like an overripe grapefruit."

Miller couldn't tell which scared him more: the dust storm, the rough sea slapping the dinghy and drenching them to the bone, or the battleship poised to blast them out of the water.

Doyle giggled and pawed for his mask like a kitten after a string.

Grimacing, du Trieux let him have it. "You're a lightweight," she said, helping him put it on.

"Eazhe up, Cactus Flower," Doyle said, snapping his gas mask in place.

Morland stifled a laugh, then coughed uncomfortably as Hsiung and du Trieux glowered at him.

Miller pulled a compass from his combat vest and eyed it nervously. An island to the east—once a ridge on Jacksonville's outskirts, now cut off by the rising seas—was fully engulfed in the red dust cloud. It had to be kilometers wide. At this rate, the storm would pass over the battleship first, then engulf the dinghies; the *Tevatnoa*—sitting just east of the Hart Bridge—would be struck last.

Miller would have much preferred to be aboard the *Tevatnoa* when it hit. He wasn't certain the rubber dinghy could withstand the wind if it topped forty knots. They'd just have to make a run for it and hope for the best. Given the sputtering noises from the dinghy's motor, he wasn't hopeful.

Hsiung cursed at the fungus covering the engine controls, wiped the blooms off with a gloved thumb, then kicked the motor with the heel of her combat boot, causing it to gasp and revive again—but victory was fleeting. After a few seconds, the engine popped, spat out a puff of gray smoke, and died.

Miller picked up a pair of paddles and tossed them to Morland and du Trieux. Hsiung snatched up the one at her feet, tucked under Miller's grenade launcher.

"Stroke!"

It was futile. White caps and two-meter crests struck the raft from behind, lurching them up and tipping them down. They were drenched and paddling against the wind on a river with virtually no current, making no headway.

Miller cussed under his breath. They could have stayed in Jacksonville when they'd spotted the battleship, left the *Tevatnoa* to its own fate. They could have hunkered down in an abandoned building and waited out the dust storm. Instead, they'd tried to outrun it in a rubber dinghy. They'd burned out their engine and would now either suffocate or drown. Hell, they *deserved* to die, for being so stupid. Bravery only got you killed.

The wall of red dust struck like a hammer, swallowing them whole. The wind lifted the stern of the dinghy half a meter out of the water, jolting them forward in their seats and sending the grenade launcher, the long-range radio and the medical kit tumbling into the murky water.

Miller looped his wrist around the safety rope and wedged the tip of one boot into the bottom seam. The dinghy bounced out of the water again, flying headlong across the waves.

The engine, probably the only thing keeping the raft from taking flight altogether, caught a gust of wind, twisting the craft in the air and spinning it around. Doyle, du Trieux, and Hsiung were the first to go; Morland and Miller, closest to the water, were able to hold on for a few more seconds until they too tipped over, the raft landing upside down on top of them.

Miller came up and out of the water under the dinghy, one hand still clasping the safety rope. Having no idea where anyone else had gotten to, he ripped the gas mask from his face and gasped for air, coughing at the effort. The air under the raft was thick with dust and sand, feeling like glass in his throat.

The raft bucked on one side, threatening to flip again, and Miller reached across, stretching his body the width of the raft so he could grab the rope. Behind him, du Trieux surfaced and grabbed hold of the safety rope with her right hand. With her other hand she lifted Doyle, still wearing his gas mask.

Miller reached over and pulled the mask off Doyle's face, dropping it into the water. Doyle coughed and sputtered, but then heaved and vomited. Du Trieux popped the flotation collar on his vest and looped his arm through the safety rope. Then she drew a deep breath and went down into the water again.

Beside him under the raft, Doyle mumbled something about a flower. Miller grimaced and hit the flotation device on his own vest. Soon thereafter, du Trieux and Hsiung emerged, followed by Morland.

"I've got a plan," du Trieux said, panting. "But you're not going to like it."

Miller spat foul-tasting water from his mouth. "I'm all ears."

"We're closest to the battleship," she said.

Morland shook his head. "Not a chance in hell."

Just then Doyle's arm slipped from the safety line and he bobbed in place, held afloat only by his flotation collar.

Hsiung suddenly jerked to one side, knocking the sniper like a pinball around the inside of the overturned dinghy. "Something just brushed against my leg."

Morland adjusted his grip on the safety loop as the raft bucked in the wind. "Let's hope it doesn't have teeth."

Du Trieux moved Doyle to one side so she could look Miller in the eyes. "We need to get out of the water. The *Tevatnoa* is too far."

"They could be the Infected," Miller said.

"You saw what they did to those bridges," du Trieux argued. "If they wanted the *Tevatnoa* sunk, they'd have done it already."

"Maybe they don't want it shunk sho they can kill ush all and take our shtuff," Doyle slurred.

Morland nodded. "Most bloody likely."

"There could be communications going on between them right now," du Trieux kept on. "Without the long-range radio there's no way of our knowing."

"I'm not kidding, guys," Hsiung said. "There's something moving underneath us."

"Let's hope it doesn't have a scaled dorsal fin," Miller muttered, instantly regretting it.

Hsiung's face turned ashen.

The wind bucked, causing the raft to shudder. "We have to do something," du Trieux said. "We can't stay like this."

"We have to wait until the dust storm passes, our gas masks are sodden and we'll suffocate," Morland said.

"Did anybody else feel that?" Hsiung asked.

The fanged mouth and bulbous head of a tusk-fiend broke the surface in the center of the dinghy. The enormous tusks pierced straight through the underside of the rubber raft, lifting it into the air before everyone let go of the safety ropes and scattered.

When the beast came down, its teeth still stuck in the rubber, the only one still near it was Doyle, floating less than a half meter away.

Miller and du Trieux swam in from opposite directions, their knives at the ready.

The tusk-fiend thrashed around in protest, entangled in the remains of the dinghy.

Du Trieux reached Doyle first. Wrapping her arm under his chin, she swam backwards, kicking and grunting, knife still clutched in hand.

Just as the tusk-fiend managed to shake off the raft, a shot rang out. The creature's brain matter was scattered into the dusty wind.

The battleship loomed to their right, the shadow of a sniper draped over the side.

Miller looked wildly to his left. The *Tevatnoa* lay at least a full kilometer away, still engulfed in the dissipating storm. Miller swam, one arm over the other, toward du Trieux and Doyle. "To the battleship, then," he said.

"You're the boss," du Trieux answered.

THERE WERE FEW events in Samantha's life that she truly regretted. It was her choices, even the bad ones, that had led her to the Archaeans, and her true calling; how could she wish any decision undone, when she was so happy with the result?

Now, however, as she pulled yet another mushroom off the trunk of a felled pine tree, she deeply regretted that she had ever joined the commune at the dairy farm. If she'd listened to her gut, steered her group away, they'd never have been roped into the kidnappings. And they wouldn't have been hunted and enslaved in turn, had they kept to themselves and continued their journey south.

With any luck, they could have got all the way to Florida and been basking on some warm, soft beach, drinking coconut milk, rather than stuck in the middle of a Northeastern forest in the middle of winter, freezing their asses off and working their fingers numb.

In fact, Samantha wasn't sure how things could *be* any worse.

The humans had the Infected under armed guard at all times. Working in packs of five, the Infected were spread across a heavily wooded area west of Old Forge; as far as Samantha could tell, they were deep into the Ha-De-Ron-Dah forest, in Adirondack Park. Even before the collapse, the area had been off the grid.

From what she could tell, these humans—fifty, maybe more—had established some sort of isolated settlement. They had a marketplace, a mayor, a forge, all in log houses. But for their automatic weapons, and the modern clothes, it looked like something out of the Old West.

The region had plentiful natural springs and an abundance of rain and snowfall, and the humans farmed their own food and lived without electricity. They probably hadn't seen a drop of the bottled Archaean water since its discovery five years before—there simply wouldn't have been a need, or desire, for it.

And since the people of the Adirondack mountains were known for keeping to themselves—suspicious of authority as it was—it made perfect sense that they'd survived, even thrived, in the rough environment.

In fact, they'd apparently done so well, they'd begun to build a second log settlement, only a quarter of a kilometer from the first. The need for fungus-free lumber, Sam guessed, was what had inspired them to start using Infected slaves.

After being dragged from the truck on arrival, Sam and the other Infected were untied, shoved down a fenced path and dragged to a log barn.

Far back in the line, Sam craned her neck, peering at the head of the queue. She spotted a forge, then smelled burning flesh. A few of the others—who had come to the same conclusions—tried to run, climbing over the fence and sprinting for their lives, but they didn't get far. The fort swarmed with guards, and it didn't take long before the Infected were tackled and dragged to the front of the line to be immediately branded.

Horror rippled through the new Infected like a shockwave, freezing many of them in position. The man in front of Sam pissed his pants. Those who stopped in line only got smacked with the butts of hunting rifles for their troubles. Terror floated in the air like a fog.

One by one, Sam heard the screams. When it was her turn, she felt weak at the knees, her head swimming as she hyperventilated.

The human holding the brand was young, hardly eighteen. He was missing his two front teeth and wore wooden dentures, making his smirk even more disturbing.

"Come on, now, don't make this worse," the boy said. He pulled the branding rod out of the forge with a heavily gloved hand. At the end gleamed a red hot circle with an 'I' in the center. "Ready when you are, guys."

Two large men grabbed Sam by the arms and pulled her toward a blackened but solid wooden block.

"No!" she screamed, panic taking over. She dug in her heels and locked her knees, grabbing hold of the fence.

The men cussed, then yanked her loose.

The man on the right stopped and flinched, frowning at his hand. "It's bleeding. Damnit, I just got Infected blood on my new gloves."

The man on the other side shook his head. "Damn shame. You'll have to burn them, now."

The man with the brand squinted at them. "Why's it bleeding?"

The man on the right stuck his finger into Samantha's bullet wound and wiggled it around. Despite her best efforts, she screamed.

"It's been shot."

The man with the brand waved them forward. "Well, today is its lucky day."

"Let go of me!"

Dragging her toward the block, they bent her at the waist, forced her chest onto the wood and held her down. The man on the left grabbed the hem of her shirt and pulled it up, dragging it over her wounded shoulder.

"Hold still," one of them said.

She couldn't breathe. Hot air burned her throat and she tasted bile. Kicking and flailing did no good. Strong arms held her in place as the man with the brand approached.

"Hurry up," one of them said. "It's stronger than it looks."

Twisting her head to one side, she flipped her ponytail out of her face just in time to see the brand descend onto her bullet wound. The boy pressed the 'I' into her flesh and held it for five seconds.

Searing pain blazed through her arm and shoulder, down her elbow and into her fingers. She saw white stars and fought to stay conscious as blackness filled her vision and weakened her resistance. She screamed at the top of her lungs, the pain tearing its way out of her.

When the brand came away, scraps of skin peeled off, stuck to the red-hot metal. The boy shoved it back into the forge, and Sam sobbed, helpless.

Just when she had begun to see clearly, the man pulled the brand out of the fire again and stuck it on her left arm. "And one more for good luck."

Sam shrieked holy hell but lay as still as a corpse, wishing for it to end. Death seemed a welcome idea.

"I just cauterized your wound for you," the human boy said. "You're welcome."

Spit dripped from Sam's mouth into the dirt. "Fuck you."

Strong hands lifted her off the block and dragged her. The toes of her worn boots ploughed the dirt.

Behind a two-and-a-half-meter-tall wooden fence, more Infected stood in clumps, grouped together in a holding pen. The men dropped Sam to her knees and closed the gate behind her, locking it from the outside.

She wanted to pass out. The pain in her shoulder and arm was insurmountable. She dropped onto all fours and choked out a few more sobs before gentle, sympathetic hands helped her to her feet and onto a pile of pine needles.

"Don't touch the burns," someone said; a woman. Through her tears and the fog of pain Samantha managed to nod, then sat on the pile.

"Drink this." The woman handed her a tin cup.

Sam drank it greedily. It was water, but tasted of pine and something else, something sweet that left an aftertaste.

"It's white pine tea. Wipe this on your burns," the woman said, handing Sam a cloth with a sticky glob smeared on it. "It's honey."

Sam touched the goo to her wounds, wincing through the agony. She heard screaming back at the branding station and shuddered.

She handed the wash cloth and cup back to the woman, who looked to be about fifty years old. Her wiry hair, twisted into dreads, was grayed at the temples, and she had lichen and fungal growths up both arms and on her face. Her eyes sunk into her face like black rocks. "Give some to whoever comes in next," she said. "And try to sleep. There will be a lot to do tomorrow." The woman looked over her shoulder at the armed humans patrolling the terrace.

"Who are these people? What is this place?" Sam asked.

The woman looked back at her, sadly. "It's a labor camp," she said. "And they own us."

When Sam opened her mouth to ask another question, the gate to the holding pen opened and another Infected—a man, short and stocky—fell inside. He'd been one of Brother Paul's right-hand men back at the dairy farm. Off the top of her head, Sam couldn't think of his name.

"You'll see," the woman said, as two able-bodied Infected helped the newly branded man to his own bed of pine needles beside Sam's.

Sam handed him the cup and wash cloth and explained what to do. The man nodded absently, looking bewildered.

Feeling slightly better, Sam blinked through the throbbing pain and scanned the holding pen. The woman who had helped her had moved off toward a group of sickly-looking Infected. They were gathered around a circle of pine needle beds, whispering amongst themselves and scratching their lichen growths. The brand-scars on their arms had scabbed over, leaving raised pink welts on their skin. Old-timers, she guessed.

She figured the transport carrying her had held twenty-five or so of her fellow prisoners; it couldn't have been many more. She had no idea what happened to the others at the farm, and tried not to think about it. Her eyelids grew heavy and she lay down.

At some point the sun set. The screams of the brandings eventually ceased, and Sam was able to capture a few hours' sleep. For a few hours, she was at peace.

The feeling didn't last long. The next morning, in the dim pre-dawn, she was awakened with the others in her pen. Armed humans fastened crude manacles to the new arrivals' ankles, secured them with bolts, then chained them together in groups of five. After handing one of each group a handmade basket woven from bark, they were marched, at gunpoint, through the forest.

Just as the sun peeked bright on the horizon, Sam and her chain gang were shown to a pile of tree trunks, covered in fungal blooms and wild mushrooms.

Two men on the end of Sam's chain started picking off the blooms and caps, dropping them into the basket at their feet. Following suit, the two beside them—a women and another man—did the same, leaving only Samantha.

She looked around, where other gangs worked on other log piles. Far off behind them, a group of ten humans made a clearing on the forest floor, chopping down trees and levelling the soil. Another team was starting on a wall: digging holes, dropping in previously-cleaned logs with pulleys and man-powered cranes, filling in the holes with excess dirt. It was a massive production.

At first, Sam couldn't understand why the humans had slaves at all. There were certainly enough of them that they could be doing this themselves. Then she realized: fungus, particularly the blooms which had sprouted after the birth of the Archaean biome, was harmless to those who were Infected, but deadly to humans. She doubted they had enough gas masks for all of them, either, much less thought to use them to clean lumber. Why bother, when you could round up some Infected to do it for you? And certainly the fungus and mushrooms wouldn't stop growing on the logs, even after the cabins were built. That meant the humans required a slave force, year round, to keep their homes clear of the toxic growths.

This didn't go on to explain how feeding, guarding, and taking care of a group of slave Infecteds was worth the hassle for such a simple job, but then she understood that the humans just weren't *bothering*.

There were no bathroom breaks; you squatted where you stood. There were no water breaks, no food. Technically, aside from a pile of pine needles, there was no shelter, either.

With snow storms coming and going at any given moment, Sam had to wonder: what good was a slave force if they continually died from the elements? Although it went some way to explaining why the humans raided Infected communes. But the turnover had to be *immeasurable*.

Just then a rifle butt struck Sam's wounded shoulder, making her flinch.

"Get to work!" a human man said, motioning to the logs with the barrel of his rifle.

Gingerly reaching forward, Samantha pinched a mushroom cap between two fingers and pulled it off the log. The cap came off, but the stalk remained lodged in the bark. After tossing the cap into the basket, Sam went back for the stalk, then pulled a fungal bloom off, accidentally dropping them both to the ground.

The Infected beside her jabbed Sam with a bony elbow. "Hey, be more careful," he said. "That's dinner."

Her stomach twisted. "Sorry." Reaching down, she picked up the mushroom stalk and tossed it into the basket. That answered that question.

Later, when the light of day had faded and the humans deemed it time, the Infected were marched back to their enclosure. Using a homemade bow drill fashioned from hair and sticks, the old-timers lit fires, then took the baskets of mushroom caps and fungal blooms and boiled them in water in tin cups. These cups were then passed around, everyone getting three mouthfuls. Then they made pine needle tea, and took turns with that. The water they collected from a muddy hole in the pen, and from melted snow.

When it was Sam's turn, she passed the mushroom cup along without taking a single sip, and only drank the tea.

She knew the Archaean parasite granted her an immunity to the majority of the fungal infections associated with it, but she'd seen how covered these Infected were, and assumed eating the fungus was contributing.

It would only be a matter of time before she was in the same condition, but if she was to ever devise an escape, she needed full mobility, and no distractions. That included itchy growths.

Her eyes scanned the crowd and rested on Binh, who she hadn't realized until then was among the new arrivals. Their eyes met as he hungrily gulped from the cup in his hands and he nodded to her as he passed it along.

She balled her fists and felt her eyes fill with tears, but not from sorrow.

From rage.

21

DOYLE WAS HOISTED aboard the battleship via a
stretcher lowered from the port side. Upon closer
inspection, it had proven not to be a battleship, but
a Bay-class dock landing ship, about one-hundred-
eighty meters long and thirty meters abeam. With
two large cranes between the superstructure and the
flight deck, and an arsenal of cannons, miniguns,
GPMGs and CIWSs, it looked a monster compared
to the *Tevatnoa*, which, while larger, was not nearly
as well-armed.

The *Tevatnoa* offered no help to Cobalt, currently
a kilometer away off the landing ship's port bow,
stationary and quiet on the St. John's River.

As the rest of the team climbed a cargo net
obligingly dropped by the ship's crew, Miller could
only guess as to what communication, if any, had
taken place between the two vessels. He imagined
Gray and Lewis in the *Tevatnoa*'s bridge, cursing
Miller's name for boarding the unidentified vessel,

but what choice did he have? Given Doyle's condition, and the threats from the water below, he saw no alternative other than to follow du Trieux's suggestion.

Once on deck, Miller watched the medics tend to Doyle, accepting an offered heat blanket.

"Get your handzz off me, you wankerzz," Doyle spat from his stretcher. "Who the hell are you anyway?"

"He's had fifteen milligrams of morphine," Miller told the medics as they whisked him away. "And his knee is shattered."

The crew wore wrinkled dark blue Royal Navy uniforms. Given their lack of fungal growths and alert expressions, Miller's first guess was that they were uninfected. The sailors stood impassively over Miller and his team, keeping their Glock 17s trained on them until an officer approached, stomping down the deck with heavy steps.

He was a commander, going by the rank insignia in the middle of his jacket. He wore a navy blue baseball cap so low on his head his ears stuck out like satellite dishes. Putting a hand on his holstered Glock, he eyed Miller up and down as if appraising a prize pony. "Name, rank, and serial number, please."

"My name's Miller and that's all you're getting."

"American, then," he said, pursing his lips. "Uninfected?"

Miller saw no harm in admitting that much, and nodded. "What are your intentions with that cruise ship?"

"We mean to marry her," the officer said, before puffing out his cheeks and breaking into what Miller supposed was some sort of laugh. Once the officer noticed no one else was joining him, his toothy smile fell and he cleared his throat. Then, with hand extended, he added, "Weapons, please."

There was little point in resisting, so Miller unholstered his Gallican and handed it over as another sailor reached for the strap of his M27.

"Knives, too," the commander said.

Morland grumbled and du Trieux muttered something in French, but their weapons were taken by three seamen, who disappeared across the deck and down a stairwell.

Gesturing to his left, the commander said, "This way."

Urged forward by the armed sailors, Miller and the others followed him across the deck and up a ladder, stopping on the main deck. Down a long corridor lined with confused-looking seamen in various states of dress, they stopped in front of a doorway. Inside was an empty bunk room, cots stacked atop metal rails like bunk beds. A stack of fresh linens rested on the end of each cot, and a weighted bucket sat in the corner.

"And if we refuse?" Miller asked, pausing.

"It's either here or the brig," the commander said. "Your choice. But it's a lot more comfortable here, I assure you."

Miller stepped inside, followed by Hsiung, Morland, and then du Trieux. "And my other man?"

"Perfectly well tended to," the commander said. "That's a promise. We are not your enemy."

"We appreciate the... hospitality," Miller said carefully, "but I'd like to send word to my ship. Let them know we're alright?"

"That's already in hand. In the meantime, there's fresh bedding and a privy. Enjoy!" With that, the commander closed the door. There was a loud metallic clank from the door as it was locked from the outside.

The moment the bolt was in place, Morland balled his hands into fists. "Tossers. We should have taken our chances in the water."

"Would you rather be wrestling that tusk-fiend?" Miller snapped. He turned to the rest of his team.

Du Trieux sat on one of the cots and tucked her knees to her chest. Wrapping herself in a woollen blanket on top of the silver emergency wrap, she shivered, but nodded.

Hsiung, standing beside Morland, merely shrugged and moved to the bunk next to du Trieux.

"We're going to just sit here?" Morland ranted. "We're prisoners! Who knows what they're planning for us, for the *Tevatnoa*?"

"There's nothing more we *can* do," Miller said. "Our mission failed."

Morland spun on his heel and cursed. "This gets better and better."

"We should not have gone to the lab," du Trieux said, surprising Miller. "At the very least, we should have waited out the storm."

Miller grabbed a sheet from one of the bunks and wiped his face and hair dry.

"And for what?" Morland said. "Four dead and a glob of mold that got washed away with the rest of the sodding kit."

Miller peeled off his inflated combat vest and hung it on a bunk to dry. It was crusted over with salt and sand, heavy and dripping.

Morland glared at Miller. "They could be back at any moment."

"There's no sense of dying from pneumonia before that, then."

Hsiung and du Trieux followed suit, hanging up their vests on empty bunks, kicking off their boots and wringing out their socks to dry. Finally, when an hour passed and no one had come back, Morland—blue-lipped and shivering—peeled off his gear and did the same.

Just as Miller had lain down and prepared himself to get a few minutes of shut eye, the door cranked open and the commander stood in the doorway.

"Miller," he said sharply. "With me."

Miller got to his feet and slid into his damp gear. "What about my team?"

"They'll wait here."

He froze. "Can you guarantee their safety?"

The commander raised an eyebrow. "I couldn't make that promise from the moment the Archaean parasite was discovered." He laughed loudly, slapping his knee a few times before resting his hand on the sidearm at his hip.

Miller stared.

"*Mon dieu*," du Trieux said.

Irritably, the commander waved him into the corridor. "No sense of humor, you lot. This way."

With a last look to his team, Miller followed the commander into the hall and watched as the door was locked from the outside.

"I can understand your hesitation," the commander said. "But like I said, we are not your enemy."

"We'll see about that."

Miller followed the commander back through the corridor and up another ladder. Men and women worked at various stations about the vessel, scrubbing the hull and railings clear of fungal growths. The crew, perhaps a hundred by his estimation, looked well-fed and clean—which was more than he could say for the occupants of his own ship. Given their condition, he had to wonder—how was a crew of this size sustaining themselves? Food rations and fresh water had to be in limited supply. Surely they couldn't have been at sea for long.

"Is this for the proof-of-life call?" Miller asked, causing the commander to stop mid-step.

"If that's what you wish to call it. I would prefer to think you'll be the voice of reason."

"I've never been called that before."

The commander cracked a smile and continued down the corridor. "If this war has taught me anything, it's that there's a first time for everything."

He led Miller to an office where a tall man in full formal dress, with a grizzled beard, dark skin and dark eyes, stood beside a woman as pale and young as he was black and aged.

The captain held a radio microphone in a tight fist and glared at Miller and the commander as they entered. Puffing out his cheeks, he let out a slow, deliberate breath. "This Miller?"

"Yes, sir," answered the commander.

"Captain," Miller said, not bothering to salute. "Are you in communication with my ship?"

The pale woman raised an eyebrow, but said nothing.

"Tell me the truth, soldier," said the captain, tugging on the hem of his jacket. "How many humans are aboard that cruise liner?" He dropped the mic beside the receiver, which sat on a long table behind an ornate desk, then sat in a large leathery chair, crossing one long leg over the other and resting a hand on his knee.

Miller stood, tight lipped. "With all due respect, sir, why do you need to know?"

"How long has your ship been at sea? How are you maintaining two cruise liners full of people? Who are all those other, smaller ships across the island? Are they with you? What is your current course and destination?"

Miller fought to keep his expression neutral. "I don't intend to share this information with you until I know what you plan to do."

"I don't have time for a contest of wills, Miller. Either tell me what I need to know, or watch as I blow the *Tevatnoa* from the water. It's that simple."

Miller gritted his teeth. The captain had a point; Miller had no leverage. "The *Tevatnoa* is privately owned by Schaeffer-Yeager International, and sails with the permission of the United States government. An attack on that ship or any of the S-Y fleet would be a direct attack upon the United States of America."

The captain hardly blinked. "Are you saying the fleet is currently following orders directly from President Fredericks?"

"No, sir," Miller said, the hairs on the back of his neck rising. "With all due respect, why are you asking me? Why don't you ask *them*?"

"I've tried," the captain admitted, dropping his leg and sitting forward in his chair. "Why do you think I'm talking to *you*?" He waved at the microphone. "*They're* not answering."

Miller's stomach rolled. Why wouldn't Lewis answer? If anything, he should be *initiating* communication with an armed warship within range of attack.

Possibilities swirled through Miller's head. Unless they didn't know he and his team had been picked up? Perhaps the communications dish had been damaged in the sand storm? Worse, maybe the flu had breached Lewis's forced isolation, and the entirety of the ship was riddled with pneumonia?

He must have gone pale. The woman standing beside the captain uncrossed her arms and squinted at him with an air of concern. "Do you need to sit down?"

"Save the melodramatics," the captain scoffed. "You saw what we did to those bridges. Unless you can verify that ship and all its fleet are uninfected, and don't intend to *become* infected, I cannot allow any of them to pass. Am I making myself clear?"

"Sir," Miller answered. "We are a privately owned fleet. I'm not infected. The ships inhabitants aren't infected. I don't understand..."

"When was the last time you were in contact with your ship?" the woman asked.

"Clark..." warned the captain.

"Sir," she said, stepping forward. "He doesn't *know*."

"I spoke with the Schaeffer-Yeager CEO last night, ma'am," Miller answered.

"And the commanding officer?" Clark asked.

"Lewis. We spoke this morning," Miller said.

"Have any of them indicated they've been in communication with President Fredericks in the last forty-eight hours?" Clark asked.

"No," Miller said, growing more confused by the moment. "Or they didn't inform me, if they had."

"Why were you in Jacksonville?"

"My mission was to retrieve medical supplies from a research facility."

"For what purpose?"

"Antibiotics, ma'am. We've got an influenza sweeping the lower decks, and many have been stricken with a secondary bacterial infection. Sir," Miller said, turning his attention back to the captain, "what is going on?"

"You weren't scouting a potential dock? The fleet isn't returning to land under Frederick's orders?" the captain asked.

"No," Miller said, a bit sharper than he intended. "Why would he—?"

"Show him," the captain said, waving his hand at the computer on his desk.

Clark stepped forward to the console, typed for a few seconds, then spun the screen around to face Miller. On the monitor was a video of President Fredericks, sitting behind his desk in the Oval Office. The time stamp dated it at less than two days before.

"*My fellow Americans,*" Fredericks said, sounding calm, although he looked ragged. His customary three-piece suit was wrinkled and loose, and his tie hung slack around an unbuttoned, un-ironed, soiled dress shirt. "*For years, we have battled against the Archaean Parasite and those who would use it to usurp the freedom and safety of every American citizen. I thank those who fought and sacrificed so bravely to combat what was once believed to be an evil force of nature.*

"*But now, I call upon the people of this country to stop fighting. I have been brought into the light of the Archaean. Knowing and understanding more fully the peace and tranquillity of it, I urge all humans, be they on land or sea, to lay down their arms and present themselves to the nearest commune so we may be unified. A nation is more powerful as one mind, one family. Come with me into the light of understanding, and there will be peace.*

"*God bless you, and God bless the United States of America.*"

Miller fought to breathe for a moment. His heart pounded in his chest, deafening him, pressing on his head until he saw stars.

This was beyond rage or fury. He took a step back, distancing himself from the computer monitor, only to bump into the commander, who stood behind him beside the office door.

"Miller?" Clark said.

He stilled, his eyes focusing on the woman's face, and then the captain's. "Who else has seen this?" he asked.

Clark answered, "Most global communication satellites have been either disabled or unresponsive for months. It went global, but with the irregularity of internet connections, and the emergency broadcast system permanently damaged, there's no way to tell how many saw it—or who will comply."

"And you thought we—?"

"Yes," snapped the captain. "And now you understand why we must communicate with your commanding officer."

Miller swallowed. "I do."

"Great," the captain said, leaning back into his chair to retrieve the CB microphone. He held it out to Miller. "Now that we understand one another, either contact your ship and convince your commander to surrender to us, or watch as we sink it to the bottom of the river. The choice is yours."

22

W<small>ITH EVERY PASSING</small> day Samantha became more and more ill. Her first lichen growth appeared after a few days: a scaly, gray-green fungus spread up from one of her hips, covered half of her ribcage, and within a week had sprouted out of her sleeve and covered the scarred, burnt wound on her right shoulder.

The itch was unbearable. Underneath the growth, her skin was being eaten away—decomposing. If she tried to peel off the growth or scratched too vigorously, chunks of flesh came away.

And she wasn't alone; the fungal growths bloomed across the new Infected workers *en masse*. The lumps covered faces and heads, growing over eyes and nostrils, obstructing ear canals and enveloping scalps. The Infected of the labor camp hardly looked alive anymore; they were like creatures from a cheap horror movie. Sam frequently had to hide her revulsion. She was in no position to judge—she was one of them.

But the growths, however horrific, were less pressing than the blackouts. A wave of narcolepsy swept the workers, striking them at odd moments throughout the day and night. It was not uncommon to have a member of a chain-gang drop unexpectedly and cause the rest of the group to tumble like fleshy dominos. When this happened, the human guards were merciless, beating entire gangs with billy clubs and whipping them with tree branches. The rest of their gang would have no choice but to prop up their limp team-mate and drag them along until they regained consciousness, never knowing when it would be their turn to pass out.

This system proved effective enough until, one day, two members of Samantha's gang blacked out at the same time.

They stood before a pile of freshly fallen tree trunks in the snowy chill of a wintery afternoon. Pinpricks of light cut through the forest canopy like tiny rays of hope, but did little to warm the air or melt the mounting snow on the forest floor. As other groups trudged off to retrieve more logs, Sam's slogged forward to pick the mushrooms and growths, their fingers numb and bony.

Working at the rightmost end of the five-person chain, Samantha felt the shackle dig into her ankle as she reached for a mushroom; then the chain sharply yanked her leg out from under her. She smacked her face against the trunk, bounced and caught herself on the ground with her hands, blinking away the darkness and licking the blood from her lips.

"Get up!" someone shouted.

Pushing herself up, Sam got to her feet. The two men next to her on the chain lay on the ground, unmoving, face up and sprawled out. One of them, lichen covering half his face, struggled to breathe through his one nostril and half-sealed mouth, which lay crushed into the snow.

A human wearing brown hunting pants and a tattered sweatshirt approached, raising a wooden switch, and proceeded to thrash the two unconscious Infected with such force Samantha felt a breeze. "*Get! Up!*" he bellowed.

Sam's first instinct was to cover her face, but when the switch came down a third, then fourth time, leaving bloody welts across the men's faces and bodies, Samantha threw herself over them, covering their bodies with her own.

"What the—" the man said, switch held high.

"Leave them alone!" Sam snapped, wrapping her arms around one of the men. "Can't you see they're unconscious?"

The whip struck her hard, cutting through her flimsy shirt and lashing her skin until it tore.

"Get up, all of you!" the human repeated, raising his arm again.

Samantha didn't move, but bit down on her lower lip.

The next blow came harder, cutting deeper. She felt hot blood trickle down her back. There was nothing to be done but let the whip come, bite back her cries, try not to black out herself. Four, five, ten lashes; she lost count.

Eventually, the men under her arms stirred, opened their eyes, gathered what had happened. Sickened, remorseful, disgusted, they helped Sam to her feet.

The human stood behind her with his blood-stained branch and glowered at them all. Red-faced and puffing, he spat onto the ground and wiped his lips with the back of his hand. "You goin' to regret that, missy," he said. "You hear me?"

When she didn't reply, he walked a few meters and met up with another guard—a woman in black sweats with a hunting rifle. They whispered together for a few moments, and then both sets of eyes turned to meet Samantha's.

A creeping dread crawled up Sam's starved belly and settled in the back of her throat.

THE SUN SET like the blink of an eye, and the work day was done. In single file, the chain gangs marched back through the forest, to be unshackled and let loose back into the holding pen. Guards gathered on the overhead walkway, keeping a watchful eye.

As with each night, after the fires were started and the fungi boiled, stories of the day's horrors trickled through the pen.

One woman named Margaret had been shot after she'd broken her own ankle to slip her chains and tried to run away.

Aside from Samantha, six others had been whipped for blacking out.

A gray-haired man named Howard had broken out into a thick sweat, grabbed his chest and died at the coldest part of the day from a presumed heart attack.

A woman, Sabra, had had her head ripped off by a terror-jaw before the beast was shot by the guards.

Samantha wasn't certain how much longer any of them could survive in these conditions. Their numbers were diminishing daily and every opportunity she saw for escape was usually tried by someone else—who ended up dead. She saw no options, no way out. If the cuts on her back didn't become infected and kill her, she would eventually starve or freeze to death, or simply weaken to the point the guards put her down.

The humans were nearly halfway through building the second fort's wall. Once the lumber for the cabins was cleaned, they'd have no more use for such a large work force; and Samantha didn't have to guess what would happen to those who were deemed too ill to keep alive.

"Hey, three mouthfuls!" someone shouted, drawing the crowd's attention. "Three!"

Over in the corner beside a fire, the woman with dreads stood over Binh, who was holding a tin cup to his mouth and dumping the entire contents into his mouth. Chewing furiously, he tipped the cup higher.

The woman reached for the cup, but Binh twisted his torso to keep out of reach, shaking the cup. A small woman sitting next to him grabbed the cup and yanked it free, splattering mush across the awaiting crowd.

The crowd of workers climbed to its feet with a chorus of outrage. Shaking their fists and raising their voices, the crowd surged forward, enveloping Binh as he cowered in place.

The uproar rippled across the crowd, like a rock dropped into a puddle. Before long, Binh had been wrenched to his feet and dragged to the center of the holding pen, slapped, punched, and kicked the entire way.

Sam watched, torn between anger and horror. It had started again—the rage. The suffering of the work camp was twisting into fury and violence, and she knew, before long, Binh would be mauled or stomped to death. She was watching the incident at the farm all over again.

Samantha stood and grabbed hold of the nearest person, one of the men whom she'd shielded that day. He looked up from the fire and softly grinned at her. Soon, she was pulsing peace and forgiveness through him. The man reached out and grabbed hold of the person next to him, and from there the empathy grew.

Arms reached out and took shoulders. Hands clasped hands. One woman laid her head on another woman's shoulder and they both reached out, finally reaching the circle pressing around Binh. The shouting stopped.

There was calm.

With a loud bang and the familiar clank of the

noisy bolt, the gate into the holding pen swung open. Five heavily-armed humans stood at the entry, all in camouflage. They stepped inside and ploughed through the crowd like the a bulldozer. The mood broke as people scattered, skittering and scampering away, some on all fours.

They headed straight toward Samantha and grabbed her. She dug in her heels, tried to wrench her arms away, but she was too weak, and no match for their numbers.

"I didn't do anything!"

They ignored her, dragging her from the pen and relocking the gate behind them. Through the fort they went, humans gawking from their cabins. They took her past the guards at the gate and out into the forest, two men dragging her as the others walked ahead, lighting the way with torches.

Her first thought was that they were going to shoot her and leave her corpse for the terror-jaws. One of them must have seen what she'd done in the pen. Surely they knew about the powers of the Archaean Bishops, and their ability to control and manipulate the Regulars. What had Alex called them once? Charismatics.

These humans were smart enough to have survived this long in the middle of the Adirondack forest; they weren't idiots. They'd be smart to get rid of a Bishop.

But a bullet to the head wasn't what they had in store for her.

Instead, they took Samantha to a secluded

clearing in the forest, laced a short chain through her manacle, and hammered a metal stake into the ground, securing her in place.

Beside her, on one side, were the rotting corpses of other Infected, frozen solid and covered in snow. On the other side was a pile of tree stumps, branches, and tree roots, stacked in a giant heap, presumably for use as firewood. Across from that was a heap of stones and rock, likely pulled from the ground where the humans had been building.

Sam considered begging the humans not to leave, but she saved her breath.

When they moved off, taking their torches with them, Samantha listened to their footsteps crunch across the forest floor, and then cringed, despite herself, when they were gone from view.

There was no moon, or none that Sam could see. The only light was the dim glow from the fort, a quarter of a kilometer away.

Crying out for help would only attract predators. If she tried to sleep, she'd freeze. If she stood up and paced to keep warm, she would likely collapse from exhaustion, *then* freeze.

As she stood, contemplating her survival, the bite in the air worked its way through her thin long-sleeved shirt and pants, chilling her to the bone. Her feet grew numb in the light snow. If she didn't do something, she'd end up on the stack of rotting bodies beside her.

Okay. First things first.

She pulled on the chain, stretched as far as she

could to the edge of the scraps pile, and dug through the heap of branches and logs. She made a small pile of dry twigs and sticks, then found two thick sticks and a fat branch, each about a half meter long.

To start, she scraped each piece against a jagged rock, removing twigs, leaves, and bark. Taking up the thicker of the two sticks, she rubbed the end hard against the rock, rounding it into a dull point. Once satisfied, she put the wood aside and untied her hair, loosening the dirty waves from the leather thong.

Gritting her teeth, she wrapped her forefinger in a thick lock of her loose hair and yanked. It came off surprisingly easy; her hands shook more from adrenaline than pain.

With trembling fingers, she tied the end of the lock with the leather strip, held it in her teeth and went to work, twisting the hair into a thick, tight braid. She secured the tip with a glob of tree sap, then tied the ends of the braid to the thinnest stick. Now she had a crude bow. Holding the fat branch between her feet, she looped the hair around the pointed stick and pulled the bow back and forth, grinding the improvised spindle in a knothole in the branch.

It took several minutes and a few false starts, but eventually smoke began to rise from the knothole; a trickle at first, then a continuous plume.

She removed the central stick. At the contact point, a small red ember burned. Dropping a handful of pine needles in the hole, Samantha picked up the branch and blew into the tinder, bringing more smoke with each breath until the pine needles burst into flames.

Samantha dumped the burning needles into her pile of dry twigs. The wind kicked in, causing her a brief moment of panic when the flames flickered, but the sticks took, the flames steadily rising until the heat started melting the snow around her.

Surely, with all these branches around her, she had enough firewood to stay warm throughout the night. She was saved, for the time being—

But saved for what?

Perhaps those who had died of exposure had been the lucky ones, she realized, eyeing the pile of bodies. Their suffering had, at least, ended. Hers could continue for days, assuming the guards didn't just come back and shoot her in the morning.

She stared into the flames and frowned—then a thought crossed her mind.

She snatched a long branch from the fire and pushed the burning pile closer to the stack of logs. It took a little while in the cold, but eventually the tree sap caught and the stack was gradually engulfed. Then the fire spread across the trunks of the trees and then set fire to the branches of the surrounding forest.

Samantha smiled. "There," she said. "That's better."

Standing in the center of a forest fire proved oddly satisfying. The warmth alone was soothing, the dry heat cracking and flaking the lichen on her arm. Sam felt warm to the core, a sensation which had eluded her since her days at the dairy farm.

It wasn't long until the fire became a genuine threat, however. She had to move.

Lying on her side in the muck, Sam kicked the stake with both feet half a dozen times, seeing it shift slightly in the hard ground. She did the same from the other side, then again, feeling it move more and more each time, until she climbed to her feet and wrenched it out of the ground with her hands. Free from her chain, she grabbed a pair of blazing branches from the burning debris and ran toward the fort.

Shots rang out as the walls came into view, hitting the ground near her feet and whizzing past her face. She zigzagged through the trees until she was close enough to toss the burning branches at the base of the wooden fort.

Turning back around, she slunk into the dark forest, heading for the spreading fire. She snatched two more burning branches and returned to the fort.

This time they were ready for her. More shots rang out, one grazing her arm. She never lost a step. Nothing short of a bullet to the head was going to stop her.

She threw more burning branches at the base of the fort, gratified to see that her first brands had caught. She ran back into the darkened forest to watch it burn.

There was shouting within, gun shots. She saw smoke rising from the fort's interior, heard whoops of delight from the Infected holding pen. When the howls of revolution came, she felt them in her chest.

The front gate swung open. Humans spilled out, mostly women clutching children—perhaps a dozen. They ran at a full sprint, stumbling in the dark and scattering into the forest, their babies squalling. A few of the men followed closely behind.

The fort gate remained ajar, and unguarded. Taking a breath, she cut across the forest and ran straight inside.

The west and south wall were both burning, where the Infected has set their own blazes to join the fires Sam had started. She scanned the pen, with a notion of sneaking past the guards and releasing her fellow captives, but they were already on top of it. Sam watched as some of the fittest inmates climbed on top of one another, forming a human ladder. A handful of them reached the top of the fence, then jumped down to the other side to open the gate.

The Infected quickly overcame the panicking humans, confiscating their weapons and knocking them out with the butts of their own rifles.

As Sam stood at the fort gate, dumbfounded, the woman with the dreads stood at the entrance to the holding pen, waving her arms over her head.

"Close the gate!" she bellowed, pointing at Samantha.

"Close the...? What?"

"Don't let any more humans escape!" she shouted.

Sam turned on her heel and grabbed the edge of one gate and pushed, and was surprised to find Binh across from her, closing the other side. One last human man darted through before the gates were closed; Sam watched as two changed direction and tried to climb up to the walkway, only to be pulled down by a crowd of Infected.

At the back of the fort, by the pen entrance, the woman with the dreads had formed a bucket brigade to put out the fires. Samantha barred the gate, then took one of the ladders to the walkway, to join them.

By sunrise, the Infected had doused the flames, secured control of the fort—including a barn full of food, a fresh well, vehicles, and weapons—and were holding approximately a dozen human hostages.

Satisfied the worst of it was behind her, Samantha got in line at the barn with the other Infected and gladly accepted a cucumber-radish and a hunk of jerky. She paced herself, eating slowly, then sat on a scorched log to watch the sunrise. For the first time in months, she felt alive.

"MILLER TO THE *Tevatnoa*, come in *Tevatnoa*. Over."

Lewis's reply was almost immediate. "*In the name of all things holy, son. What are you doing over there?*"

"Our dinghy flipped in the sand storm, sir. We were..." He paused for a moment. "Rescued."

"*I'm glad to hear it,*" Lewis replied, quickly adding, "*How fortunate they were able to swoop in and save the day. And I suppose now they want to return you to your ship, no strings attached?*"

"Not quite, sir."

"*That's what I figured.*" Almost as an afterthought, Lewis asked, "*Did you find anything in Jacksonville?*"

"Negative, sir. The lab was cleaned out and abandoned some time ago."

The line cut short with a brief burst of static, then reopened. "*That's unfortunate.*"

"Yes, sir. Have you received any communication

from President Fredericks in the last forty-eight hours?"

After a brief pause Lewis answered. "*No, but our long-range communications have been down for weeks and the sand storm knocked out our short range for a couple hours. We just got them back on line. Why? Who's in command over there? What do they want?*"

Looking to the captain, the commander and Clark, Miller cleared his throat and continued. "*Sir, it appears President Fredericks is infected.*"

The line cut out again. Ignoring the quizzical looks from the RN officers, Miller gave a twitchy shrug and nervously fingered the receiver. Minutes later, there was another burst of static.

Gray Matheson's voice came on the line. "*Miller, repeat transmission.*"

"I said, it appears President Fredericks is infected."

"*How is this...? How do you...? Where did you get this information?*"

"There was a long-range communication video uploaded to the..." He looked over at the officers watching him.

"Emergency broadcast network," Clark said. "And the internet."

"Well, what's left of them," the commander said, chuckling.

"To the EBN and the internet," Miller said into the radio. "Two days ago. I've seen it myself, sir. It looks legitimate. He's asked all humans to surrender to the nearest commune."

The line cut again for a few seconds, then, "*Who's got you and what do they want, Miller?*"

"It's the RN, sir. They want to be sure we aren't infected, and don't intend to become so."

"*Tell them we don't.*"

"I did, sir."

"*Good. Thank them for their concern. We're sending a transport to retrieve you and your team.*"

The captain cleared his throat.

"I suspect the captain has a thing or two to say about that."

The disgust in Gray's voice was apparent when he spoke again. "*I'll put Lewis back on.*"

Miller held out the microphone and waited for the captain to take it.

After tugging on the hem of his jacket, the captain squared his shoulders and cracked his neck with a sharp twist. "This is Captain Jefferson Corthwell of the Royal Navy. To whom am I speaking?"

"*This is Commander Brandon Lewis of the* Tevatnoa. *Thank you for rescuing our security team. We'd like to dispatch a transport to retrieve them so we can be on our way.*"

"Nothing would make me happier, commander," the captain replied. "In exchange for the rescue of your team, we would gladly accept an operational desalination unit as a token of your appreciation."

Miller's mouth dropped open. "Hold on a minute."

Lowering the mic, Corthwell frowned at Miller. "By our estimation, given the size of that ship and the depth of its drag, you have approximately five thousand people on that boat alone, not to mention the other cruiser. The blast in New York City was over six months ago. For you to be at sea that long without stopping for supplies means you have multiple desalination units aboard each ship, *and* a sustainable food source. Am I wrong?"

Before Miller had the opportunity to reply, Lewis responded from the receiver. "*That's quite an ask. Is there something else that would interest you? A refrigeration unit, or perhaps some fresh fruits and vegetables?*"

"No," Miller barked, more at Lewis than at the captain. "Do *not* take food from that ship, captain. They're starving as it is."

The captain raised a disapproving eyebrow. "Is that so?"

"Yes, sir," Miller said. "You would be putting lives at risk with that demand."

"Sounds to me as if you've been mismanaged." Turning to the commander, the captain nodded toward the exit. "Escort Mr. Miller back to his team. Mr. Miller? It was a pleasure meeting you."

"Sir?"

"Everything will be dealt with accordingly, I assure you," the commander said. He stepped in front of Miller, hand resting on his sidearm.

Seeing no other alternative, Miller stepped into the hall, face hot, palms clammy. He followed the commander below.

What *bullshit*. He wasn't going to play along with any negotiation if it involved taking food out of the mouths of those aboard the *Tevatnoa*. They'd just have to think of something else.

Inside the bunk room sat du Trieux, Hsiung, Morland, and now Doyle, who was snoring on a bunk beside Hsiung. His left leg, wrapped tightly in a gelatinous compression bandage, was propped up with an extra pile of bedding.

The three others sat gripping steaming cups of tea.

Seeing Miller, du Trieux rose to her feet. "What happened?"

"We're hostages. Lewis is negotiating our release."

"Well now," the commander said. He stood in the door, bristling. "That's not quite the way I'd phrase it."

Miller frowned at him. "How would you put it?"

"A mutually beneficial exchange of resources," he said, smiling. He stopped abruptly when Miller took a step forward.

With a slow, steady hand, Miller reached out to the door behind the commander and moved to shut it. The officer had no option other than to step into the hallway and get out of the way.

"I'll see to it you get some tea as well," the commander said.

"Don't bother." Then he shut the door in his face.

"What a wanker," said Morland.

The door locked from the outside. Miller gritted his teeth. "The captain is all right, I think." He stepped away from the door and slouched onto a bunk.

"What if they can't reach an agreement?" du Trieux asked.

Miller shook his head. "I don't know. They want food, water. Everything we *can't* spare. If they can't figure something out, my guess is we'll be absorbed into this crew."

"Either that or they put us on a raft and push us out to sea to die," Hsiung said.

Miller ran his hands through his greasy hair. He'd have loved a shower and a shave. He felt sticky, crusted, like the inside of a rotting ship, and suddenly exhausted. What he would have given for a few hours of uninterrupted sleep. "I don't think they'll do that. They're not cruel."

Du Trieux lifted her chin. "A cup of tea doesn't make someone decent."

Miller rubbed his eyes with the heel of his palm, then shook his head. "They shared information with me they didn't have to." When he was certain he had all their attention, save Doyle's, he dropped the bomb about Fredericks.

There was a moment's shocked silence.

"That's it, then," Hsiung said. "We've lost."

Morland spat. "It's not over yet."

"We have no country," Hsiung snapped back. "We're *done*."

"We're not without allies," du Trieux said, looking to Miller. "You think the captain will return us to the *Tevatnoa*?"

"I can't say for certain, but I think so."

Du Trieux checked Doyle's pulse, then slumped back onto a bunk. "If he thinks we're weak, he could attack."

Morland shook his head. "I can't believe we've gone through all this, done all the shit we've done—and Fredericks turns into a fucking bug head. What are we going to do now?"

The words hung in the air. Doyle mumbled something in his sleep and du Trieux's face fell.

Miller squinted at her. "What'd he say?"

Du Trieux frowned at the locked door. "He said, 'Rats in a cage.'"

IN THE HEAT of the second day of their 'rescue,' Miller and his team sat silent and stone-faced in a Royal Navy rubber dinghy, empty weapons laid on their laps.

Waves slapped the sides of the raft, spraying their faces and dampening their uniforms.

Less than a kilometer away sat the *Tevatnoa*, still on the St. John's River. Three of the ship's mega-lifeboats approached, laden—as far as Miller could tell—with his team's ransom.

Behind their dinghy, the Royal Navy ship had launched a Landing Craft Utility Mk 10 from their well dock. Designed for transporting men, stores, and armored vehicles, the thirty-meter-long ship had stern and bow ramps for fast loading and unloading, and could carry over a hundred tonnes. Miller shuddered to think how much the *Tevatnoa* had had to promise in exchange for their release. It rose and fell with the waves, silent and unmoving, halfway between Miller and the RN ship.

When they were less than a half kilometer away from the *Tevatnoa*, Miller felt his heart swell. For better or worse, he was headed 'home,' as it were. He wondered if James Gray had survived his bacterial infection, and how the other ships of the S-Y fleet had gotten along—if at all—in the *Tevatnoa*'s absence.

Who knew how many messes Miller would have to clean up upon his return? Oddly, he found the thought comforting. Battling the elements, the sea life, and each other was vastly preferable to being held hostage aboard another ship, even if they were Royal Navy, and presumably one of their allies.

Miller shot a look over his shoulder at the awaiting Mk 10 and frowned. *Presumably.*

It was too bad they couldn't come to a mutual arrangement, Miller mused, and work and travel together. It would have been nice to have some added muscle, especially when pirates and ships of Infected got in their way.

"Miller," du Trieux gasped.

He looked away from the *Tevatnoa* and followed her gaze. The Mk 10 had dropped its bow ramp. It wasn't empty, awaiting a king's ransom, but full of more rubber dinghies, manned with sailors in full tactical gear.

"What the hell?" Morland gaped.

They watched as the dinghies launched from the Mk 10 and skimmed across the water, passing the mega-lifeboats headed toward the *Tevatnoa*.

"They don't think they can take a cruise liner with

a bunch of dinghies, do they?" Doyle asked, leaning over the side of the raft to peer into the Mk 10.

Just then there came an echoing roar from the RN ship behind them. Water fountained into the sky near the *Tevatnoa*'s port side.

"That's bloody cannon fire!" Morland shouted, rising in his seat.

Miller shouted to Hsiung in the stern of the dinghy. "Cut the engine!"

Slowing the dinghy to a crawl, Hsiung stopped the boat and let it idle. By then, the dinghies had surrounded the *Tevatnoa* on all sides.

"We have to do something," Morland said.

"Do what? We don't have any ammo," Doyle pointed out.

"I can just hear Lewis on the bridge right now," Hsiung said. "He's got to be shitting bricks."

"They could fire the railgun," Morland suggested. "See how the Navy boys like it."

Du Trieux shook her head. "It's still untested. Firing that thing could capsize the *Tevatnoa*, for all we know."

"What do we do?" Hsiung asked Miller. "We can't stay out here on the water. We're sitting ducks."

Miller pressed his lips together and eyed the commotion at the *Tevatnoa*. The sailors on the dinghies had shot grappling hooks onto the ship and were crawling up the cruise liner's hull like roaches. Soon, the *Tevatnoa* and all its occupants and resources would be under RN control.

Three-quarters of a kilometer behind them sat

the RN Bay Class ship. The *Tevatnoa* was well within range of their DS30B cannon. They'd missed on purpose, of course, but Miller had no desire to return to either vessel until the hostilities subsided— one way or another.

The other option sat like a swampy goitre on shore. They had enough fuel in the dinghy to make it to Jacksonville. They could avoid capture and call for help to rescue the *Tevatnoa*, but with the US government now under Infected control and the whole of Jacksonville controlled by communes, the idea was fruitless.

Miller nodded at Hsiung and she re-started the engine.

"Take us to the *Tevatnoa*. I don't think they'll stop us."

"They could shoot us out of the water!" Morland snapped.

"We aren't a threat. Besides, if I'm going to be held prisoner, I'd like to do it aboard my own ship."

Hsiung revved the motor and steered the board closer to the cruise liner. No-one spoke.

Miller blinked at the approaching vessel and ran the pads of his fingers against the stubble on his chin. If anything, he was hoping for a nice shave before they were taken into custody—if that was what the Brits had in mind.

It's the small things in life, he mused silently.

Small things were all they had left.

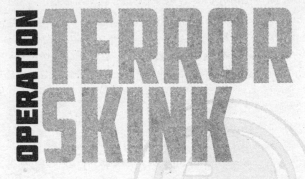

THE ROYAL NAVY took seventeen minutes to assume control of the *Tevatnoa*.

Miller saw no sense in running away. His people—for better or worse—were aboard that ship, and he wasn't going to abandon them. He hadn't back in Astoria when Harris had gone nuclear. He wasn't about to now.

They arrived some ten minutes later and docked via the davit system, which emptied Miller and crew onto the second floor deck. RN troops in full tactical gear greeted them.

Miller saw the heads and faces of his shipmates popping in and out of doors down the corridor. They looked equal parts curious and petrified.

"You Miller?" a lieutenant asked.

"I am."

"Come with me."

Miller looked back at his team, eyebrow raised, and they followed the officer up the stairs to mid-deck and past the stern hydroponics station, half a dozen armed sailors trailing them. In front of a storage closet, the sailors came forward and confiscated their empty weapons, then motioned them inside.

"You can't be serious. Just let us back to our quarters," Miller said.

"Where I'm sure you've stashed weapons and ammunition? I don't think so. You stay here until the captain and the commander reach an agreement," the lieutenant said. "Shouldn't take long."

Miller remained rooted in position outside the door. "I'd like a word with Commander Lewis. He needs to know we're aboard."

The lieutenant nodded briskly. "He's aware. If you wouldn't mind?"

Frowning, Cobalt entered the windowless storage closet, Doyle limping along with Morland's assistance. Miller opened his mouth to speak again, but the lieutenant closed the door in his face.

"So much for the voice of reason," Miller grunted.

Doyle hopped atop a pile of cardboard boxes and arranged his leg, propping it up. "Come again, boss?"

Miller frowned and paced the room in three strides, swung around on his heel, then paced back. "Forget it."

Du Trieux sat on the floor in the corner, arms propped on her knees. "Where's the rest of the security squad?"

Hsiung nodded from her spot beside her. "Good question."

"I'd forgotten about the smell," Morland said, drawing everyone's attention. "You haven't noticed? This ship stinks of body odor and sauerkraut." He sat beside Doyle on the boxes and sniffed.

Doyle raised his nose into the air and inhaled loudly. "Oh, yeah."

"It's got to be the hydroponics," Hsiung guessed. "Combined with the fungus in the air. There's a pipe right there." A large metallic cylinder, secured with an aluminium bracket, came up the wall from the floorboards by the back wall, ran across the ceiling, then out the other side of the room.

When no one immediately replied, Miller said, "Maybe."

"What's the play?" Hsiung scratched behind her ear. "Wait this out?"

"I don't see we have any other choice," Miller answered.

"I say we bust out and go find Lewis," Morland said.

Du Trieux raised an eyebrow. "There's likely a guard outside our door."

"They'll come and feed us, right?" Doyle asked. "Bring us water? I don't think there's anything in these boxes but pool toys."

Miller shrugged. On the RN's ship, they'd been brought tea, along with cured sausages and instant mashed potatoes, but they were prisoners aboard the *Tevatnoa* now. It wouldn't take the captain long to discern the severity of their food situation. No telling what he would do then.

Miller turned and paced again, lost in his thoughts. The storage closet was lit by a single, softly buzzing wall sconce. The entire space couldn't have been more than two meters deep. Morland and Doyle sat on a heap of cardboard boxes, stacked waist-high to one side. On the other, with du Trieux and Hsiung, was an open box of snorkel gear, two corroded oxygen tanks, and a pair of bent, rusted spear guns. A plastic trash bin sat in the corner behind the door, overflowing with child-sized safety vests.

The ship felt oddly motionless. After the rocking of the turbulent ocean, the tranquillity of the St. John's River was a nice change. For once, Miller could stand in the middle of a room and not have to hold something for support. He was about to mention it when the entire room shook, tipped to one side, then slammed back down with a jolt.

Miller, the only one on his feet, tumbled to the floor and landed in du Trieux's lap.

"They're firing at us!" Morland cried.

"I didn't hear a blast," du Trieux said. She struggled to extricate herself from under Miller and a drift of safety vests.

"Are there any reefs around here?" Hsiung asked, also getting to her feet.

Warning bells went off in Miller's head as he stood. "Yes, but they're south, near Key Largo," he answered. "We haven't moved. I don't think that's what that was."

Another jolt, this time from the stern. The whole ship tipped forward, then fell back with an audible splash. Miller heard cries and screams from the decks below.

With a pop and a snap, the pipe at the back of the room groaned and burst. Water gushed into the closet.

"Can't we stay dry for a whole bloody day?" Doyle hollered, scrambling out of the way.

Miller and the others flailed for the exit, only to find it locked from the outside. The handle, a tiny brass knob, wriggled in Miller's palm, but the door wouldn't move. He piled his shoulder against it, but the sailors had reinforced it. It hardly budged.

"Get back," Miller ordered them. He wiped water from his face and splashed across the room. The water was up to their ankles already. "Away from the door." He grabbed the two rusted oxygen tanks and laid one on the floor, the valve and nozzle pointed to the back wall. He then picked up the other one and raised it over his head like a mallet.

"Are you crazy?" Hsiung shrieked.

"Trust me," he snapped.

The memory was clear as day. Billy had been complaining about Miller's wall-to-wall work schedule back in his early bodyguard days, and had *insisted* they have a romantic get-away. Something sporty and fun, to keep Miller from getting bored. He'd arranged for the both of them to go scuba diving off the Molokini Reef in Maui.

Despite Miller's extensive experience in the water, the instructor on the tour boat had given a long, terribly rehearsed safety speech regarding the oxygen tanks, warning them that the tanks were highly explosive.

That wasn't true, of course. In fact, oxygen isn't even flammable, although it acts as an accelerant. It's the compressed carbon dioxide in the tank that does the damage. The one thing Miller *had* learned was that if a tank was dropped and the valve was forcibly broken off, the tank would fly through the air at sixty-four kilometers per hour and could not only kill a person instantly if struck, but could puncture the boat's hull and endanger all those aboard.

The instructor, a tanned, beach-blond former stock broker who'd come to Maui on vacation and never gone home, bugged out his eyes and waved his palms at Billy and Miller with a deadly serious expression. "Like, dudes," he'd said. "Whatever you do—don't drop your tank."

Miller eyed the oxygen tank in the water at his feet, gripped the other tank in his sodden arms, and struck the valve with all his strength. The nozzle popped off and the tank shot across the floor like a missile, smashing clean through the door, leaving a perfectly round hole the exact diameter of the tank.

Sloshing across the room, Miller then leaned down, reached through the hole and groped around, knocking something long and skinny from under the door handle.

Morland heaved up the other oxygen tank and brought it down on top of the brass handle, breaking it loose.

Back out in the hall, there was no guard. Hsiung helped Doyle and the five of them made their way past the sloshing hydroponics station to the railing, just in time to see the end of a large, scaly fin, like the one he'd seen back at the *Dunn Roven*, cut across the ship's starboard side and sink below.

"Did anybody else see that?" Hsiung blinked, her eyes wide.

"How is something that small rocking a ship this size?" Morland asked.

Miller squinted at the shadow in the water, a few meters off the ship's starboard side. It hadn't been a dorsal fin, he now realised. It was the tip of a fluke. This thing was about twice as long and wide as a California Blue Whale. The tail was more than ten meters long all by itself.

Morland must have seen it too. "Fuck me."

"It's a monster," Hsiung breathed.

Miller looked to du Trieux. At the same time they said, "Railgun."

Leaving the limping Doyle to fend for himself, Miller, du Trieux, Hsiung, and Morland took off for the stairs to upper deck. They climbed them two steps at a time and sprinted past the exhaust ports, right by Gray Matheson's office and another hydroponics station, before barrelling up another flight to the bridge.

Two heavily armed RN sailors stood in the doorway, cradling AR-15 assault rifles. One look at the four of them and they opened fire. Miller saw the flash of the muzzles and dove headfirst over the stairwell railing. The others, hearing the shots, ducked down below the landing.

Hanging onto the railing by one hand, Miller shouted, "Launch the railgun!" he shouted. "That *monster's* going to poke a hole in the ship!"

"Show me your hands!" one of the sailors shouted. They advanced to the top of the stairs, rifles at the ready: one aimed at Miller's head, the other at the remainder of Cobalt on the stairs.

Du Trieux, Hsiung, and Morland, all crouched at the base of the stairwell, raised their hands out in front of them. Miller, still flapping on the breeze from the stairwell railing, grunted by way of reply.

"Guards?" a female voice shouted from the bridge. "Report!"

From Miller's vantage point he could just make out the pale, blonde head of Clark, the captainerpses of other Infecteds's assistant, also in full tactical gear.

"Miss Clark," he said, finally able to get a foothold and pull himself up. "We need to fire the railgun before that thing..."

The entire ship rocked to the port side, tipping momentarily before crashing back down. Water crashed the *Tevatnoa* on both sides, spraying all the way up to the bridge. Screams and cries from passengers echoed underneath. From inside the bridge, Miller heard shouting.

Clark, who had grabbed hold of the railing to keep from falling over, holstered her Glock service weapon and motioned to the RN guards. "Bring them up."

At the top of the stairwell, Lewis's voice cut

through the air. "Firing your weapons at an unidentified biological this close to my ship leaves too much room for error, and is quite possibly the stupidest thing I've heard come out of your mouth yet, captain. I'm more inclined to weigh anchor and make a run for it. We can be pretty fast when needs be." Holding the communications microphone, Lewis squinted at Miller, then waved him in.

The radio burst with static. "*And allowing a ship I've just commandeered,*" the captain shouted back, "*to fire their untested weapons system when my ship is within firing range is also a stupid idea, commander.*"

"We're not interested in starting a war, captain..." Lewis kept on.

Corthwell scoffed. "*Forgive me if I don't believe that, coming from an American.*"

"The longer we wait," Miller interjected, "the more likely they'll be pulling three thousand civilians out of the water and jamming them onto their ship."

Lewis relayed Miller's thought into the radio. "Unless you've got enough food and fresh water and places for all three thousand of us," he said. "I suggest you allow us to do our jobs."

"I've seen the creature, sir," Miller said, addressing both Clark and Commander Lewis. He couldn't help but notice each station inside the bridge was double-manned, with one member of the *Tevatnoa*'s crew and one shadowing RN officer. "It's the creature from the *Dunn Roven*, sir. It's looking for a soft spot to crack us open."

Lewis nodded. "It's on radar, we've got a fix on it."

"Then you've seen it's attacking from the starboard side," Miller said. "The RN ship is on port. There's no feasible way they could get off a clean shot. We *must* use the railgun system."

"Our men have no experience with such a weapon," Clark said.

"Let my men defend our ship, captain." Lewis spoke into the mic through clenched teeth. When no immediate reply came, Lewis pressed the microphone button again. "Captain, do you copy?"

"Distress signal coming from the RN ship, captain," said the guard beside the communications seaman.

All eyes inside the bridge looked out the observation window to the ship across the river. The Phalanx close-in weapons system on the RN ship fired a salvo off their starboard side. From the water, the tentacles of what looked like a giant squid were crawling up the hull.

Miller squinted into the distance and grimaced. It was easily four times the size of any giant squid he'd ever heard of.

In a matter of seconds the creature had skulked up the hull and was laying waste to the upper deck of the RN ship. One of its tentacles had gripped one of the cranes, tilting the ship sideways, while another grabbed a crew member and flung him wailing into the water.

"Bloody hell," Clark breathed.

Lewis shouted into the receiver. "Weigh anchor, captain! Get out of here!"

Clark turned crimson all the way to the tips of her ears. "Why doesn't he use the L7s?"

Just then the entirety of the *Tevatnoa* bucked like a bronco, shoving the occupants of the bridge to one side. Warning alerts and alarms sounded across the positioning and navigations stations, illuminating the central alarm console like a Christmas tree.

"We've taken damage below deck, commander," announced one of the seamen. "Fusion reactor is offline."

Miller grabbed the back of the captain's chair for balance and glared at Clark. "We're wasting time."

Clark shot one more look at the RN ship. The tentacles of the squid had warped the crane and bent it backwards. "Go," she said. "But if you damage my ship in the process, I'll shoot you myself."

"That's a deal," Lewis said. "Mr. Dermer, get me coordinates on that whale!"

"I think it's more of a giant crocodile, sir," replied the radar tech.

"Shut up," said Lewis, then to Miller, "Get a squad to the observation deck, use whatever we have to keep it in position long enough to give the railgun a clean shot. And move fast, before we're all sunk!"

Miller turned to his team and waved them out the bridge door, shouting over his shoulder, "Yes, sir!"

It took Samantha and the Infected three weeks to repair the fire damage done to the fort. By the time the restoration was finished, and the forest fire had moved off to the east, a routine formed among the inhabitants.

Firewood was collected, food was distributed, warmer clothing and shoes were passed out. Living and sleeping arrangements were made. Away from their all-fungal diet, those affected the worst by the lichen improved. By the end of the first month, Samantha knew what was coming.

Snow had begun to fall in sheets, rising from an inch or two of powder to drifts a foot deep and climbing. It set people on edge. Fights broke out over blankets, socks, and shoes.

At Jan's urging—the woman with dreads—the Infected gathered around a central fire pit in the largest of the log cabins in the hopes of discussing matters and setting rules. As Samantha suspected, it was a hotbed of shouting and near-riots within minutes.

"The humans will come back and attack!" someone bellowed.

"No, they won't!"

"Most who escaped were women and children, and they probably died from exposure."

"We have their weapons!"

"They don't need weapons. All they need is a match."

"Or a bow drill," Samantha agreed. She crossed her legs and stared into the flames. As she listened to the shouting, she felt the anger and frustration building around her, filling the room like smoke.

"Let's go back to the dairy farm," Binh suggested. "There's safety in numbers! They have plenty of food, and shelter. The brothers will welcome us back."

Samantha shook her head. Thankfully, she didn't have to speak; someone took the words right out of her mouth.

"It's a cult," another man spoke.

"If they hadn't organized those raiding parties, we never would have been captured by the humans in the first place," a woman said.

"It was because of that," another man spoke, "we ended up here."

Samantha found herself nodding. She wanted to bring up the numbness, the feelings of detachment and impassivity created at the dairy farm, but she felt eyes upon her and looked up across the fire.

Jan stared at her, her head tilted to one side, her mouth open as if she were about to speak. While the crowd debated, yelled, and tossed ideas and accusations across the room, the two women met eyes.

The two Bishops, Samantha realized. In a crowd of drones, they were the only two who could resist the crowd's emotions.

"Where do we go?" the woman asked her.

"South," Samantha suggested. "Someplace warmer?"

"But not too warm."

Samantha nodded. With the planetary environmental shifts, it would be a handy trick to find someplace temperate. Samantha had spent so many months feeling cold; she'd forgotten the scorching, at times unbearable, heat that had blanketed New York City before its ultimate demise.

Perhaps they *should* stay at the fort? The cold wasn't bad as long as they had control over it. There was still forest left to keep the campfires burning for a few months, maybe more. And when their resources dwindled, they could build another fort a few kilometers away in another part of the forest, just like the humans had begun to...

A chill ran up Samantha's arms. She'd come full circle.

The humans knew where they were. They knew where to attack. They knew more about the fort than the Infected did. If the Infected grew complacent, they were doomed to repeat the same mistakes Samantha had seen at her first farm, and again at the dairy settlement. The best way to keep from in-fighting and violence was to stay on the move. A nomadic life, however uncomfortable, kept them active and distracted. It gave them purpose and drive. The more Samantha thought about it, the more she was certain.

She wasn't sure Jan would agree, but the woman nodded nonetheless, as if sensing Samantha's thoughts.

"There's the transport trucks," Jan said.

"Provided there's enough fuel," Sam added.

"To a town or a city, to start," Jan suggested. "A few more creature comforts might still the beast."

"I think we should head west," Samantha said. "It will be rough for a bit. But once we pass the Bible Belt, there are more opportunities for open land."

"Plenty of territories to explore," Jan said.

"Exactly."

They stood together. A ripple of silence quieted the room. All faces turned to Jan and Sam.

Sam shrugged and nodded at her new partner. "Seems we've been elected."

A wry smile pursed Jan's lips. "Bully for us." Then, to the crowd she said, "Meeting adjourned. Everybody to their sleeping quarters. In the morning, we pack the vehicles and travel west."

Around her, Sam saw perplexed expressions and heard murmurings of confusion, but the majority of the crowd quieted and filtered out toward their respective cabins.

Sam waited until the room was empty, then

followed suit. She felt oddly optimistic at the prospect of travel. A life of adventure—isn't that what she had always wanted?

She grinned softly to herself. Not really.

SAMANTHA PRESSED THE clutch with her left leg, then turned the key to the transport truck. To her delight the truck roared to life. Cheers from the hold made her smile. They'd been stuck at the fort all morning trying to find enough experienced drivers to handle the vehicles. Now that they were packed with supplies and people, it'd taken the better part of three hours fighting with the transmission of the old Army transport van. Kudos to Alex for insisting Sam learn how to handle a stick all those years ago.

Binh, sitting next to Samantha in the passenger seat, slapped his knee. "Take that, you nasty stick shift."

Samantha laughed. After checking the mirrors for the umpteenth time, she slammed the truck into reverse and backed it out from behind the fort's barn.

Jan stood at the gate, waving and guiding her through the opening. Sam was so focussed on the older woman's silhouette in the side mirror, she didn't notice Binh as he reached forward and twisted the dial on the radio.

Immediately, the cabin of the transport was filled with loud, grating static. Quickly, Binh reached over and twisted the other knob. To Samantha's utter shock, she heard the voice of the President of the United States and immediately slammed on the brakes.

"*My fellow Americans,*" Fredericks said, sounding composed. "*For years we have battled against the Archaean Parasite and those who would use it to usurp the freedom and safety of every American citizen. I thank those who fought and sacrificed so bravely to combat what was once believed to be an evil force of nature.*

"*But now, I call upon the people of this country to stop fighting. I have been brought into the light of the Archaean. Knowing and understanding more fully the peace and tranquillity of it, I urge all humans, be they on land or sea, to lay down their arms and present themselves to the nearest commune so we may be unified. A nation is more powerful as one mind, one family. Come with me into the light of understanding, and there will be peace.*

"*God bless you, and God bless the United States of America.*"

"Holy shit," Binh whispered.

All Samantha could do was gawk at the radio. From the driver's side window, Jan appeared.

"What's the hold up?" she barked. "You're wasting fuel."

On a loop, the radio fluttered with static for five seconds, then repeated the President's message.

Samantha said nothing, watching Jan as she listened. There was a mix of revulsion, then pride, and then a disbelieving joy swirling across Jan's face as the words sank in.

Afterwards, during the next five-second burst of static, Jan reached over the steering column, grasped the keys, and turned off the truck's ignition. Moving off the step bar, she smacked the driver side door twice. "Everybody out!"

Binh frowned at Samantha. "What?"

Samantha pressed her lips together in a tight, thin line and snapped off her seat belt.

"Change of plans, I guess."

26

MILLER ROTATED THE round spring-driven revolver-style magazine on his MGL Mk 1 grenade launcher, and shot six rounds into the water in rapid succession. To his left and right, Hsiung and Morland did the same.

From the opposite end of the *Tevatnoa*'s observation deck, du Trieux gripped the railing with one fist and held her binoculars in the other, eyes trained on the water on the starboard side.

The grenades detonated in the St. John's River, and Miller stared at the water's surface. If all went according to plan, the detonations would send shock waves around the port side, pushing the attacking sea creature to starboard, where the railgun could get a clean shot, away from the RN ship.

The Navy ship had fired their close-in weapons system at the giant squid, wounding it but apparently not killing it. After bending one of the freight cranes in half it had receded back into the depths of the river, hopefully to find easier prey.

But Miller doubted that was the end of the battle. Chancing a look over his shoulder, he shouted at du Trieux, "Anything?"

"Negative," came her reply.

"Anything on radar?" he asked through his com.

"*We see it,*" Lewis answered. "*But it's too fast, and it keeps swimming under the ship. We can't get a clean fix on it.*"

Morland spoke up. "Is that supposed to happen?"

Hsiung grabbed another shell from the crate at their feet, then nodded toward the river. "Miller?"

Back out on the water, the corpses of fish and tusk-fiends—even a couple goliath-brutes—floated to the surface. "It's the shock waves," Miller explained, reloading. "Ready?"

Morland hitched his MK1 to his shoulder. "Ready."

Another eighteen grenades detonated under the waves. More corpses rose, although fewer than before.

Miller looked over his shoulder. "Trix?"

"I'd tell you if it turned up," she snapped.

"There!" Hsiung shouted.

Back on port side, the scaled tip of the creature's fluke cut across the water's surface, then disappeared into the green, murky river.

"Why is it over here?" Morland asked.

As if in answer, the beast reared up from the water and opened its cavernous snout, lined with jagged crocodilian teeth.

"Reload!" Miller shouted, already knowing it was too late.

The beast wrapped its jaws around the corpse of a goliath-brute, snapped down with an audible smack, and dragged the body underwater.

"Good God," Morland gasped.

"*Miller, what the hell is going on out there?*" Lewis barked over the com.

"Sir, I think we've miscalculated," Miller said, hurriedly reloading his grenade launcher. "Instead of driving the creature away, we've brought it port side to feed on the dead sea-life."

"It's a seafood buffet," Hsiung said.

"*Hit it again,*" Lewis said. "*If the blasts are killing the behemoths, it's at least hurting the big one. Do it quick and don't stop.*"

"Yes, sir."

Another eighteen rounds, another slew of dead animals. Miller didn't bother to ask du Trieux if she saw anything on her side. The crate of ammunition was nearly empty.

In a gout of spray, the creature broke the surface, snatching a tusk-fiend a few meters off the port bow.

Miller heard a loud shot over his shoulder, and twisted to see Doyle, his rifle perched on a tripod. He crouched, his splinted leg sticking out in front of him, between two communications antennae on top of the bridge.

Lewis's voice shouted over the com. "*What the hell was that?*"

Doyle answered, "*Just tagged it with a tracking beacon right in the schnoz. That oughtta help.*"

"*Stand by, we're searching for the signal,*" Lewis

said. After a moment he added, "*It's under the ship again.*"

"Hold your fire," Miller told his team.

Across the river, the RN ship had opened fire again, machine guns ripping up the water's surface and puncturing the squid's tentacles as it fought to regain a hold of the ship. The beast had wrapped itself around the stern, right at the well dock—if it broke in there, it could enter the cargo hold and attack the ship from within. After being hit with a few rounds, the squid released the boat and disappeared below the water again.

Miller saw the RN sailors on deck raise their arms in celebration.

"*It's on the move,*" Lewis reported. "*Coming to starboard. Ready the railgun.*"

At the bow of the *Tevatnoa*, the railgun turret rotated and levelled, grinding with the strain. The support chains securing it aboard clanked and clattered, but held. The entire turret, from tip to deck, was covered in fungal blooms. It was a miracle it was moving at all.

"*Automated load procedure complete,*" a seaman spoke over the com. "*Standing by.*"

The ship suddenly jolted sideways; caught off-guard, every member of Cobalt jostled in position. On top of the bridge, Doyle toppled over, grabbing hold of one of the antennae to keep from sliding off the roof.

"*Railgun off-line,*" a seaman reported over the com.

Lewis swore. "*Get it back up. Track the bogey.*"

"*Tracking signal lost, sir,*" another seaman reported. "*It must have knocked off the tracker when it hit the ship.*"

"Smart sucker," Hsiung commented.

The railgun turret, now slightly askew, cranked and turned, moving back into ready position under loud protest.

Back on his feet, Miller stared over the edge of the ship. "Anybody got eyes on this thing?"

Across the water, the RN's CIWS popped off another fusillade. The massive squid had pulled itself back onto the upper deck and wrapped itself around the ship's second crane.

"Target has breached!" du Trieux shouted from the starboard side.

"*Railgun standing by.*"

"*Cobalt!*" Lewis bellowed over the com. "*Hit the deck.*"

As Miller dropped to the observation deck floor he heard Lewis shout over the com. "*Fire!*"

The railgun rang like a church bell, and Miller lay on the deck and smiled at the sound of it. With an audible surge of electromagnetic power and a hypersonic *crack*, the huge slug shot down the center of the parallel rails at the sea creature.

Miller watched the starboard side for proof of impact and was greeted with the sight of hunks of flesh splattering through the air in all directions.

Du Trieux, hunkered on starboard side, was sprayed with water and blood. She cursed in French.

"Wahoo!" Morland cheered. "Meat chunks!"

Miller climbed back to his feet and gripped the railing for support. The entirety of the ship rocked with the aftershock. Down in the water, tiny waves slapped the side of the swaying ship, jostling the corpses of the dead marine-life. For a few seconds, the world was eerily silent.

Across the water, the RN ship's machine gun had stopped. Somehow, during the action on the *Tevatnoa*, they had prised the gigantic squid off their hull and it had slipped below the surface.

About a half-kilometer to the south, a large explosion threw water high into the air. The giant squid came clean out of the river in pieces—a tentacle here, a portion of the head there.

Miller gaped. "What the *hell?*"

"*Mark 44 torpedoes,*" Lewis said over the com. "*Clark's idea. They just needed to get the squid far enough away. All right, Cobalt, everyone, well done. Clark is talking with the captain and wants to broker an agreement between the RN ship and us— just for a little while. We're high-tailing it off this fucking river and meeting up with the rest of the S-Y fleet out at sea. Get cleaned up and rested everyone. You've earned it.*"

The coms went dead.

27

IT HAD BEEN the worst spell of global warming ever recorded on the planet Earth, and snow pounded the Adirondack Mountains. It was a sick joke. Having missed the window to escape the fort, Samantha and Jan gathered the commune inside the largest log cabin within to discuss the 'change of plans.' Once again the fire pit burned almost to the ceiling.

Samantha stared into the blazing fire and scratched at the patch of lichen still covering her ribs. She'd hoped that after a brief discussion about President Frederick's new decree, the rest of them would be even more eager to vacate the fort and travel west— but to her surprise, Jan had had a change of heart.

"This changes *everything*," she argued, sitting beside Sam. "If we go to a main city, we'll have governmental support. Do you know what that means? Health care, schools, utilities... the Infected are rebuilding America. We *have* to be a part of that."

Samantha shook her head. "You have no idea if that's true. And we both know what will *really* happen, we've seen the pattern. Small groups of Regular Infected can be governed as long as they are kept busy and active, but if we drive into a large city, with thousands upon thousands of them? We might as well turn our group loose now. There will be no stopping the mobs, the violence. That's how it went in New York City, and it'll be no different now."

Jan rubbed her face, making no effort to hide her disapproval. "We'll have things to keep us busy—rebuilding! As for the Regulars, we'll find more Archaeans, more Bishops. We'll assign one to every few dozen Regulars."

"We've tried that," Samantha snapped. "The moment my farm hit hard times, it unravelled. Bishops *died*, Jan. Regulars might not harm one another normally, but when pushed... We both saw what almost happened to Binh. Rules we thought applied are irrelevant now. It'll be a thousand times worse in a big city."

"New York City happened when Infected were in the minority," Jan argued.

"That's not what happened at all."

"With help from the government, things will be different."

"What if they organize human hunts and expect us to participate? Is that what you want? President Fredericks has told them to surrender; you know what comes next. That's the kind of violence we should be running *from*—not toward."

Jan waved her hand in the air dismissively. "We should go to Syracuse. Let the commune decide if they stay or go."

Samantha squinted at the woman. "They'll do whatever you or I want them to."

Jan glared at Samantha, then stood from the fire pit. "It's decided." To the crowd, she raised her voice. "Get some rest. We leave for Syracuse at first light, regardless of weather."

The crowd roared their approval.

Samantha listened to their cheers and felt sickened, but stuck.

AT FIVE THE next morning there was a break in the snowfall. With lightning efficiency Jan organised another caravan—this time, destined for the city of Syracuse.

Sam, seeing no option but to follow along, volunteered to drive the second truck, as the stick shift was gummy and they still needed an experienced hand.

By six, the trucks were rolling at a steady pace south on Route 28 away from the old town of Thendara. Once a junction on the Fulton County railway, the town had been listed as a Historic District and served as a tourist destination well before the war between the humans and the Infected had begun. Now, it was a broken ghost town.

Samantha popped the clutch, cranked the transport into third gear and pressed on the accelerator to keep pace with Jan's van in front.

There were maybe a hundred of them, in four trucks. Armed and on high alert, the energy in the commune felt wild, and expectant—as if waiting for the fuse to be lit. It set Samantha on edge, too.

On her right sat Binh. He'd taken it upon himself to serve as 'co-pilot,' which to him meant messing with the radio, continually turning the dial in search of more transmissions from President Fredericks, or anyone else. So far, all he could find was the message from the President they'd already heard, but that didn't stop him from trying. The static didn't help Samantha feel any calmer. She knew they were driving straight into trouble, but what choice did she have?

She couldn't stay at the fort alone. That was a death sentence for sure. She couldn't leave the group on foot while they were in the middle of the Adirondack forest either. Her best bet was to stick with the group, for the time being—at least until they made it to Syracuse. Perhaps then she would have the chance to grab Binh and a few others and head out on their own before the violence started. She still liked the idea of heading west, and as she drove, she daydreamed about warm Southern California winds and moderate temperatures.

The CB radio spit a burst of static and jarred Samantha from her thoughts. *"There's some debris in the road,"* Jan said from the vehicle ahead. *"Everybody slow down, but don't cut the engines. We're coming to a stop to clear the way. Shouldn't take long."*

"*Copy that,*" said the driver behind Sam, echoed by the last transport.

Samantha gripped the CB in her palm and responded in kind.

"How long will this take?" Binh asked. "Suppose there's time to pee?"

"Why didn't you go before we left?"

"There was coffee."

Sam shrugged, looking into her side mirror at the transports behind them. One of them had steam coming from the radiator grill, but that could have just been the cold. Jan's transport blocked her view of the road ahead and whatever debris needed to be cleared.

On either side of the two-lane highway, trees and mounds of snow surrounded them. With no-one ploughing the roads, Sam had assumed there'd be stops to clear the way, but she had hoped—at least—that it wouldn't have been this early into their voyage. They'd been on the road for less than an hour.

As the truck idled, Binh wiggled in his seat and continued to play with the radio.

"If you need to go, just go," she said.

Binh frowned, gave the tuning knob one last twist, then reached for the power. Just then a man's voice cut through the air and Sam grabbed his wrist, stopping him.

"...*They do not have the right to do this,*" the man said. "*Our research belongs to the whole of the world, and I plead with whoever may be listening—*

help us. Johns Hopkins Medical School has been one of the leading research hospitals in the world for decades, and we have made an incredible break-through in finding the cure for the Archaean parasite. Additionally, we've developed an anti-fungal aerosol solution that not only stops the fungal blooms and lichen skin growths spreading, but in some cases reverses existing growth.

"The United States government doesn't want you to know about these advancements and has attempted to seize our research facility—and us—by force. We've barricaded ourselves into the University Research Center and have a militia protecting us, but we need help to get our research to other world leaders, not under the control of the Archaean parasite. Please, if you're listening and you can help, come to Johns Hopkins University in Baltimore and stop the United States of Archaean from destroying us and the only hope for humanity."

After a brief burst of static, the message began again, *"This is Dr. Anthony Wooster of Johns Hopkins Research Hospital, and I lead a team which is now under siege by the United States government. They do not have the right to do this. Our research belongs to the whole of the world, and I plead with whoever may be listening—help us..."*

Sam released Binh's wrist, but neither of them moved. Their eyes widened as they listened.

For a moment, Samantha wasn't sure what she was feeling. Why was her heart pounding? Why did she have to stop herself from smiling? She should feel horrified—nay, stricken—that the humans had found a cure for the Archaean parasite. This could mean more airdrop bombs, like the ones that had failed in NYC. This could begin another war—one even bloodier than before. Yet, in the depth of her belly, Samantha felt her stomach churn and her palms slick—not from fear—but from something else.

Dare she admit it?

She felt hope.

She was simultaneously disgusted and proud of herself. She was tired of the hive-mind. She was sick to death of the lichen growths and the constant pull of other people's emotions. Yes, humans were flawed; yes, they had so many destructive tendencies, but as the Archaean people had evolved, so had they—and there were too few Bishops to reel them in.

This was what she had been wanting for months, she realized. A cure. And it was in Baltimore, behind lock and key, about to be destroyed by President Fredericks and the United States Army. Who knew how old that message was, or how long ago it had been recorded? For all she knew, Fredericks had blown up the whole of Baltimore with missiles and bombs weeks ago, and there was nothing left of Dr. Wooster, his militia, or his research. But what if they were still there, hunkered down in the basements of the research center, just waiting to be rescued? What if they could cure the Archaean parasite and end this war?

Sure—there would always be battles. The new Archaean ecology wouldn't simply cease to exist just because they removed the parasite. Would it? The planet had suffered an immeasurable blow. There was no telling how many generations it would take to repair the damage—how long it would take just to spread the cure. But there was a chance. Not two minutes before, Sam had thought everything was hopeless—but now?

Her fingers hung in the air in front of the radio. The volume had been turned low; the passengers in the back hadn't heard. Only she and Binh had caught the message. She twisted the power knob and cut the radio, then eyed Binh to gauge his reaction.

He swallowed once, eyes still wide, almost panicked. "What do we do?" he asked.

Sam kept her joy in check and tried to look solemn. "Jan should know," she said. "I'll be right back. You should go pee."

Binh nodded, nostrils flaring. "Yeah. Okay." He snapped off his seat belt and opened the door, then hopped off the seat and used the step to lower himself into the snow. He closed the door behind him with a gust of frozen air.

Sam took off her own belt, then shot over her shoulder, "Be right back!"

Samantha's worn leather boots sank into the snow all the way up to her knees. She'd found a winter coat at the fort and a pair of lined leather gloves, but the chill was still enough to make her catch her breath. Ahead, she heard the voices of those who worked to clear the road.

"Grab that end and lift."

"Got it."

"Peg, if you could grab the middle? Okay. Toss it to the left. On three: one, two, three!"

As Sam approached she saw a large branch fly through the air, landing on the side of the road. As she rounded the corner, she spotted Jan and four others clearing the way. A tree had cracked clean in half under the weight of the snow, sagging over the road. It would seem Samantha had shown up just in time to see the last limb fly.

Jan frowned at Sam as she trudged through the snow back to her idling van. "I told you it wouldn't take long. It's done. Let's go."

"There's been another radio message," Sam said, trying to keep her voice low.

Jan ran her tongue along her gums. "From the President?"

Sam shook her head. As she relayed the message, she saw with a sinking heart that Jan's reaction was the exact opposite to hers. Yes, she was excited, nodding with enthusiasm—at the prospect of joining the United States government in battle against the evil researchers in Baltimore.

"This can't go global," Jan said. "Not if the Archaeans are to survive."

Samantha chose her words carefully. "That is true."

"We must head south," Jan said. "We'll skirt by Syracuse and head to Baltimore. We have weapons, trucks, bodies. We can help."

Sam swallowed the bile burning the back of her throat. "Agreed." Without another word, she turned and stepped high through the snow back toward her transport. The tips of her boots had soaked through, and her feet had begun to freeze. She felt cold and numb, inside and out.

"Samantha," Jan called, stopping her.

She turned, saying nothing. What was there left to say? If she spoke too much, she feared her emotions would betray her. Jan was a Bishop, and no doubt sensed Sam's frustration. Hopefully, Jan took her to be disappointed at the longer haul, but there was no way to be sure.

To her relief, instead of confronting Samantha about her feelings, Jan tilted her head to one side and whispered, "Did you hear that?"

Clumps of snow fell from the branches on Sam's left. The crack of wood, and the rustle of pine needles; could be the wind—or something else.

The hairs on the back of Samantha's neck prickled as she scanned the surrounding forest. They'd been stationary for at least five minutes, probably more. They were wasting fuel, and open targets.

"Go," Sam breathed to Jan. Then, retracing her steps through the snow, she half jumped, half ran to her transport. She got to the door and yanked back the handle, looking up through the cabin to see Binh, running through the forest on the far side, fumbling to zip his fly. Behind him, a pack of three terror-jaws followed through the trees.

He'd left his rifle on the floor of the truck, right beside Sam's.

Cursing her stupidity, Sam heaved open the cabin's

door and dove inside, snatching up her hunting rifle. Then, closing the door behind her, she flipped around and went feet first out Binh's door, rifle at the ready.

Even at a full sprint on flat land, Binh didn't have a chance in hell. As it was, he was knee-deep in snow. The beasts spread out in a half circle around him and started to close.

Sam loaded a shell in her rifle, peered through the scope, found her target, hitched the butt of the rifle tight against her shoulder, fought to control her breathing, and squeezed the trigger.

On Binh's right, a terror-jaw collapsed mid-step. Another rifle shot rang out from the cabin of the front transport, taking out the 'jaw on the left.

The center terror-jaw, the farthest from him, hesitated just a fraction at the rifle shots, giving Binh the time to clear a fallen tree and make it to the road.

Sam desperately pulled another shell from her pocket and loaded again. She barely had time to put the butt against her shoulder before she fired, hitting the third terror-jaw in the skull. It hit the ground, sinking like a bloody stone into the powder. Binh, pale and sobbing, sprinted to the truck and hugged Samantha, rifle and all, nearly toppling the both of them onto the snowy ground.

"Thank God," he gasped, coughing at the effort to speak. "Thank *you*."

A scream erupted from farther back in the caravan.

Sam propped Binh back onto his feet, loaded her rifle again and turned toward the chaos. At least five more terror-jaws were crawling over the top of the last transport, battering the doors with their bony heads.

As the windows shattered, the pack clawed their way into the back of the truck. Rifles fired, the horn blared, screams filled the air. Sam ran toward the noise.

The rearmost transport, with a hard shell top, carried an extra five people, freeing up space in the ragtop in front of it for food and supplies. The metal canopy shredded like paper under the terror-jaw's claws; several holes had already been ripped through.

Taking aim, Samantha took out the terror-jaw on the roof, then plunged through the snow to reach the tear in the side wall. The Infected were spilling out from the hold through the connecting threshold to the cabin and into the road, blocking her shot.

On the other side, Jan shouted, "Move! Where are your rifles?"

Panic had taken hold of the Regulars, who were scattering like sheep from wolves. Most ran off into the forest or up the road to the foreward vehicles. Only a few, including Jan and Samantha, stayed to fend off the terror-jaws.

Sam aimed through the gap and took out one of the terror-jaws inside, then pushed towards the back doors.

Rounding the end of the truck, she saw a terror-jaw holding the limp body of a woman in its mouth. Sam reloaded and took aim, but before she could get the shot off, the beast squeezed backwards out of a hole in the far side, dragging the body along with it. Sam ran after the 'jaw as fast as the snow allowed, but the animal skidded across the forest floor with surprising agility, pulling the limp body over fallen trees and broken branches. Fifty meters out it turned around, as if to check if Sam was still in pursuit.

She stopped and reached for another shell in her pocket. Empty. Instinctively, she reached for her sling in the waist of her pants, but it had been lost months before, and she'd never replaced it.

The terror-jaw somehow sensed her helplessness. It dropped the body into the snow and bared its teeth at her, crouching low. It stalked slowly forward.

Sam's stomach dropped and she cursed herself. She'd separated herself from the safety of the group and given away any advantage she may have possessed. In the forest, the terror-jaws were in their element.

She could run, like Binh had done, but she was a good distance from the caravan now, and there was no way to alert the others without drawing more of the creatures.

Sam gripped the rifle in her gloved hand, and slowly turned it around, holding it like a club. It might buy her a few seconds.

As the beast advanced, Sam felt strangely calm. It was just as well that she die here, she thought; she didn't want to go to Syracuse anyway. She didn't want to be among these people any longer. Her treacherous thoughts regarding the cure in

Baltimore had sent karma to her doorstep. Not that she believed in that, or any sort of god, but if she did, she doubted He or She would come to her rescue anyway. She was on her own, as always, struggling to find herself in a sea of other minds. It was better this way. Better for it to end in blood, in control of her own faculties, than as a cog in a massive Infected machine bent on twisting the whole world into one confused mind.

Her fingers relaxed. The rifle sagged in her palms. She steadied her breathing, never taking her eyes from the beast as it advanced upon her.

A shot rang out and she flinched, half expecting the bullet to pierce her own head; but the skull of the terror-jaw burst like a piñata.

She turned to see Jan and Binh a few meters behind her. Binh lowered his rifle, smoke rising from the tip, but Jan stood with icy stillness. She squinted at Sam, glared even, as if she'd heard every word of defeat that had passed through Samantha's mind.

"Jesus, Binh," Samantha breathed, her lungs stinging in the frozen air. "Good shot."

He grinned, despite himself, and nodded. "You're welcome."

"Come on," Jan said, glowering at Samantha with the heat of a burning forge. "We've got wounded."

With one last look at the limp body of the Infected, Sam turned and followed the others, using her footsteps in the snow to help her back through the forest and toward the road. She tried to feel relieved at her rescue, but felt only disappointment.

She was so tired of this—of running. Always moving. Always at the mercy of the parasite. Of the cold. Of frozen toes and numb fingers. Of feeling hungry. Back in New York she had only wanted to cooperate and be one with the planet, but now—it felt as if the Earth itself had tricked her. She never should have helped Alex and the humans destroy the city. She should have stayed. Yes, the Exiles were horrible and the wasps were destroying everything, but things had only gotten worse since then.

Back at the caravan, it was hard to know how many Infected had been lost. Severed limbs, blood, and bodies sat piled inside the last truck. The terror-jaws had shredded the whole interior. Benches, seats, and crates of supplies: everything was crushed and scattered.

At the sight of it, Sam had a hard time to think of what to do. Beside her, Jan frowned, sighed heavily, and took command.

"Siphon the gas," she said. "Save whatever you can. Pile the wounded with the others in the second transport. We've got to move."

"What about the truck?" Binh asked.

"Leave it."

"One down," Sam said, suddenly feeling chilled to her bones. "Three to go."

Jan audibly growled and stomped off to assist the others, mumbling to herself. Sam only caught the last few words:

"...shitty thing to say."

28

MILLER SLEPT FOR twelve hours and awoke feeling as if he'd drunk an entire bottle of Jack on an empty stomach and then passed out.

If only.

After clawing himself out of bed and using the better portion of a week's water ration to shower and shave, he still felt like hell. His quarters, a single compartment no larger than a walk-in closet, hadn't been touched or cleaned since he'd left for Jacksonville more than a week before. The room smelled stale and his body felt as if he'd been run over.

And it showed. It proved difficult to look at his own reflection to shave. His cheeks were hollow, sunken; the bags under his eyes were a deep, dark purple and looked so swollen he wondered how he didn't have issues blinking.

He wasn't yet forty years old, and he looked twice that. His muscles hurt and his joints crunched like puffed rice with every agonizing step. He needed a few weeks' rest, at the minimum—some serious R-and-R—maybe a starchy meal and a roll in the hay. Given the lack of pasta, potatoes, and sexual partners, Miller slouched back onto his twin-sized bed and groaned. Something had to give, he just didn't know what.

Torn between going back to bed and going to the bridge for a status update, Miller untied and retied the laces of his combat boots. His debate was answered, however, when on a whim he slipped his com into his ear.

"*Is it mandatory?*" Doyle asked.

"Oui," answered du Trieux. "*The whole ship is receiving the injection. Not just those who have the virus.*"

"*That's a bit overkill, don't you think?*" Morland said.

"*We've lost two hundred and forty-five passengers,*" Hsiung said. "*Including Matheson's son.*"

"Oh, Jesus," Miller said.

"*That you, boss?*" Doyle asked. "*Didn't think you'd ever wake up.*"

"When did James die?"

"*Who?*"

"Matheson's son!"

"*While we were gone, sir,*" du Trieux said. "*There was nothing you could have done.*"

Miller's eyes burned and his breath quickened. He ripped his earpiece out and flicked it across the room. It bounced against the wall and snapped in two.

No wonder Matheson wasn't on the bridge during

the attack. It hadn't occurred to Miller to wonder why until then.

After rinsing his face a few times, Miller stepped out his quarters and into the corridor. The sea breeze was a bit fresher than on the St. John's River. They must have moved away from the mainland. He wasn't entirely sure where he was going, but by placing one foot in front of the other, he figured he'd end up either on the bridge, or perhaps in line at the food distribution center. Better idea.

He cut across the central courtyard, using the walls as support on the rocking ship, and hooked a left to the stairwell, trying not to imagine James Matheson on his deathbed. He'd known the kid since he was young—since before he was in the double digits. Shaking the memories from his head, Miller stomped down the stairwell, his palm skimming the railing.

The area was surprisingly empty. Usually, passengers gathered in groups, traded, clogged the walkways and loitered in any available open space—but there was no-one in sight as Miller achingly made his way down to the next floor. That was when he found them.

Lined up single-file down the left side of the hallway, and wrapping around the entire length of the ship, passengers wearing various sorts of face coverings stood in a queue headed straight into the infirmary.

At the infirmary door stood Jennifer Barrett, her clipboard clasped in white knuckled hands, a stained silk scarf wrapped over her nose and mouth and tied at the back of her head. She took one look at Miller and glared. "I suppose you get to cut in line?"

"I don't know. Do I?"

"Part of your team did. I'm assuming that means you as well."

"I guess so, then." He paused at the infirmary entry to ask, "What's this, exactly?"

"Think of it as a mandatory flu shot," she said. "If I get any more scientific, I'll hear a ton of anti-vaxxer bullshit from the masses, so I'll just leave it to the British doctors to explain."

"Sounds as if you've been having fun," Miller said.

Given her expression, she didn't appreciate his sarcasm. With a quick wave she motioned him past the passengers clogging the entry, then blocked the way behind him with her own body.

"What the hell?" a passenger hollered.

"Essential personnel," Jennifer explained.

"Essential, my ass," someone else snapped.

Inside the infirmary, the queue wrapped around like a theme park line, up and down the center of the room in rows, finishing on the stage. Four folding tables had been placed downstage, equally spaced. Each table was manned by a masked, lab-coated man or woman, and behind them, smaller tables held glass vials, syringes, rubbing alcohol, and ultra-violet sterilization units. RN crew and medical staff bustled between tables, wiping each patient's arm with an alcohol swab and injecting them, passing the syringe back to be sterilized and refilled. It was a veritable assembly line.

With surprising efficiency the line moved forward, one step at a time. The passengers, looking a bit ragged and skinny, trudged along with all the grace of a herd of cattle—and smelled about the same.

Skirting around the heart of the queue, Miller pushed his way to the stage stairs and made his way to the first lab coat. He was dark-skinned, with a closely trimmed crew cut and sharp eyes. After washing his hands in a basin (quickly taken away by one of the techs and replaced), the doctor snapped on a pair of rubber gloves and reached out. A syringe was placed into his palm by another tech.

Beside Miller, a technician arrived with a dampened square of gauze. He couldn't have been more than twenty—a red-headed tech, wearing a dress uniform and a surgical mask over his freckled face. "Roll up your sleeve, please."

As he did so, Miller asked, "What's this exactly?"

Waiting at the table, the doctor pinched the top of his mask against the bridge of his nose, tightening it. "A flu shot."

"No," Miller said, pulling away so the tech couldn't sterilize his arms. "No, really. What is this?"

The doctor sighed loudly and raised an eyebrow, then turned to one of his techs. "Did you give him the pamphlet?"

"No."

"Todd!" the doctor barked. One of the other techs stood up straighter. "Hand this soldier a pamphlet, will you?"

Todd, a muscular brute with a thick cockney

accent, squinted at the doctor from behind his mask. "We ran out of pamphlets, sir."

"Out of...?" With a great sigh the doctor rolled his eyes. "Fine. It's a shot of therapeutic microbiomes which fight off the flu virus and any secondary bacterial infections."

"Fight them off how, exactly?"

The doctor's face reddened. "Todd, could you explain things to this soldier? Over there? He's holding up the line."

"Yes, doctor." As another tech returned with a fresh washbasin, Todd motioned Miller behind the table.

In the meantime, the doctor impatiently waved the next person forward from the line.

"Now, what's your concern?" Todd asked Miller.

"My concern? Look, I don't think I'm asking too much to want to know what you're shooting into my body."

"Like the doctor said, therapeutic microbiomes."

"Yeah, I heard that. But what's a microbiome?"

"Humans depend on a variety of microbes to function," Todd said. "One microbiome digests food, another yields nutrients, another set protects us against bacteria and viruses. The microbiota we've isolated is one of the latter. It both attacks the secondary bacterial infection striking influenza patients, and weakens the virus for the body's natural immune system to fight."

"So you're using the body's own bacteria to fight off other bacteria?"

This seemed to fluster Todd. "I—well, no," he scratched his head. "Okay. Sort of."

"And Lewis and Matheson approved this?"

Todd's face contorted for a moment, but then relaxed. "Yes, sir. They were the first to get it."

Miller inhaled and eyed the crowd of people waiting below him in the queue. If only they hadn't wasted all that time in Jacksonville, could they have gotten the solution to the ship faster? Would James have been saved?

Miller had known investigating the old labs was a long shot—desperate, even. Gray wasn't in his right mind, and was in no position to give orders. Then again, after Miller had watched James vomit all over his bed and nearly choke to death on it, he hadn't been in any position to *take* orders. He should have stayed. He shouldn't have gone to Lewis with the idea. He should have...

The room went blurry. Miller pursed his lips and swallowed. Then, turning back to Todd, he nodded. "All right. Let's do this."

The tech's eyes brightened. He motioned back to the doctor and the first table, stacked high with syringes. "Doctor? He's ready."

The doctor jabbed a passenger in the arm. "Hallelujah. Alert the media." Pulling out the needle, he held it aloft for a tech to remove it from his hand, and then pulled off his rubber gloves to wash again.

"Seems awfully wasteful," Miller said. "All that water and the new gloves each time."

The doctor patted his hands dry on a paper towel, tossed it into a trashcan beside the table, then snapped on new gloves and held out his hand. Todd placed a syringe into it.

With a quick motion the doctor jabbed the needle into Miller's arm and compressed the plunger. He snorted under his mask. "Yes, well, what you see as wasteful is necessary. A bit more cleanliness could have jolly well avoided this whole epidemic."

Miller tried not to wince as the doctor pulled the needle out of his skin and a tech pressed a piece of gauze over the injection site. It throbbed. "Thanks, though," Miller said, meaning it. He grabbed hold of his arm and moved ahead in the queue. "If this works, we owe you, big time."

The doctor shook his head. "I think that's the point, isn't it?" Turning back to the line he shouted, "Next!"

ON THE BRIDGE, Miller was unsurprised to find Commander Lewis and Clark standing side-by-side beside the captain's chair, deep in heated discussion. What caught him off-guard was seeing Gray Matheson with them. He stood by the pilot's chair, looking sickly.

"Sir," Miller gasped, feeling as if every ounce of blood had drained from his head.

Gray nodded, expression blank. If Miller didn't know any better, he'd say Gray didn't look as if he felt anything at all.

Lewis sat in the captain's chair and dug his thumb into his thigh, scratching with vigour above his prosthetic. "Good, I'm glad you're here, son. Clark has just brought something to our attention."

"Yes, sir?"

Clark gestured to the communications console on her left. "We've intercepted a message from the Johns Hopkins University Research Center in which they claim to not only have an effective anti-fungal solution, but also a cure for the Archaean parasite."

Miller dropped his hands from his hips. "Do we have access? How soon can we get to them? Is this verified?"

Lewis shook his head. "I'm afraid it's not as simple as that."

Clark said, "The United States government is attempting to seize the facility, and the message we found was an S.O.S. from the main researcher at the facility. They're under attack and need reinforcements."

Miller's mind was already on track. Any muscle aches or joint pain he'd experienced when awakening clouded over with adrenaline. "How long ago did you 'intercept' this message?"

Clark frowned. "Five days ago, but we don't know how long it's been broadcasting."

"You knew all along," Miller said, realization dawning. "That's why you wanted to commandeer the ship. You need bodies, soldiers. To invade Baltimore."

If he'd hit upon the truth, Clark didn't give any clue. She squared her shoulders and set her jaw as tight as a vice. "Our ship is well-equipped with landing gear, ammunition, and weaponry, and we possess plenty of surface missiles—but yes, for a full-scale military operation to assume control of the university, search and rescue of the medical staff and their research, and to evade the whole of the United States Infected Army—we needed people. You have approximately fifteen hundred able-bodied men on this ship alone, another thousand on the other cruise liner."

Miller shook his head. "Civilians, Clark."

"I don't know if you've noticed, Miller," Clark said, glaring. "But humans are *losing* this war. We're spread out and dispersed so far and wide we're no use to anyone. If we don't band together and *fight* for our existence, we might as well curl up into a ball and die now. Our *only* chance is to find the cure."

"*If* this is truly the cure," Miller said, "why didn't they broadcast the formula? Why make us send thousands of people to their deaths, just to save a couple of scientists who aren't smart enough to figure that out? It doesn't feel right."

"It doesn't *feel* right?" Clark asked. "You'd let Fredericks destroy the last chance we have at saving the human race, because it doesn't *feel* right? Civilians are *already* dying, Miller. There are reports of human hunts, labor camps, mass exterminations."

Gray cleared his throat. "This is our last chance, Miller."

"You don't know that."

"I'll lead the strike," Lewis said, digging into his thigh with added force. "If Miller won't, I'll take Baltimore myself."

"Sir!"

"I don't think you're hearing what Clark has been saying, son. If we miss this chance, we may miss our only shot to save us. All of us. Every. Single. Human. Being."

"I understand that, sir," Miller said. "But we don't even know if this broadcast is legitimate. It could be a trap. What if Fredericks set this whole thing up just so we'll come running?"

Gray shook his head. "Stockman could have come up with something that smart, but Huck? Please."

"He has a point," said Lewis.

"Great. It has to be true because our President is too dumb to think of it?"

Gray shrugged.

"A full frontal assault with civilians would be a disaster," Miller said.

Lewis raised his eyebrows. "We're not planning to just walk in, son."

Clark nodded. "Our crew will engage the US military. If the university is truly under siege, then Cobalt will slip in, rescue the team and their research, and get out. We'll withdraw to the ship once we know the solution is safe."

Miller pursed his lips. It wasn't the worst of plans. "What do we do with the cure once we have it?"

"The British government is prepared to enact mandatory inoculations..."

"We're getting ahead of ourselves," Gray said. "Retrieve it first. We can argue what to do with it once we have it."

Miller shifted his weight. A low throb pulsed under his left kneecap. When he lifted his arm to rub his face, his elbow popped. The injection site beat with every thump of his heart, and it felt like his brain was pushing out through his eyes.

He found it hard to stand all of the sudden. He was in no condition for this. How was he going to operate point on a search and rescue into the heart of a literal Infected army? Or ask his team to, after everything they'd been through?

They'd done it before. In New York, Cobalt and the security squads of Schaffer-Yeager Corporation had fought and defeated a rogue battalion of Infected recruits. But that had been at the beginning of the war, when Miller and his team were fresh.

Now, Doyle could barely walk. Morland had easily lost fifty pounds of muscle. Du Trieux and Hsiung seemed okay on the surface, but he wasn't blind to their fraying tempers, their snide comments and sarcasm. Cobalt was crumbling.

Miller ran his hands over his scalp and sighed. "When do we launch?"

Lewis gave up scratching his thigh and placed his palm on the arm of his command chair. "Four days."

THEY DROVE FOR hours, bypassing Syracuse and driving south through Utica. They took Interstate 8 to the 88 through Binghamton, and then merged onto the 81. The roads were desolate.

Sometime after they passed the Pennsylvania border, the radiator on the third van started spewing thick black smoke and choked to a halt. It was dark, with a sky full of dust clouds and no visible moon. There was no sign of terror-jaws, but rather than risk camping out in the open, they pushed the dead transport off to the side and piled into the two remaining vehicles. Just north of the 84/81 interchange they exited the highway and stopped in the parking lot of an old school.

After a quick sweep of the school's interior, they found evidence of an old commune. Samantha's first clue was the waste area: with no running water, the inhabitants had resorted to using an out-of-the-way classroom. It reeked to high hell, but given the circumstances, Sam couldn't really blame them. And it was common Infected practice.

Mountains of stinking blankets, bed sheets, and filthy pillows were scattered down the hallways, and there was evidence of cooking fires—but no bodies. None. Whoever they'd been, they hadn't died of starvation or sickness; they had simply left. It was a modern-day Machu Picchu.

Seeing as how it was night, dark, and more than a little suspicious, Jan and Sam helped the others barricade themselves into an auditorium, with plans to either fix the broken radiator, find an alternative vehicle to commandeer, or cram into the two remaining transports and make for Baltimore at first light.

The group had scavenged the cleanest of the blankets and sheets and were cuddling together in small clusters for warmth. The lot of them were content, even comforted, by being indoors, locked in, and most importantly, together.

Samantha wasn't sure how they could stand it. She curled her body into itself and huddled at the back of the auditorium, alone. Despite her exhaustion, her mind raced.

Somewhere in Baltimore, only a few hours away, was the cure for the Archaean parasite. The mere idea of being free from the weight of everyone else's emotions made Sam want to get to her feet and start walking.

How could they bear it? These people. Every moment of sadness was shared. Every hint of shame, intolerance, and yearning swirled around the heads of every member of their group. Sure, the happiness and joy were also collective, but in this world, on this planet and among these terrors, how much of those was there? She could count the happy moments on one hand.

Even now, the cautious optimism and contentedness were fleeting. She knew by the morning the crowd would be full of wanting, of trepidation and anxiety. An unease would rise in every soul in the auditorium, smothering Samantha like a blanket.

She would be glad to be free of it, truly. If she could have cut the others' emotions out of her head by hand, she'd have a knife through her ear in a heartbeat.

Soon, and near, an opportunity approached. Baltimore was her last hope. If all failed there, she had no other reason to continue this pitiful existence.

Sam blinked away her anger. She felt someone watching and spotted Jan, across the room. She had just finished walking the perimeter of the auditorium.

Jan came up and sat in the next seat over. She set her rifle on the floor, pulled the edges of her jacket tighter across her chest and buried her hands in her armpits. After staring at the ceiling for a few moments, the older woman turned her head toward Sam. "They're so happy. It's tempting to stay here, isn't it? But what's happening in Baltimore is too important. Wouldn't you agree?"

Sam pursed her lips and pulled her legs against her chest. "I agree," she said.

Jan nodded.

Disgusted, and with an uneasy churn in the depths of her belly, Sam turned her back on her and closed her eyes.

AT FIRST LIGHT, Samantha and a few others set out to explore the school campus in search of supplies, while the rest of the group went back for the third vehicle. After wandering the halls for a few minutes, Sam found a cafeteria, and beyond it, an industrial kitchen.

Stainless steel cabinets and countertops lined the long room. There was a double oven—broken, covered in fungus—a six-burner stove and grill, also broken, a whole line of cabinets—all empty—and a pantry with a broken light switch, which at first glance appeared to be bare.

Unwilling to admit defeat, Samantha stepped into the dark pantry and fumbled blindly around the barren shelves. The bottom shelf was empty, as was the one above. At chest level she found a large can of something—she couldn't be sure what. She set it beside her feet on the floor and moved into the darkness. In the back of the pantry she found a pair of nylon trash bags, a large roll of industrial cellophane wrap, and another can. She checked the shelves on the right, but found they were bare.

Satisfied, she snatched up the two cans, draped the trash bags over her shoulder, and cradled the cellophane in the crock of her arm and turned to leave. She found Jan standing at the pantry entry, one hand resting on the door.

"Oh," Sam said, "are you back with the third transport?"

"You're not the only Bishop," Jan said.

"Huh?" It was hard to see Jan's expression in the shadows, but Sam heard the anger in her voice. "Did something happen to the group who went back for the third van? Is everything alright?"

"No." Jan shook her head. "But it will be."

"Okay... Found some stuff here," Sam said, making an effort to keep her tone sunny. "Not sure what it is, but it's better than nothing."

"You forget who you're talking to," Jan said.

Sam paused, still gripping the loot in her arms. "Jan, what's going on?"

"I can sense your feelings," she said. She drummed her fingers on the door, raising a hollow, metallic thumping noise. "I know what you *really* want."

"What I want is to get out of this pantry and back on the road to Baltimore as soon as possible," Samantha said.

"But not for the right reasons."

Sam felt her skin prickle. "What do you know about my reasons?"

"Enough to say that you shouldn't come with us."

Sam swallowed the lump in her throat. "Of course I'm coming with you. We don't have time to debate this. It's time to go." She stepped forward.

With a fluid motion, Jan moved to Sam's left, closing the door slightly and blocking it with her body.

"If you pace yourself with rationing," Jan said, "you can live here until winter passes. It'll be easier once the snow melts. You can head west like you originally wanted. You're resourceful, you'll be fine. This is for the best."

"Get out of the way," Sam said, temper rising. "We need to pack these cans of"—she checked the labels and frowned—"ketchup for the trip."

"Sorry," Jan said, darting out and closing the door, "but you leave me no choice."

Sam barely had time to react. Darting forward, she thrust her foot into the gap.

Jan tried to slam the door closed again, only to have Sam shove her back, the cans giving her fists weight.

Stumbling backwards, Jan fell into the kitchen, grabbing the edge of a counter to steady herself.

Still clutching the supplies, Sam rushed her, crashing into the woman and sending both of them to the cracked tiles below, with Sam on top.

Jan's head hit the floor with a wet *thunk*, but it did little to slow her. Eyes wide, she grabbed Sam by the shoulders and rolled her over, climbing on top of her and clutching her by the shoulders. As Jan struggled to stand, Sam realized she intended to drag her into the pantry.

Swinging her hand upward, Sam cracked Jan over the head with one of the cans, splitting the lid and splattering ketchup all over the both of them.

Under the blow, Jan lost her grip on Sam and toppled to the floor, smacking her head against a cabinet. Momentarily stunned, Jan blinked and shook her head.

Seizing the moment, Sam dropped the other items in her arms and grabbed up the roll of cellophane. Pulling a long strip across her chest, Sam flattened the plastic wrap over Jan's nose and mouth and pressed the woman to the floor, her chest over the woman's face.

Jan was not a slight woman. She was easily an inch taller than Sam, and in her prime, could have snapped Sam in half like a twig—but she'd also been at the labor camp twice as long as Samantha, and in her weakened state, was no match for her. She kicked and flailed, but Samantha pressed down with all her might, anger and frustration lending strength to her arms.

Jan screamed and bucked. She pushed off her feet, raised her hips and tried to twist away, but Sam held fast. She clawed at Sam's face and attempted to jam her thumbs into her eye sockets, but her strength was fleeting, weak from months of eating nothing but fungus. Within minutes, Jan's body went slack, and then she stopped moving.

Sam could hardly breathe. She waited a few seconds, paralyzed. Eventually, she crawled off the body and slid backwards, her shoulder blades banging against the cabinets as she choked on air. The back of her hand, smothered in ketchup, went to her mouth and all at once her adrenaline failed her.

Holy Christ. What had she done?

She'd *murdered* Jan.

How the hell had she done that?

She hadn't even felt Jan's fear. What was happening to her?

What the hell was she going to do? Show up covered in scratches and ketchup, with no Jan, and drive to Baltimore like nothing happened?

The others would ask questions. What was she going to do? Kill them all, to cover her tracks?

There was almost one meter of snow outside. She couldn't take off on her own. She wouldn't get a kilometer without freezing to death or being chomped by a pack of terror-jaws or husk-mutts. Any moment, someone could show up in the kitchen, searching for them both, and then she would be toast.

She had to do something. Fast. The others would appear before long.

Shaking from head to toe, Sam grabbed a counter and pulled herself upright. Then, stumbling forward, she grabbed Jan's body by the arms and dragged her into the pantry, closing and locking it behind her.

Using the rest of the cellophane and the trash bags, Sam attempted to wipe herself clean of ketchup, but her hands shook and she just seemed to smear it around. Finally giving up, she made her way back to the auditorium, where Binh and the others were gathering up whatever loot they had managed to find and collecting it on some of the blankets and bed sheets, to lug back to the trucks.

"Jesus," Binh breathed. "What happened?"

"Terror-jaws," Sam said, not really knowing where the lie came from. "In the kitchen. We've got to hurry!"

Binh's eyes widened in terror.

"We've got to evacuate," Sam said. "*Now!*"

Binh nodded, his face having gone pale. "What about Jan? She went to find you."

Sam shook her head. Her eyes filled with tears. "The terror-jaws..."

Binh looked stricken, but resolved. He adjusted the strap of his hunting rifle on his shoulder, and handed another to Sam. She took it with a steady hand.

"Let's go," he said, raising his voice to address the crowd. "This location's been compromised. We're moving out!"

Sam blinked slowly and grabbed a corner of a bed sheet. They exited the auditorium with calm precision and loaded up the three transport trucks. All the third truck had needed was to cool off and have the radiator refilled. Sam wasn't sure how long it would last before overheating again, but it was only a few more hours to Baltimore.

With a heave, the group loaded up the supplies. Binh patted Sam on the shoulder, then ran ahead to drive Jan's truck.

How was he to know her tears were from guilt, and not fear? She watched them rally and move, suddenly impressed with how efficient Infected could be when properly motivated and directed. She was the only Bishop among them, now. There would be no way they could resist her, she realized, if she pushed them.

Sam closed the truck door, compressed the clutch and popped the ignition. A thought crossed her mind and she bit her lip to keep from smiling.

There was no one to stop her now.

30

As much as they would have liked to sail up to the Cruise Maryland Terminal in Baltimore and drive straight toward the Johns Hopkins Research Facility, Captain Corthwell and Commander Lewis figured there'd be too many US military troops. Looking at the map, Miller didn't disagree.

"If we had a hundred thousand troops or so, then maybe we could storm the port and take it by force," Lewis said, "but we don't."

"It would be a fool's errand," agreed the captain. He stood in the dingy room with a dignified air.

"Besides," Lewis added, "what with the rising sea levels, we're not one hundred percent certain it's still there, much less operational."

Miller eyed the charts and maps laid out across Gray's ping pong table desk and nodded. "What about this river?"

Lewis grimaced. "The Back River is industrial waste and city run off; it'd be like swimming in sewage.

Besides which, it's only about ten meters deep."

"We thought it best," the captain said, pointing to the northeast on the map, "to enter here, at one of the Gunpowder River's outlets. There's a national park, or what's left of it—most of it's under water now. We think you're unlikely to find too many troops stationed that far from the target."

"You will, however," Lewis added, "find more wildlife to contend with. So keep a sharp eye."

"You'll move north here, up this peninsula," said the captain. "Dundee National Environment Area. Then you'll pass north of this airport. Once you're by, you can get on a highway—things will move much quicker from there."

"It's awfully far," Miller observed.

Lewis frowned. "It's about a four-hour walk, if you go slow. But if we bring you in south of the target, we run a bigger risk of your being seen. We have to swing wide and drop you north. I know it's not ideal, but it's the best we've got."

"Separate from the troops once you pass Interstate 95," the captain said. "They'll proceed directly to engage as you slip in from the northwest."

"Black-ops shit," Miller said, grimacing.

Only Lewis caught the reference. "Some things never change."

Miller smirked. "Nope."

DOYLE SNAPPED A mag into his combat vest and sheathed his knife. His knee, currently held together with pins and an exo-skeletal brace, sat propped on an ammunition crate in front of him.

Hsiung, watching from her nook across the room, slid out of her parachute hammock and cleared her throat. "What have you taken for the pain?" she asked him.

Behind the bar, sitting on his favorite stool, Morland scoffed.

Du Trieux, sharpening her knife on a whetstone in a chair by the door, continued stroking her hunting blade with rhythmic motions.

"Nothing," Doyle said. "I refused it, if that's what you're worried about."

Hsiung pressed her lips together.

"You sure that's wise?" du Trieux said, not missing a stroke.

Doyle shrugged and snapped another mag into his vest.

"Won't the pain slow you down?" Hsiung asked.

Doyle raised an eyebrow.

Du Trieux stopped sharpening. "*Mon dieu.*"

Hsiung's face reddened. "You're a liability. You should sit this operation out."

"And do what?" Doyle retorted. "I'm no good to anybody here."

"It's not your call," du Trieux said to Hsiung, her words sharp.

"Miller wants us all. The choice is made," Morland said. He hopped down from his stool to where his rifle lay spread in pieces across the bar and began reassembling it.

"Maybe Miller isn't thinking clearly," Hsiung said. "Have you seen him lately?"

"I'm just fine, thanks for your concern," Miller said. He stood in the Crow's Nest door. He fought to keep his voice level. He knew he looked like shit—hell, they all did—but if this wasn't a case of the pot calling the kettle black, he didn't know what was. "And so is Doyle. Am I right?"

Doyle pushed off the arms of his chair and stood. If he was in any sort of pain, which Miller was fairly certain he was, he hid it well. "You bet, boss."

"That's settled, then." Miller frowned and eyed each member of his team. He wished he could have given them more time to rest—or at the very least, a pep talk—but there wasn't any time left; and besides, Miller wasn't sure he had any pep to give. After four days at sea they'd reached their drop location. It was go time. Any misgivings had to be put aside. "Our transport is ready. Move out."

Doyle was the first out the door, hardly a limp in his step. "Yes, sir."

THE RN BATTLESHIP had loaded three hundred sailors onto their Mk 10 transport and sent them to land at first light on the fifth day. Once they had cleared an area of wildlife and deemed it secure, the Mk 10 returned to the ship. It arrived again on land with two fully equipped Foxhound armored vehicles.

The Foxhounds, Britain's solution to the IEDs from desert wars past, was a light-weight protected patrol van—smaller than most mine and ambush resistance vehicles, but larger than a Humvee or a Bravo. The plan was to house the RN commander in the frontmost Foxhound, and Miller and Cobalt would take up the second in the rear. Each vehicle could hold up to six passengers.

From the *Tevatnoa* they'd rustled together almost a thousand S-Y security troops, some who hadn't seen battle since the evacuation of the Astoria Peninsula almost a year before. Armed with L85A2 assault rifles provided by the RN, another thousand civilians from the *Princess Penelope* had volunteered for the operation—men and women. All were transported to land via the mega-lifeboats and then taken into the RN's command.

Leading the troops, to Miller's utter shock, was the captain's assistant, Sarah Clark.

"Don't look so stricken, Miller," she said, after seeing his expression. She climbed into the passenger side of the front Foxhound cab. "I was a major in the Royal Marines before I set sail with the RN."

"I'm not stricken," Miller said.

"Look at you. Would you rather have had the commander?"

Miller frowned.

"I thought not."

"You mistake me," Miller said. "Your mission entails engaging in front line combat with the whole of the Infected United States Army. My concern is that you're too valuable to lose—and Cobalt will be unable to help you once we have the laboratory staff and research in tow."

"I understand the risks," Clark said. "I'm not looking to die anytime soon. We'll distract them enough for you to get in and out—then we roll. There are over two thousand humans under my command and we've become an endangered species. I don't want any more loss of life than is necessary."

"Don't wait for us, if it comes to that," Miller said. "My team has been in scrapes like this before. We'll find a way back to the ship somehow."

"Just get to the rendezvous point," Clark said. "Let me do the rest."

"Yes, ma'am."

Clark slammed the door and nodded to the driver. With the roar of the engine the armored car thundered to life and rolled forward.

At the tip of the Dundee Natural Environment Area sat the sunken remains of two separate plant nurseries. With Clark on point, the troops in the center, and Cobalt driving the second Foxhound at the rear, the small army travelled up the central road on the peninsula, then hooked a left onto a two-lane highway, leading west. After passing a church to the south, they marched barely five kilometers before all hell broke loose.

To their north, a wooded area loomed. Clark, with her RN troops just behind, had passed under the 43 overpass when the trees on the right rattled and groaned from within.

From his vantage point in the driver's seat of the Foxhound, all Miller could see was rustling trees and branches. If he hadn't known better, he would have sworn the forest had come alive and was moving forward to protest their presence in Baltimore; but the truth was much worse.

A wild pack of bird-like dogs came bounding out of the woods. They were chasing a small herd of thug-behemoths—four adults and one calf—who were barrelling toward the civilian militia at neck-break speed.

Like an avalanche, the behemoths ploughed through the center of the group, scattering and trampling anyone too slow to get out of the way.

Once the behemoths were across the highway, the dogs followed: perhaps five or six of them, by Miller's estimation.

"What the fuck are those?" Doyle asked from the passenger seat.

The salamander-esque predators had a ridge of hair up their spines. They slunk around the evading behemoth herd, encircling them, following them south.

"I've heard of them, but never seen one," Hsiung said, talking over Doyle's shoulder while peering through her binoculars at the carnage. "I think they call them husk-mutts."

One mutt deviated from formation—distracted by the pack of humans so readily available for chomping. It pounced on a man, grabbed him by the throat and attempted to drag him away. The beast got only a few meters before one of the civilians had the good sense to shoot it.

"*Braiser cette merde*," du Trieux swore.

Clark, who had swung around in her Foxhound, hung out the passenger side window and shouted orders at her RN troops to intervene. They encircled the civilians, closed ranks and then tended the wounded.

The entire ordeal had taken less than five minutes. Miller and Cobalt, at the far end, could do nothing but watch and wait as the RN took care of the injured, removed the dead from the road, and moved on. The herd had moved south and then east, by Miller's estimation, but who knew where they would be headed next? It was best to get out of the way as fast as possible.

When they reached Interstate 95, Clark led the troops straight, toward downtown, while Miller and the Cobalt Foxhound turned right and headed north up the 95.

"*See you on the other side*," Clark said, before cutting communications.

Miller switched off the Foxhound CB and tapped the com-link in his ear. "This is where the fun begins."

31

SAM PRESSED HER foot against the accelerator and gritted her teeth. They were mere minutes from Baltimore. Somehow, she had to convince almost a hundred people to betray their own kind and facilitate obtaining the very substance that could make them lose the core of their identity. It was going to be a hard—an impossible—sell. Her first thought was to pulse something through the group—she was the only Bishop left among them, after all, and they would be powerless to resist her. But she remained conflicted on which feeling would get her what she wanted.

She considered giving an inspirational speech— some sort of rip-roaring *Henry the Fifth* we-band-of-brothers oration—but she felt more like Brutus from *Julius Caesar* than any sort of inspiring king.

The closer she got to the Johns Hopkins, the more her hands sweated and her heart raced. Her nervousness seemed to rub off on the others: the thirty or so Infected crammed into the back of the truck were restless. They snapped at each other and picked fights of the dumbest sort, over legs touching or loud breathing. There were ten more people in the transport than it was designed for; of *course* they were uncomfortable. Still, Samantha couldn't help but wonder if her own emotions weren't influencing the masses.

Ahead, Interstate 83 was wide open. They passed the 695 and what was once the Johns Hopkins University—not the medical school—without another soul in sight. There was the occasional abandoned car, and evidence of communes and human settlements could be seen in the campfires and occasional glimpses of movement, but for the most part, the outskirts of Baltimore looked deserted.

Had there been some sort of war here, like in NYC? Where the hell was everyone?

"Here we go again," said a voice over the CB.

Sam shot a quick look into her side mirror and spotted the issue. The third truck's radiator was steaming. The sun was high in the sky. The temperature had easily hit the low hundreds. Away from the snow of the mountains, the ground baked and the sky seared. It was no wonder the transport had only lasted a few hours.

Sam snatched up the dangling receiver. "Ok, pull off at the next exit. We'll lay low until tonight."

"Seems a shame," Binh said over the CB. *"We've come so far. We've got to be close. Shouldn't we just keep on until it dies?"*

"It's best if we get a lay of the land and assess the situation before we drive into a battle."

"*Good point*," Binh said, pulling off at the next ramp.

The ramp banked to the right, passed a sludgy lake on one side, a residential street on the other.

"*We should pull into the neighbourhood*," Binh suggested. "*There's bound to be a commune in there. We can find out what's happened from them.*"

That was exactly what Sam *didn't* want. "Keep going. I see what looks like a power plant? Next to a basketball court. Just ahead."

"*Why there?*"

"Parts for the van, of course," Sam said, shaking her head. Her logic was sketchy at best. If Binh put up even the slightest hint of resistance she would have a problem, but luckily, he didn't.

"*I see it*," he said.

"*Make this fast*," said the woman driving the third truck. "*The gauge is on the H. The truck is going to catch fire if we push too much farther.*"

Sam shifted her transport down into second gear and prepared to slow. "Copy that."

They pulled into the complex and spilled out of the transport vehicles. The facility, some sort of government maintenance building, was surrounded by a tall concrete wall and enclosed by a metal rolling gate. Perfect for Samantha's needs.

"Set up camp here," Sam instructed Binh. "Search for supplies and fill up the truck's radiator again."

"Wait, what are you doing?"

Sam crawled back into the cab of her empty transport and re-started the engine. "Don't commune with any other Infected until I figure out what's happening. Binh, you're in charge until I get back."

This idea seemed to horrify him. "You're not going out there alone! What about predators? What about *humans?*"

Sam gave a small nod. "There's a lot to be said for being sneaky," she said. "Everything will be fine."

"We go together, or not at all," Binh insisted.

Sam had to appreciate his loyalty. If she didn't know any better, she'd think he was evolving into a Bishop, but all thoughts of that were put to rest the moment she placed a hand on his shoulder and pumped him full of tranquillity. His entire face relaxed and he yawned, covering his wide mouth with his palm.

"Stay here. This won't take long," she said.

From the maintenance yard, Sam drove back out onto the highway, then exited off Oliver, heading south, and then turned east. She took Preston St. past a cemetery—completely overrun with goliath-brutes grazing on the overgrown weeds—and through a residential area—crawling with communes as far as the eye could see. She then took Wolfe Street south.

That was when she saw them.

She had noted during her drive that there were no military aircraft in the skies. No fighter jet fly-bys, no combat helicopters searching the area with spotlights. In fact, she'd begun to doubt the United

States military was still there at all, until she noticed a giant tank roll by, south of her position off Wolfe.

After parking the transport and locking it tight, she proceeded on foot. As she neared the corner of Wolfe and Madison, she came to a complete stop and hid behind a row of abandoned cars parked along the fungus-covered curbs.

There wasn't just the one tank, but four. One was parked at each corner, as far as she could tell, surrounding an entire block to her left. Three buildings, linked by glass walkways, straddled the junction. A temporary barrier of wooden pylons and barbed wire ran down the center of the boulevard, manned by soldiers in full-blown tactical gear—helmets, goggles, assault rifles, the works. They paced back and forth on either side of the pylons in five-minute intervals.

After sitting and watching for a good half hour, she came to the conclusion that this was not an active military operation. In all likelihood, the formula from the research facility was already gone. What she saw here was a battalion of guards holding a position—and probably waiting to catch some fool trying to infiltrate it.

With no desire to be that fool, Sam waited for a break in the patrol, then crossed the street behind the parked cars. Just south, and down a barricaded dark alleyway, there was another entrance to the last of the three buildings that lined the city block. The door was chained shut, and more pylons and barbed-wire stood in the way, but it wasn't anything a pair of bolt cutters, a hundred or so people, and a little luck couldn't remedy.

Inside the facility, perhaps she could still find an old hard drive, a sample of the formula, or research papers—anything left behind. She had not come all this way to *not* look, and she would never forgive herself if she slunk away like a dog with her tail between her legs just because it looked difficult.

After driving back to the maintenance facility where she had left Binh and the others, she listened to their list of finds: some tools, one can of diesel fuel, a lot of electrical wire and gas meters, and about three hundred neon orange vests.

"There wouldn't by chance be any wire cutters in that pile of tools, would there?" she asked.

Binh pursed his lips and shrugged. "Yeah, I think there are a few."

Sam smiled and fought the urge to rub her palms together. "Excellent."

AT DAWN THE next morning, Sam instructed Binh to get the group ready.

"We need to know what's going on, what the U.S. troops have in there," she said. "I propose we break into the facility and find any evidence of the research by ourselves."

"Why don't we just send someone to *ask* the troops if they have the research?" Binh suggested. "Like an envoy, of sorts. They're Infected, aren't they? We're on the same side."

If Sam were actually interested in finding that out, it would have been a good suggestion. She shook her head. "It could be a trap. We can't risk a single life until we know for *sure* that they're with us."

She cleared her throat. "There's an alleyway that leads directly into the research facility. We have to get through a patrol, a pylon barrier, and a lot of barbed wire, but even so, it's our best bet. Have your weapons ready, and do not hesitate to shoot the soldiers if they try and stop us."

"All this could be avoided," Binh said, "if we just contacted—"

"This is for the best," Sam said, placing a hand on Binh's arm.

He blinked slowly, then said, "All right."

Samantha led the small army down to the intersection she'd found the previous day. She broke them into groups of ten, sticking to the shadows and skirting the patrols behind the cover of the abandoned, fungus-draped cars still lining the curbs. It took a bit of time, but once she had them safely inside the alley, she set them to work in getting through the pylons and the barbed wire. Sam and Binh waited in a stairwell across the way as they worked.

Perhaps it would be faster if they sent someone back for one of the transport trucks, and they crashed their way into the door? But the entry was on a raised platform—it was unlikely the transport could make the jump—and the idea of sneaking a transport by the battalion was laughable. They were lucky to have snuck past them as it was.

"Shit. We have incoming," Binh said, pointing down the alleyway.

Sam squinted into the dark tunnel; down the way—approaching in a two-by-three combat formation—were five soldiers. Unlike the others, in their full black tactical armor, they didn't wear helmets, and looked a bit the worse for the wear. One had his leg in an exo-brace and walked with a slight limp. Another of them, a woman with dark skin and a silent step, glared about her surroundings with a ferocious scowl. A shorter, angrier woman cautiously walked next to a tall, lanky Caucasian man, who in turn looked around as if confused.

At the sight of the fifth soldier, Sam's breath caught in her throat.

"Hold on," she said to Binh. "I know these guys."

There was no denying the swagger of the man on point, or the closely cropped brown hair and the weathered, sharp jawline. Samantha had to fight to keep herself from calling out to him. She stood up.

Binh looked horrified. "What are you *doing?*"

"I worked with these humans in New York City. We can work this to our advantage."

"They're human?" he whispered harshly.

"These aren't your typical humans, Binh. You'll have to trust me."

"They've seen us. Shit, there's a laser pointer. Get down!" Binh shouted.

The whole of the Infected band followed Binh to the asphalt and cover—all but Samantha. Instead, she stepped forward and walked into the middle of the alleyway. She kept her face expressionless, her posture confident and assured. Her heart pounded in her chest like a jackhammer.

At the sight of her, Cobalt took cover behind a concrete stairwell farther on the opposite end of the alley. The one with the brace aimed a sniper rifle at Sam's chest. She looked down at the red laser dot over her sternum. Only Alex remained in the middle of the road.

Sam continued her walk toward him, her boots echoing off the concrete walls. She saw the moment he recognized her. Despite himself, a smile crossed his lips.

Sam felt her face warm. She stopped and met Alex midway. His smile fell as he got closer—damn, she must look like shit. Come to think of it, so did he.

She tried to keep her voice light, her posture unassuming. When he got within earshot, she cleared her throat and said, "Fancy meeting you here."

Alex raised an eyebrow. "I'll be damned."

OPERATION KING RAT

32

"Hold your fire!" Miller said, bringing his fist over his head.

The red laser danced across Samantha's chest, then disappeared. She swallowed thickly, and then, to Miller's astonishment, laughed.

Her amusement spread across her group like the embers of a forest fire. Soon, the Infected were all eerily cackling from their pathetic cover positions in the alley behind her. One man, a young fellow of Korean descent, stood and pointed to Sam as if they shared in some hysterical private joke.

Miller's face grew hot.

Samantha shot a weary look over her shoulder at the boy and rolled her eyes. When her merriment burned out, so did the others.

Behind Miller in the enclave of the alley, du Trieux coughed; the sound echoed off the silent concrete walls.

"I should have known you'd show up," Samantha

said, putting a hand on her bony hip. She'd changed dramatically since last he'd seen her. Before, she'd been terribly thin, even gaunt; now, she looked starved. Deep hollows lined her mouth and under her eyes. Her skin hung off her like shredded fabric. As before, her once long, full hair was tied back into a loose braid, but it looked as if chunks of it were missing. Samantha shook her head at Miller with a bemused grin. "You're like the sick punch line to a bad joke."

He wasn't sure if that was meant as a compliment. "Is this going to be a problem?"

"Depends," she said. "Why are you here?"

Miller shifted on his feet and felt his left hip pop. "Well, I'm *not* here under the command of the United States Army," he said. "Are you?"

"Definitely not."

"We have that in common, at least."

Samantha ventured a look at the research building to her right, Miller's left. "Is what you're after in there?"

He fidgeted with the M27 in his hands, then nearly cursed himself when she grinned at him again.

"I propose a deal, then," she said.

"I don't see how this is going to work if we both want to leave with the same thing."

"You needn't worry. Our interests lie with the anti-fungal solution," she said quickly. "Only."

"I'm here for both."

She considered this, her dark eyes darting back and forth as if she were calculating equations in her head. "If we work together, you can have the cure. I'm assuming you're here because you don't want the President to destroy it?"

"You're not here to make sure he does?"

She pursed her lips before speaking. "No. It would seem we have no choice but to work together. Besides, there's a hundred of us, and only five of you. Seems a prudent choice, don't you think?"

"We didn't come alone," he said. "But seeing as how I don't want to start a firefight in this alley and draw the Army's attention—I'm willing to work out a deal."

Sam nodded. "We get the anti-fungal. You get the anti-parasitic."

Miller bit the inside of his cheek and tasted blood. "Agreed."

Sam's face brightened. She absently scratched at her shoulder. "Then let's get moving."

Miller tapped the com in his ear. "We're going in together."

"Of course," Doyle said, standing from his position in the enclave and resting his rifle on his shoulder. "What could possibly go wrong?"

A shot rang out and a bullet whizzed by Miller's face. He spun in position and dropped to his knee, his rifle aimed straight at Sam's head. When another shot spun past Sam, causing her to crouch down, he realized it wasn't the Infected who had fired. The shot had come from behind her.

A patrol had found them. There were only three or four soldiers, but they'd positioned themselves behind pillars of cement and were shooting through the Infected troop, straight at Cobalt.

Miller's team dispersed, leaving the exposed enclave and taking up positions around the alleyway. Du Trieux took down the soldier on the far right with a well-positioned shot to the face. Sam—hiding behind a pylon to Miller's left—aimed with her hunting rifle and took out another soldier with a single round to the chest. Afterwards, her Infected minions twisted and mowed down the other two guards in a barrage of bullets.

For a moment, Miller watched in awe. This wasn't right. After another second, the echo from the gunfire died in the alleyway, and he realized the change. These Infected had killed other Infected. How was that even possible?

"Binh! Through the barrier!" Sam bellowed, tossing the Korean boy a tool from her pocket.

Samantha's Infected made quick work of the barricades and barbed wire. Equipped with a handful of wire-cutters, the group methodically passed down the tools, unwound the wire, then moved forward to the next barrier with meticulous precision.

At the center of it all, Samantha barked orders and occasionally pressed her palm onto someone's shoulder. When she did so, it seemed to create a burst of energy. They snapped to attention, moved faster, sharper than before.

The alleyway was cleared within minutes—just in time for another handful of soldiers to arrive and open fire. Behind them, an MGS Stryker rolled down the jagged boulevard, turret turning in their direction with a grind.

"Get inside!" Miller shouted.

"Go!" Samantha reiterated, and the herd of Infected scrambled in unison toward the chained double doors. Using their bare hands and the bolt cutters, the mob ripped the corrugated steel covering the entry, then bust into the building like a wave.

The Stryker's turret came to a grating halt and fired once into the mess of pylons and barricades. An explosion of fire and shrapnel rippled across the back of the crowd. Some of the Infected found cover, or rushed into the door, spilling over the top of their comrades. Others whipped around and ran toward the vehicle as if to swarm it. The Stryker discharged another canister—a M1040 antipersonnel round, by the looks of it—and blew them away before they even got close.

Cobalt moved into action. Behind Miller, Morland shouldered his MK1 grenade launcher and sent a round straight onto the top of the Stryker's hull. A plume of fire and metal shards burst from the vehicle, momentarily disabling the turret.

With the main gun out of the equation, the Infected in the alley surged forward and swarmed the vehicle, ripping open the top hatch and shooting the soldiers in their seats. Cobalt shot down the foot soldiers surrounding the vehicle, clearing the alleyway.

It wouldn't be long before the next wave approached and flagged Miller's team. "Go!"

Sam turned and shouted at Miller. "Quickly!"

The rest of the Infected and Cobalt piled into the research building, then dragged the barricades and pylons in behind them to block the door.

Inside the building was an open foyer, littered with trash. The white linoleum floor was gray with grime and dirt. The walls, white and sterile in their prime, were covered with fungal blooms.

The Infected circled the room, as if unsure where to go, and uncertain how to act. The walls outside rattled with the impact of the newly arrived Army reinforcements.

"Miller!" du Trieux barked, pointing.

There were three hallways off the foyer. The one on the right was barricaded with pylons and barbed wire all the way down the hall as far as the eye could see, until it abruptly cut to the left. The hall in the center went straight back and sat wide open, unencumbered by debris and suspiciously inviting. The passageway on the left sat stacked floor-to-ceiling with abandoned office furniture, allowing a narrow, twisting route through the obstacles. The fluorescent ceiling lights blinked an eerie strobe effect down the corridors, making it hard to focus.

"Door number one, two, or three?" Samantha asked, brushing a strand of hair from her face.

"Obviously not the middle," Doyle said.

In the center hallway, just past the threshold, a single dented soda can sat on the floor. An Infected, a woman with a single-shot hunting rifle slung over her shoulder, reached down and gripped the can.

Miller raised his hand in the air. "Don't!"

Too late. As the woman lifted the can, there was a snap of a pressure-release explosive device.

On instinct, Miller jumped on top of Samantha as an explosive charge shot fire and shrapnel across the room, peppering the walls with shards and rubble.

The Infected nearest the woman went flying through the air in a wave of fire, knocking others back and down like bowling pins. A surge of heat filled the air from ground to ceiling, warming Miller's back. Beneath him, Samantha shrieked.

When the dust settled, all eyes opened and turned to where the woman had once stood, now reduced to a smear of blood and a charred oval on the floor. Bodies were strewn around the area, missing limbs and heads, showing cavernous torso wounds. At the sight of the carnage, the remaining Infected scattered.

They scrambled around the foyer and into the hallways, and discovered to Miller's horror that the whole space was trapped; the piles of trash and wrecked furniture were riddled with pressure-release mines. The Infected set off two, three more blasts in their frenzy, with more deaths each time.

They fled, flailing, in all directions: down each hallway, back out the main door, and crowding around Samantha like drones to a queen.

"Wait!" Miller shouted after them. "Stop!"

It was futile.

The panicked whimpering echoed down the three corridors, along with another string of explosive blasts.

"The whole place is rigged!" Hsiung said.

"Get down!" Sam shouted, grabbing the front of Miller's combat vest and yanking him back to the floor.

"Stop running!" Hsiung bellowed. "Hold still!"

"These prats are going to get us killed!" Morland shouted. He looked up from his crouched position beside the door then immediately hit the floor again when another blast blew from down the right hallway.

"Pull your people back!" Miller said.

"Let them go." Sam lay underneath him on her back, her palms still gripping his combat vest. "Follow behind them. They'll clear the way."

Miller was too shocked to reply.

Sam moved out from underneath him and signalled to the rest of the Infected in the foyer. There were only about three dozen of them left. Lining them up around the building entry, she waved her hand at Miller. "Go. We've got your back."

Du Trieux raised an eyebrow, but Miller didn't hesitate. He moved to the far right hallway and grabbed at the first pylon to inch the battered, smoldering thing out of his way.

"You," Sam said to a group of her followers, "surround them." Shots peppered the entry from outside and struck the wall behind them. One Infected was hit and went down. Samantha didn't even flinch. "Get them through," she told them.

Like clockwork, ten Infected stepped forward. Using their wire cutters, working together without talking, they cut back the pylons and wires blocking the right hallway and pushed the debris to the side for easier passage, allowing Cobalt a clear path.

Miller watched them work with stunned awe and horror, then urged his team into the hall behind them.

He shouted back to Sam. "What about you?"

She shot another round out the entry door at the approaching soldiers and yelled back, "I know what I'm doing! Go. We'll hold them here. Come back for me after you've gotten the formulas."

He stared at her in dumb silence.

"Promise you'll come back for me!"

The words came out without a thought. "Yes, of course."

She turned back toward the action, dug into her pocket and loaded another round into the rifle's chamber. "Hurry!"

Miller turned from her and followed the hallway back. After rounding the bend, the corridor shifted from offices to lecture halls and classrooms.

The sounds of battle, outside and in, reverberated off the walls and made Miller's ears ache. His team shared nervous looks, then looked to the Infected in front of them, then frowned at Miller.

He didn't disagree. This could possibly be the worst idea he'd had yet.

33

Shots flew through the battered doorway with alarming regularity, narrowly missing Sam and her remaining followers time and time again. She'd positioned herself between Binh and a woman named Stephanie, both returning fire from behind a barbwire-wrapped pylon just inside the entrance.

The attacking soldiers, in spite of their training, seemed unwilling to commit to an assault. Whether it was because the Infected soldiers didn't truly want to kill Samantha or her commune, or if they were just unsure of the situation, wasn't clear. As the bullets flew and minutes ticked by, the soldiers outside fell back, resorting to half-heartedly firing at the entry. It was just enough to keep Sam and the others in position, but not to particularly threaten them.

She became increasingly suspicious. Clearly, they had superior firepower and more men. What on earth were they waiting for?

Perhaps they were waiting for another of those

tank trucks? Surely, a blast from that thing would rip the research building and their pathetic barricade wide open. It wouldn't take much.

One of Alex's cronies had had a grenade launcher. Certainly, in the whole of the Infected United States Army, they had one of those, too? But where were they? Where was the tear gas, the artillery fire, the machine guns? It didn't make sense.

The answer to her question was soon answered. The ground rumbled under her feet and the walls of the foyer shook.

"Earthquake!" some idiot shouted.

Dust cascaded from the ceiling. Whole fungal blooms separated from the walls, hitting the floor with a wet noise.

Sam peered out from behind her pylon and squinted through the narrow gap, and cursed under her breath.

They hadn't been waiting for the tank truck to blast the door open, they'd been waiting for an *actual* tank. The thing was mammoth. Painted in a splotchy mess of desert tan and olive green, it trundled down Rutland Avenue, crushing everything in its path.

They weren't going to blast the door open. They were going to blow the whole building open.

"Pull back!" Sam shouted.

Running toward the right hall, Sam stopped short of the archway and urged the others to follow. Charred pylons and bodies littered the corridor. Finally satisfied that enough of her crew were behind her, she took the corridor at a full sprint down. Zigzagging her way around the obstructions, ducking and jumping wires, she turned the corner to the left and stopped short, allowing her comrades to gather behind her before shouting, "Build a wall!"

The Infected worked in groups of five, pulling back the pylons from the hallway to create a makeshift barricade.

With an audible *crack* and a colossal *boom*, the tank fired. Wind, smoke, fire and shattered masonry burst through the foyer and spread across the first floor of the facility. The very ground vibrated.

Crouched behind their barricade, Sam and the Infected were showered with drywall, ceiling panels and light fixtures. Live wires broke free from their conduits and splayed across the hallway, sparking and shocking people at random. Air ducts running along the ceiling cracked and broke, spilling clumps of dust and asbestos onto their heads. Someone screamed.

Sam dusted herself off and reloaded her rifle, fighting to keep her head clear. The fear in the air was palpable, gumming up her thoughts. It was hard not to lose her mind with all that internal chatter.

Bullets followed the burst. Sam risked a glance around the corner and spotted approaching foot soldiers. She dared not return fire for fear of exposing herself.

Binh peered up from his tucked posture with wide and glassy eyes. "They're coming!"

"What do we do?" someone else bellowed.

Stuck between snapping a sarcastic reply, fleeing, and staying to hold back the horde for Alex's sake, Sam pressed the butt of her rifle against her shoulder and urged others to reload.

"When they come around the corner, shoot them down!" she instructed.

The Infected followed suit. What choice did they have? She was pulsing so much energy at them that they couldn't resist. Sam felt the weight of their terror, but they were no match for her. She pushed a pang of guilt down and took up position at the forefront of the barricade.

The first soldiers came down the hall and rounded the corner in a two-by-two formation. Sam, Binh and the others opened fire, and the soldiers were ploughed down in a barrage of bullets.

One man, wounded but still alive, got off one round in their direction, missing entirely, before Binh pulled an automatic pistol and shot twice into the soldier's chest.

Sam pulled back from the barrier and reloaded her rifle, a line of Infected behind her stepping forward. As the second team of soldiers came, then the third and fourth, the Infected rotated back and forth, firing, and reloading; they cut down the troops with efficiency and limited casualties.

Sam was just thinking they might pull this off when a grenade rolled around the corner with a clunk and landed in the pile of dead soldiers.

"Gren—!"

She never finished the sentence.

The pile of bodies helped some to stifle the blast: blood splatter, body parts, shrapnel, and unspent ammunition burst directly in front of the pylons.

By sheer luck Samantha wasn't on the front line. Ducking down, she covered her face and twisted just in time to take the brunt of the blow on her back.

Those who had been directly behind the pylons didn't fare as well. Some had been blown clean back, burnt or shredded beyond hope. The survivors cowered behind the pylons, ignoring the next team who had rounded the bend in the blast's wake.

Bullets riddled the hallway, dropping at least four of the Infected fast. It took several seconds for the next line to load, take position and return fire—and by then, much damage had been done.

Sam reloaded yet again, cringing at the lightness of her pocket. She'd have to ransack the pockets and bodies of the dead before too long—but first, she had to get rid of the three remaining Army troops at the end of the hall.

She took up position beside Binh at the pylons, and they took aim and fired upon the three soldiers. Two of the GIs were hunkered behind the bodies of their fallen—the other one twisted around the corner to take another shot.

Sam took out one of the soldiers behind the bodies, as Stephanie beside her took out the other. The woman standing at the bend went down with multiple shots to the torso.

A sinking feeling twisted Sam's gut when no new soldiers came around the bend. Usually, as one line fell, the Army sent another to immediately take its place. Now, half a minute passed without anything. The Army was brewing something—and if Sam had learned anything in the last ten minutes, it was that good things did not come to those who waited.

Her answer came in the form of a fully armored, fireproofed soldier wearing a flame-thrower on his back.

"Get back!" Binh bellowed.

The line behind Sam scattered like roaches caught in the light. People dove, leapt, ran, and outright screamed as a stream of burning gas shot straight over the pylon barrier where Sam and Binh crouched and set the hallway ablaze.

Men and women caught in the torrent lay on the cracked linoleum, shrieking as they burned alive.

Down the hallway an emergency fire hose, encased in a red metal cabinet, was attached to the wall. Sam bolted from her position behind the pylons and ran through the flames straight toward it.

A deluge of flame chased after her, setting the back of her jacket ablaze and scorching the end of her braid. Whipping off her jacket, she side-stepped a burning body and smashed open the cabinet with the butt of her rifle. Twisting the crank with her free hand, she waited for the release of water into the hose—nothing came.

"Sam!" Binh shouted. He'd left his position behind the pylons and was crouching inside a classroom doorway. Half of his face was blackened as he fought to reload his handgun with burnt, blistered fingers.

"Get back!" she cried at the others. "Everybody pull back!"

The flame-thrower operator unleashed again. The whole of the corridor was aflame. The Infected smashed through classroom doors, hid behind burning corpses, ran away.

As Infected ran past her, and the flame-thrower shot another stream of fire across the hall, Sam reached for her jacket pocket for another round and gasped at her own stupidity. She'd taken off her jacket when it'd caught fire. She was completely unarmed.

Ducking across the hall into a classroom, she waited for another break in the torrent of fire. Covering her mouth and coughing against the noxious fumes pouring from the burning hallway behind her, she waited for the right moment, then ran out into the flames. Fighting not to crash into burning and fleeing Infected, Sam grabbed up an AR-15 from a corpse on the ground and dropped to one knee.

Her boot caught fire on the burning floor. The skin on her face tightened in the flames and heat. The entire building shook with another violent blast, knocking Sam onto all fours. As the others ran for their lives, coughing violently, Sam clambered upright, inhaled deeply, closed one eye, aligned her vision through the rifle's site, and shot straight into the flame-thrower's gas tank.

34

COBALT FOLLOWED BEHIND Samantha's Infected cronies for a few minutes of tense silence, as if shadowing an unexploded bomb. The sound of gunfire cracked and echoed from all over, both inside and outside the building, urging them on. The whole situation stunk to high hell, but they were committed now.

There were ten Infected with them, men and women covered in lichen growths and looking like concentration camp survivors. Their skeletal bodies moved unaided down the corridor—one foot in front of the other—but Miller honestly couldn't figure how they were walking at all.

Down the passage was evidence of their former comrades' folly. The Infected who had scattered down the hallways at the first explosion in the foyer were now corpses tangled in barbed-wire—or nothing but chunks of body parts, blown to bits and strewn across the corridors.

The Army had booby-trapped the entire building.

Aside from the mines and the pylons, there were also trip wires over sharpened wooden stakes and neck-high wires attached to grenades mounted on the wall. This meant only one thing to Miller: the Army had arrived days ago, and the 'cure' the Johns Hopkins doctor had broadcast about over the radio was likely long gone.

"Boss," Doyle whispered from beside Miller.

He exhaled slowly. "If you're thinking we're too late, I'm right there with you."

"Then what are we doing?" Doyle pressed.

"Making sure."

Doyle snorted. "Of what? That we're walking into a trap?" His exo-knee brace gave an audible electrical grind with every step.

"What do you mean, *walking into* a trap?" Morland quipped from behind them. He stooped below a neck-high wire. "We're already in it."

"We have to be certain it's not here," Miller said. "Last time we found a thumb drive. Maybe we'll get lucky twice."

"And maybe this time we won't lose it in the ocean," Morland grumbled.

"The bodies are thinning out," Hsiung said from the back of the troop.

"I'm not sure how they're on foot," Morland said. "Honestly."

"No," Hsiung snapped. "Look around."

Miller glanced about the hallway; suddenly aware they'd passed through one building and were on a windowed breezeway headed toward the next.

Apparently, none of the scrambling Infected had made it past this point. There weren't any more corpses, no bloody puddles of flesh where an Infected had once stood.

"Don't touch any of the trash," Miller said at full voice. "And watch your head." He'd meant it as a word of warning to the Infected who walked ahead of them, but none of them turned or even acknowledged he'd spoken. Just what had Samantha done to these people? How was she maintaining such control of them?

Just then the building shook. Dust trickled from the ceiling and the walls vibrated. It sounded like an artillery blast. Miller doubted there would be much left of Samantha or her troops, after that. They were running out of time.

Inching on, they emerged from the trash-filled breezeway and into the second building. It had a modern, sterile feel compared to the other, and while the older building had offices and classrooms, this one seemed to be full of laboratories, on either side of the hall. There was a large common area at the center, with passages radiating off in all directions. Devoid of trash and debris and the regular booby-traps, the empty building was also missing furniture, equipment, wall or floor coverings—everything was concrete from ground to ceiling—and doors. It was as if the entire structure, down to the water spigots and the lighting fixtures, had been stripped cleaned and hauled away. But to where? And why?

"Where are we?" du Trieux asked.

"The Traylor Building," Hsiung answered, stopping in the center of the common area. "The research facility is one more building to the west."

"Why clean this out?" du Trieux asked.

Doyle shrugged. "Red herring?"

"No, thanks," Morland snorted. "I'm sick of fish. What I wouldn't give for a kebab right now..."

"Shut it," Doyle groaned. "Before I stuff my fist down your throat."

"Why an empty building?" du Trieux persisted. "If the place is a trap, what's their angle?"

"If there were mines they'd want the place full of junk. More debris means more casualties," Hsiung said, and du Trieux nodded.

"Can't be an ambush," Miller said, "for the same reason."

The Infected had stopped just ahead of them, waiting. They gathered around one another and murmured amongst themselves, casting suspicious glances back at Miller and the others. He wondered how much longer they'd cooperate. He scratched the inside of his palm, keeping his eyes trained on them.

"Where do you guess the breezeway to the next building is?" Morland asked.

"They took the maps off the walls when they took out—well, the walls," noted Doyle.

"Going right makes sense," Hsiung said. "The last one was on the north side of the building, too."

Miller nodded, then stepped toward the Infected. As he neared, they pulled back abruptly. "Hold up," he said. "Head that way." He pointed to the right.

One of the women in the group squinted at him, then sniffed. She scratched at the lichen growing up half her face and moved off to the right. The rest of her group followed, shuffling their feet.

Miller turned back toward the others and shrugged. "Maybe they didn't figure we'd get this far?"

A click from ahead made every member of Cobalt freeze in position. Miller strained his ears and heard the soft hiss of a lit fuse.

The Infected stood at the hall entry to the far right. The front-most of the group, the squinty woman, looked down at her feet, then to the side of the corridor, where Miller caught a glimpse of a thin, metal wire.

"Trip wire!"

Starting at the breezeway behind them, and then circling the circumference of the common area, charges went off in quick succession, separating the floor from the baseboards. The entire cement surface beneath their feet jolted straight down and crumbled.

The Infected at the threshold of the corridor took off running. The three still in the hub remained behind, gawking at the destruction, as Cobalt sprinted from the collapsing floor straight at them. Miller crashed through them first, lowering his shoulder like a linebacker sending all four of them to the floor. Behind him, he heard the pounding footsteps of Morland, du Trieux, Doyle, and Hsiung following suit.

Or so he thought...

Doyle's bellow was a knife to Miller's gut. He disentangled himself from the horrendous-smelling Infected and scrambled to his feet.

Doyle hung from a bent, jagged rod of rebar just below the hallway, dangling above a cavernous pit by a single hand. At least two stories below him, in the building's basement, was a pile of rubble.

Morland and du Trieux dropped to their bellies and crawled to the edge of the cavernous opening, hanging perilously over the edge to reach Doyle. It took the two of them together to lift the man clear.

Covered in concrete dust, bleeding from a gash on his head, and cringing every time his busted exo-brace moved, Doyle spat blood and cursed up such a storm Hsiung rolled her eyes.

Gripping their knees and panting for air, Morland and du Trieux fist-bumped but said nothing.

Hsiung put a hand on her hip and made to speak.

"Not a bloody word out of you," Doyle spat at her. "Not a word."

Hsiung clamped her mouth shut and turned on Miller, her face reddening.

"On your feet, soldier," Miller snapped. "If you can."

Doyle groaned but managed to stand with Morland's help. He touched the wall for balance once, testing to see if his injured knee could bear weight, and turned white with pain, but remained upright.

"Lot of bloody help they are," Doyle snapped, nodding toward the Infected.

"Can you walk?" du Trieux asked.

"If you think I'm staying behind, you're bonkers."

"All right, then let's move." Miller turned to face the Infected. Only four of them remained. He was about to ask where the others had gone when he heard another string of catastrophic *booms*. Smoke plumed down the hallway in their direction. Wherever they had gone, they'd triggered something.

Further down the hallway, they found them. All had been killed when they'd triggered a pressure-release mine hidden under the linoleum floor. Miller wasn't sure he would have seen it either.

Doyle limped along at the tail of the group and grumbled under his breath. All Miller caught was, "...good for *something*."

Moving ahead, they found the breezeway leading into the next building and increased their pace. The hall was walled with thick double-paned industrial glass on both sides. The research facility sat straight ahead, a blocky stepped structure of glass and concrete.

Outside, on their left, was a grassy area completely covered over with barbwire pylons and stationary Strykers.

And an entire battalion of troops, aiming directly at them.

Bullets starred the glass on their left, landing inches from Morland's head and taking out one of the Infected. Morland ducked down and took off ahead of them, leaving the others behind as he turned the breezeway's corner to the left and then barrelled to a stop.

More shots rang out and Morland hit the ground.

The rest of them came to the end of the breezeway at a sprint, twisting around the bend to return fire. On their left, from the grass below, shots continued to pierce the windows, striking the ceiling and hitting the glass on the far side of the hall. Shattered glass scattered across the floor.

They were pinned down. The Infected closest to the window took a bullet to the head.

"Doyle, take out that sniper!" Miller ordered.

Dropping to the ground and resting his custom rifle on the body of the fallen Infected, Doyle calmed his breathing, took aim through his sight, and sent three successive rounds through a hole in the glass.

Around the bend, Morland lay on his right side on the hallway floor, facing away from Cobalt. He was still gripping his rifle, and the Mk-1 on his back was strapped across his left shoulder. Miller couldn't make out where he'd been hit, but his head had tapped the floor fairly hard and he was bleeding from behind his right ear. There was nothing Miller could do to help him at the moment.

If only Miller could get to Morland's Mk-1, they'd be able to clear the corner and seek cover inside the building.

He had a sick thought.

"You!" he said, pointing to the last Infected. "Get me that grenade launcher!"

Without blinking the Infected ran around the corner and grabbed hold of the Mk-1's strap around Morland's shoulder.

Morland groaned in protest, which was a relief to Miller, but the Infected succeeded in peeling off the strap and tossing the launcher to Miller's awaiting hands before taking bullets to the chest and abdomen and falling on top of Morland.

Rotating the drum, Miller whipped around the corner and shot two grenades down the hallway. The blast created plumes of fire and smoke, giving Cobalt just enough cover for them to come around the bend and bust through the first door inside the building. On their way, Hsiung and du Trieux grabbed hold of Morland's feet, and dragged him behind them.

"How do we know which lab we're looking for?" Hsiung asked, checking Morland's vitals.

He slapped away her hand from his neck and sat up. He had several rounds stuck inside his combat vest. "Well, that sucked."

"We don't have time to search the whole building," du Trieux said.

"Follow their lead," Doyle said. "Wherever they try to stop us, go that way."

Hsiung frowned. "The path of most resistance?"

Du Trieux raised an eyebrow but nodded. "*Oui.*"

"If that's the case we head straight toward the barricade," Miller said.

"Wait—where's all our Infected?" Hsiung asked.

Looking about the room, there was only the three of them.

"We lost our human shields?" Doyle pursed his lips. "Pity."

Morland pushed off the ground and got to his feet. "Hardly human."

The next twenty minutes passed in a blur. After blasting through the barricade at the end of the hallway, Miller and Cobalt followed the barricades like breadcrumbs toward a lower level, where they found a sub-basement laboratory. Once they got there, however, it was as Miller feared.

The entire room, just like the second building, had been cleaned out, to the last paperclip. Even the cabinet knobs were missing. The lab, a mix of white Formica and rusted stainless steel, had been stripped to the bone.

Miller thrashed about looking for a flash-drive, a scrap of paper, *something*. He opened every drawer, scanned every nook and cranny—but they were too late. It was picked clean and barren.

"We didn't miss them by much," du Trieux said. "I can smell the disinfectant."

Hsiung sighed and flapped her lips.

"Now what?" Morland rubbed his palm against the bump on his head.

Miller's face grew hot and his hands balled into fists. Standing at the center of the lab, his frustration boiled over and he screamed at the top of his lungs with a primal fury, making everyone in the room jump. He kicked the air and punched at nothing, shouting at the top of his lungs indecipherable gibberish at full volume.

He didn't know why he had expected to find anything. Nothing had gone their way since the moment Bob Harris had taken charge of the Astoria complex back in New York City, over a year ago. Why would their luck change now? The human race was cursed. Any time they had attempted to make progress, to inch toward any kind of improvement in their situation, they were met with battles against the environment, the wildlife, the Infected, or each other.

Fucking impossible. And no matter how much they fought, nothing was achieved. Fucking *nothing*.

Miller bellowed in fury one last time.

What was the point?

They were losing. Fuck, they'd already lost. He knew he'd thought these things before; he'd think them again. He also knew that if he gave it enough time, he'd pick himself up off the floor and keep battling, because really, what choice did he have? But in that moment, on the floor of that empty laboratory on his knees, Miller pushed his palms onto the concrete floor and allowed himself to despair.

They were going to die. Maybe not today, maybe not tomorrow, but eventually, inevitably, he would lose Cobalt, and the rest of the human race would follow. Lewis. Gray. He'd already lost James Matheson. They seemed to be the only humans even trying to save mankind, and they were *failing*. Badly.

Fuck this shit.

"Boss." Doyle's voice cut through Miller's anguish. "We've got incoming."

The first thought to go through his mind was *Let them come*, but the words wouldn't pass his lips.

"We've got to go," du Trieux said. Then, "Miller. Get *up*."

Morland entered the room from the hallway; Miller hadn't even noticed him leave. "There's a whole squadron approaching from the west side of the building."

"Can't get out that way, then," Doyle said.

"Can't go back, either," Hsiung pointed out. "There's no way we'd clear the missing floor in that second building."

"We could go up two flights," du Trieux suggested.

"No, we stay in the basement," Doyle said.

Morland frowned. "We're trapped as it is."

"Emergency exits," Doyle said. "Look around. There's got to be one around here someplace. Maybe to a parking garage, or a stairwell to street level?"

They moved quickly. Morland jogged out into the hallway. Du Trieux came up alongside Miller, her fingers nervously gripping and re-gripping her Gilboa Viper. "Miller."

He nodded, pushing back up to crouch on the balls of his feet. His knees felt weak and his left hip was sore, but he stood of his own volition.

Du Trieux had an odd look on her face. She seemed as if she were about to say something, when Morland came back into the room and waved them over.

"I found the stairwell," he said.

The thought gone, du Trieux followed Miller toward the exit. Out the room, down the hall, up one flight of stairs to the stairwell landing.

It seemed to be some sort of campsite. Complete

with a bedroll, a propane-powered hot plate, and a lantern. Whoever had been staying there hadn't left that long ago; the rusted pan on top of the hotplate was still warm.

"Rat-things," Doyle said, his face contorting. "Pan-fried rat-things." A bucket sat in the corner of the landing, full of tiny cooked skeletons.

Morland grimaced. "Tasty."

"What's behind that?" Hsiung asked, pointing to one wall, where large panels of cardboard had been duct-taped.

Du Trieux was closest. She pulled back the panel, revealing a small dugout compartment, just big enough for a small person to hide inside. Curled up in fetal position on the floor was a short, skinny, petrified teenager.

Thick glasses, so chipped and dusty Miller wondered how anyone could see through them, sat on a large, beak-like nose. He was devoid of lichen growths, and had a shaggy mop of dark, dirty hair and large, dark eyes. The kid whimpered and curled up tighter, pressing his face into his knees.

"Nice hiding spot," Doyle said.

"How long you been here?" du Trieux asked.

"Just kill me. I don't want to be Infected."

"You and me both, kid," said Morland.

"Just make it quick," the kid said. "Please."

"From your lips to God's ears," replied Hsiung.

This seemed to catch the kid's attention. He looked up at them and squinted through his broken lenses. "Hu-human?"

"Last time I checked," Miller said, offering him his hand. "What about you?"

"Y-yes. I'm hu-human." The kid took Miller's hand with bony fingers, then pulled himself up. The kid wasn't a kid at all, just a very short, malnourished man. He pushed his glasses up the bridge of his nose and swallowed thickly.

The sounds of gunfire and artillery urged Miller to get to the point. "Who are you?"

"I'm Nihar. Doctor Nihar Mehta. Where are you going? What are you doing here?" His eyes suddenly widened. "Can you get me out of here? Can you take me with you?"

"We can try," Miller said. "But I'm not going to lie; it's pretty rough out there."

Dr. Mehta reached into his pants pocket and pulled out a rumpled, folded stack of lined notebook paper. "I have value," he said, handing the papers to Miller with shaking fingers. "I have the formulas. The ones the Army took. You must save me. I can help."

"*The* formulas?" Morland gaped.

"Well, that's a stroke of luck," Hsiung said.

Miller almost couldn't believe it. He took the papers from Mehta and opened them. Scratched on both sides in smudged blue ink were mathematical equations and a diagram of a molecule. "This is the anti-parasitic formula that the doctor spoke about over the radio?"

"The same," said Mehta, trembling on his feet. "The anti-fungal's on the back. You must help me. Please. I can produce it again. I swear."

"Hey, boss," Doyle said.

Miller turned toward him. The sniper stood by the topmost stair, looking deeply sceptical. The thought had crossed Miller's mind, too. They were never this lucky. How in the hell did they happen to find the only survivor, who just happened to have the formula they were looking for?

The coincidence was too great—but Miller couldn't take the risk that Mehta *didn't* have what he claimed.

"Fine," Miller said. Mehta smiled widely, which only made him more suspicious. "Take him to the Foxhound." He handed the paper to du Trieux. "Don't let him out of your sight, and don't wait for me."

She looked alarmed. "Where the hell are you going?"

Miller twisted his head to one side and cracked his neck, relieving the dull throb at the base of his skull. "I made a promise."

35

SAM PULLED THE magazine from her AR-15 and frowned. No more bullets. She blinked a few times in denial, then tossed the magazine and the rifle to the floor of the lecture hall. God, her head was pounding.

There were only a handful of Infected left. The explosion from the flamethrower's tank had given Sam and the others just enough time to get down the hallway and barricade themselves inside a lecture hall, but the building was on fire on all sides and the flames were coming fast.

For whatever reason, the Army had stalled their advance, content to let Sam and her commune die of smoke inhalation, if they didn't burn to death first. Just as well; she'd done what she set out to do. Hopefully, Alex had the formulas and was long gone, on his way to Washington to set the President straight and save the world.

She hadn't figured he'd come back to get her

anyway. She'd only said that so he'd leave and find the formulas. She'd figured on being dead by the time he returned, if he did. The one thing she hadn't figured was getting stuck in a burning building and dying by inches—but if Sam had learned anything in life, it was that you never got what you expected. Or wanted, for that matter.

What were the chances of Alex coming back for her now, truthfully? She couldn't blame him. Only a fool would risk entering an inferno, with no idea of where to find her. Alex was no fool. He was many things, but not that.

Her last few followers coughed and wheezed. The air was gray—thick with ash and hot in her rough throat. Fighting the urge to lie down and fall asleep, Sam plopped herself into a desk and swung it around to watch the only door. In the back of the room, Binh and a handful of others were fashioning face masks to cover their mouths and noses, but she saw no point in it.

Her eyelids grew heavy. It hurt to breathe, and her head pulsed with every slow heartbeat. The room turned fuzzy. Coughing, she tried to force air into her lungs, but only tasted ash.

Electrical conduits and lighting fixtures overhead popped and sparked as the fire spread across the ceiling. Outside, she heard more popping, more cracks as the building buckled.

Were those gunshots? There was another explosion, followed by eerie silence. Then more crackling fire and popping conduits.

The door burst open and she couldn't move. The smoke billowed around the lecture hall and a single shadow appeared in the doorway.

"Sam, get up!" Alex shouted at her. He held a grenade launcher in his hands. "This whole building is coming down!"

How cliché, she thought. Alex to the rescue like some knight in shining armor. She hadn't considered herself a romantic, but here she was, hallucinating her rescue like some little girl.

The shadow passed by her and wrangled the rest of the group from their huddle in the back of the lecture room. Finally, a hand grabbed her upper arm and she was pulled to her feet. Alex—or, at least, a man who looked like him. He was limping, favouring his left leg, but he still managed to drag her out of the room, her feet moving like boulders.

They scuttled down the hallway and back out the way they'd come. Stepping over bodies and dashing through the fire, they came out the crumbled foyer and into the alleyway, just in time to see the backside of the tank as it rolled down the boulevard away from them, surrounded by an entire squadron of soldiers.

Binh coughed beside her. Sam wondered what they hell he was doing away from the dairy farm before her mind cleared and she realized where she was. God, her head was pounding.

"Where are they going?" Binh asked, watching the tank leave and coughing again.

Alex spat sooty saliva onto the pavement and

wiped his mouth with the back of his glove. "We've got a battalion fighting south of here. My bet is they're the reinforcements."

"You came back for me," Sam said, surprising even herself with her sentimentality.

Alex didn't even have the good sense to look sheepish. He squinted at her like she was talking crazy and then coughed into his fist. "Yeah, well. This is where I leave you. Good luck to you. As always, it's been a pleasure."

"Hold on. Did you get the samples?"

He frowned and shot a quick glance at the Army troops as they departed a few blocks south. "Not exactly."

"What the hell is that supposed to mean? Do you have them or not?"

"We have the formulas. No samples."

Samantha's mind was suddenly rushing. She'd figured he'd find the solutions and take them to be reproduced, but this could still work. If she played this right, there was hope yet for her to get what she wanted.

Freedom.

"I'm not leaving your side until I have what you promised me," she said.

"I don't have it, Sam," Alex snapped. "And I don't have time to stand here and debate with you. I'm sorry. I got you out. That's the best I can do."

"Take me with you, then," Samantha said. "You wouldn't have those formulas if it wasn't for us."

Now everyone was looking at her like she had

lost her mind. Maybe she had, she could hardly tell anymore.

Binh's mouth had fallen open and he was gawking at her. "Sam, no."

"We can finally farm without the threat of fungus ruining entire crops," she said to him. "Don't you see? It could change everything."

Binh looked even more confused. "Enough for us to be taken prisoner? No!"

"Not prisoner." She pointed at Alex. "He's different. He's a man of his word. If he said he's going to give us the anti-fungal solution, he will." She turned to him. "Right, Alex?"

He didn't answer. He just stared at her. He was probably trying—and failing—to figure out what game she was playing.

"Take us with you," she said again. "We had a *deal*." She gave him a look, laced with a thousand unspoken words and tinged with years of personal history.

Alex's face fell. "I can't guarantee your safety," he said.

"I trust you."

He squinted at her, then looked south, running his tongue along the edge of his lower lip. "Okay. It's your funeral."

THEY'D STASHED THEIR transport truck less than a mile from the Rutland Avenue underpass, in a parking lot beside a boarded-up brick building with a mural cityscape painted on one wall. It was a ten-minute walk, and could have been half that, if the Infected had been in any condition to run.

When they arrived, huffing, puffing, scratching, and wheezing, the rest of Alex's team was waiting.

In the back of the transport, on the floor, lay the man with the electrical knee brace. He looked pale and gripped the sides of the brace with both hands, pulling and snapping and twisting the contraption, trying to get it comfortable. He was getting help with this from a dark-skinned scrawny man in a tattered lab coat and ridiculously thick cracked glasses. Another man, tall and lanky, and two women sat on seats on either side of the compartment. None of them looked happy to see Sam and her kind.

One of the women got up from her seat and jumped out of the truck. "No," she said. "We don't have the time—or the room. Whatever you're thinking, Miller, the answer is no."

"We never would have gotten out of there if it weren't for them," Alex argued. "We owe them."

"I never would have busted my knee again," the man on the floor said, in an English accent, "if they hadn't triggered the bloody explosives."

"We can't leave them here," Alex pressed. "They'll be killed by the Army in a matter of minutes."

The dark woman glowered at Sam. "We didn't *get* the solutions. It was a trap. I'm sorry about your people, but we have nothing to offer you."

Alex squinted at his team individually. "Actually, we do."

The scrawny man in the lab coat look alarmed. "We do?"

"I'm not giving you guys a choice on this," Alex said, rounding the back of the transport. He waved his arm at the door. "They're coming with us. Get in."

They folded up the seats and crowded into the back of the transport, filling every square inch of the interior. Even with the wounded man sitting between the passenger and driver's seat, and the scrawny lab coat guy curled cross-legged beside him, there still wasn't enough room.

Eventually, two of Alex's team—the lanky white guy and the Chinese woman—opted to ride on the outside of the vehicle, holding onto the side bars with their feet wedged onto metal steps.

They were finally on their way. Sam grabbed hold of a bar on the ceiling and tried to keep her balance. The interior grew particularly ripe once the doors closed, stinking of bodies and sweat. The ride was rough.

As in NYC, thug behemoths had dug up many of the streets, especially to the south, where they were headed. The highways weren't as bad, but the city streets were in many places no more than rutted tracks, piled high with asphalt and concrete rubble.

When Sam had driven the truck to Johns Hopkins from the electrical plant during her scouting mission, the roads hadn't seemed this bad, but now, standing in the middle of a British military transport vehicle, her body pressed against Binh on one side, another

Infected on her other, it felt like at any moment another pothole would send them flying, or her knees would buckle, or she'd hit her head against the ceiling and knock herself out cold. It wasn't an unwelcome thought, but she couldn't afford to lose herself now.

They rode south for a few kilometers, then hooked to the east. They drove on for five more minutes in uncomfortable silence. Eventually, the transport slowed and Miller grabbed up the CB radio.

"Cobalt to Major Clark, we have reached rendezvous location. What is your ETA, over?"

Sam squinted out the windscreen and tried to make out where they were. It was a freeway exit of some sort, an actual fork in the road.

Miller tapped his ear. "You two see anything out there...? All right, copy that."

"*Merde*," the black woman said. "What's the play?"

"We follow orders," Miller said, snapping the CB pack onto its clip with a sharp swipe of his hand. He tapped his ear again. "Hang on, you two. I'm gunning it back to the Mk 10." He chuckled and pressed his foot on the accelerator. "I'll be sure to register your complaints with my superior officer."

They drove under the freeway and down a two-lane highway. Evidence of a past animal attack zipped by as the transport's automatic transmission shifted and Alex stepped on the accelerator.

They passed a church and turned right down a single lane road, surrounded by overgrowth and shrubbery. At the end of the flooded peninsula sat a large military boat, with a ramp lowered, like a ferry. Miller drove the truck through the watery shore and straight onto the ship.

"Alex?" Sam asked. "Where are you taking us?"

"Get down!" he barked.

Several soldiers wearing desert camouflage closed the ramp behind them, and in moments they were out on the river.

"Our headquarters is on a ship," Miller said to Sam. "They can't know you're here."

Sam nodded, then motioned for the rest of her people to crouch down.

Binh frowned and whispered, "This isn't what we agreed to! I thought they had a base nearby or something."

"I did, too," Sam confessed.

The wounded guy with the knee brace nudged Alex with his head. "Get me out of here, boss. I'm suffocating."

"Can't get you out without opening up the back," Alex told him. "Sit tight. It'll just be a few minutes."

The man didn't look pleased with the answer but remained silent the rest of the way.

Across the choppy waters, the ferry took them out to sea. There were two ships around the bend: a cruise liner and a military battleship. To Sam's dismay, they were sailing directly toward the battleship. In the back of the enormous vessel was a large hanger filled with water. The ferry pulled straight in, then docked. Another ramp opened at the front, and Alex popped the truck into gear and drove it up the ramp and onto a platform.

"How are we going to...?" asked the woman beside him.

"I'm working that out," Alex said. He tapped his ear. "I need the three of you who can walk to surround the Infected and get them onto the lifeboat. Meanwhile, Doyle's about to have a seizure."

"I am?" said the man with the knee brace.

Alex opened the driver's door and stepped outside. "Hey! We need some help in here!" He reached back and tapped the wounded man's shoulder.

The man rolled his eyes, hung his tongue out the corner of his mouth, and shook himself like a maraca.

The back door of the transport opened.

"With me," the tall one said, another Brit. Binh was the first one out, the rest followed.

Lumped together and moving at a rush, Alex's soldiers surrounded Sam and the others and herded them into a large two-level boat bobbing in the water further down the dock. With orange canvas stretched across the top and benches lining the center of the vessel, it seemed to be some sort of extra-large lifeboat.

Outside and back at the transport truck, a crowd had crawled inside the vehicle and appeared to be tending the wounded soldier.

"Get down," one of Miller's soldiers barked at her.

Sam dropped below the window and hugged her knees to her chest. The boat's floor was made of finely honed wood planks, but was in desperate need of a scrubbing.

"No, really." Doyle's voice carried from behind the lifeboat. "I'm feeling *much* better! I've always been one to recover quickly." Then, in a hoarse whisper, he added, "My leg's about to give out. Help me aboard, but don't make it *look* like you're helping me, or they'll never let me leave."

The three men appeared at the boat entry. Alex had his hands on Doyle's ribs while the scrawny doctor tossed the soldier's arm over his shoulders. He hopped on one leg over the boat's threshold, then immediately sat on one of the benches. "Get us out of here."

Alex pulled the flap shut and tapped his ear. "Go!"

The motor roared to life, and quickly, the vessel drifted away from the dock and dropped backwards out into the choppy sea.

"Morland," Alex said, rushing past Sam and the Infected and bounding up the stairs. "You're on lookout for predators."

The trip only took a matter of minutes, but felt much longer. In the ferry, the ocean hadn't seemed as rocky, but on the lifeboat they rose and fell with every passing wave.

A couple of the Infected grew ill, vomiting onto the deck. After surviving the trip to Baltimore, the attack on the research facility, an escape, and now this—Sam's guilt was getting the better of her.

Disgusted, the wounded soldier—Doyle—hobbled up the steps and remained there, along with the rest of Alex's troop, for the remainder of the journey.

The boat drove right up to the cruise liner, where it was pulled up with cranes and pulleys. On deck, Alex and the others circled the Infected again and escorted them through a twisty maze of hallways, stairwells, and corridors until they reached an old bar near the front of the boat on the top deck.

Before allowing them inside, however, the two women entered and cleared a bunch of stuff out, setting a full crate outside by their feet. Then, unceremoniously, Alex ushered the Infected inside and turned to leave.

"You're going to lock us up?" Sam asked, horrified. "In here?" The place looked trashed. An improvised nylon hammock hung in one corner, and a few chairs and tables sat scattered around the area, but there was no bedding. No beds, for that matter. The bar was empty, the cabinets and shelves bare. The room swayed in the rocky ocean, and several of the Infected, Binh included, shot angry looks at Sam.

On the plus side, it wasn't a labor camp and doors on either side of the bar pointed to restrooms.

"I don't suppose those are working?" she asked.

Alex squinted at her. "No. All water has been diverted to the hydroponics and the residential sector."

"Then hide us there."

"Among the humans?" he asked, his eyes wide.

Sam cast a quick look over the remains of her commune. They were sickly, starved and covered in lichen, and probably stunk to high hell. Binh had slouched onto the floor by the door and instantly passed out with his mouth open. Two women had ripped down the fabric and were shredding it to use as blankets. One other man was behind the bar, furiously looking for whiskey. "Point taken."

"We'll bring you food and water in a bit. I promise."

He looked like he meant it. Maybe he did. Sam scanned the room's interior and buried her anxiety. "I'm trading one prison for another," she said.

Alex didn't seem certain of what that meant. He nodded.

"How long before we get the formula?" Sam asked.

Alex cast a quick look at the scrawny man in the lab coat. "Depends," he said.

Seeing that she wasn't going to get much more out of him, Sam pulled up a chair and sat. Feeling a dull ache in her shoulder, she reached absently to scratch. Her lichen growth had receded a bit since she'd last checked and she was surprised to notice that the itch was from her brand. Without thinking twice she lifted up her shirt in front of Alex and inspected her ribs. It was gone there, too.

Odd.

"Okay, well," Alex said, backing out of the room. "Try and get some sleep." He limped toward the door—his left hip obviously giving him some trouble—and then moved to close it behind him.

"Alex!" she called after him.

He stopped and gazed back at her with a sad expression. He always looked like a lost puppy when he got hurt.

"I'm trusting you," she said.

He frowned, then nodded, closing the door behind him.

Sam looked through the window, casting a wary eye on Alex's teammates as he said a few hushed words to them, then walked away with the man in the lab coat. A woman stood by the door, then glared in through the window.

Their eyes met.

Alex had called her du Trieux. Sam recognized her. In fact, Sam was fairly sure she'd set Alex and the woman up to clean out a commune back in New York after confiscating their weapons. Sam wouldn't blame the woman if she held a grudge—which, given her expression, she did.

"But it's not you I'm worried about," Sam said aloud, although Alex was already gone.

"GOOD TO SEE you, Miller," Lewis said, waving him into Gray's office. "You're just in time."

A line of sullen faces sat around the ping pong table. Beside Lewis, on Gray's left, sat Jennifer Barrett, her stack of clipboards piled in front of her. Next to Jennifer was the British doctor, Kapoor, and then Dr. Dalton, the scientist from the *Penelope*, both looking glum.

Miller sat on Gray's other side, nodding to Captain Corthwell and his annoying commander, who extended his hand toward Miller and then chuckled when Miller merely nodded at him.

"I'm sorry, captain," Gray said, "you were saying."

"Right," the captain said, rolling out a map in front of him. On the opposite side of the table, the two doctors grabbed the edge of the paper and held it flat. The captain leaned forward and pointed down the coast of what had once been the United States of America. "We currently sit here, south of Baltimore, in this alcove on the Chesapeake Bay. The U.S. Navy is no doubt on the lookout for us, so we've got to perform our repairs quickly and get back out to sea.

"The Bay Class has a hull breach—it's been patched, but needs a more permanent repair—and we have to rebuild both our cranes. Whatever that thing was that attacked us is still a mystery. Our preliminary findings show that it *wasn't* a giant squid, but some sort of hybrid—something like a cross between a crab and a squid, which would explain why our machine guns did little to deter it... the exoskeleton, you see.

"At any rate, once we know what the good doctors can cook up, we can decide where and when we launch our vaccine distribution campaign. I've updated Whitehall and have requested all available reinforcements and repairs. I await their instructions."

He released the map and sat back into his folding chair. "The Baltimore assault south of the research facility suffered massive casualties, including Major Clark. We lost one Foxhound and ninety-two of our sailors. Given the numbers of the enemy troops—who were apparently lying in wait—we pulled the troops back and evacuated the civilian survivors, then sent the Mk 10 back to the pick-up location, per our contingency plan." The captain looked to Miller. "Glad to see you made it back, sir."

"Thank you, captain," Miller said.

Lewis rested his hands on each thigh then said, "Miller?"

"Two wounded," he answered carefully. "And as you're all probably aware, our mission to retrieve the researchers in the Johns Hopkins research facility failed. The US Army had gotten there first and the building was booby-trapped. We managed to rescue one man, a doctor who had handwritten notes on the formulas. Upon our return to the ship, I escorted Dr. Mehta to Dr. Kapoor." He stopped short, clamping his lips closed.

Lewis wrinkled his brow. "Is that it?"

Miller raised an eyebrow. "Yes, sir."

Gray nodded, then motioned toward Jennifer Barrett. "Okay. What's the status report on the *Tevatnoa*, Jennifer?"

Jennifer flipped a few pages of the topmost clipboard. "We lost three hundred and twenty-six civilians during the outbreak, most of them either over sixty years old or under eighteen. Another nine hundred volunteers were lost during the Baltimore battle."

Lewis sighed and scowled. "Jesus."

"I'm having to shuffle a lot of people around," she continued, looking beaten. "We've got an overabundance of single-parent families now, so I'm doubling them up in quarters and spreading out the orphans—twenty-five of them—among them as best I can. Some singles have opted to take a few out of the sheer kindness of their hearts, which helps. I have a couple more I can't place that I might take myself, if nobody else will."

Gray raised a hand. "I'll talk with Barbara. We'll take them."

Jennifer looked close to tears. "Thank you, sir."

Dr. Kapoor rubbed his earlobe. "What about the spread of the influenza?"

"Contained," Jennifer said. "For now. There are a couple people down in the infirmary who had an allergic reaction to the microbiota injections, for whatever reason. It looks like they'll pull through. But for the most part it's stopped the spread and helped with the secondary infections—which is good, since they've got their hands full with the wounded now."

Miller cleared his throat. "How many?"

"Hundreds." She dug in the pile of clipboards and thumbed through a few pages. "Two hundred and eighty-eight. Most of them are stable, so the numbers may change."

"You've done an incredible job, Jennifer," Gray said. "Thank you."

She drew back into her chair and bit her lip, saying nothing.

All eyes shifted to Dr. Kapoor and Dr. Dalton. Gray leaned forward in his chair. "Doctors?"

"It's too early to tell if we can produce anything," Kapoor said "Dr. Mehta is working with the RN and the S-Y researchers with his notes. They're a bit usele—"

"—incomplete," Dr. Dalton said, finishing Kapoor's sentence.

Gray's face fell. "How incomplete?"

Dr. Dalton looked up at the ceiling. "Well..."

Kapoor was having none of it. "Very. To be quite

frank, I'm not certain Dr. Mehta's information isn't a ruse devised by the American government to trick us into wasting valuable time and resources."

"He's a spy?" Jennifer asked, looking mortified.

Dr. Dalton rolled her eyes. "No, he's not."

Kapoor glared back at her. "He doesn't even know the cellular structure of the parasite protozoa!"

"When you yell at people all the time," Dr. Dalton shouted back at him, "it's hard to remember anything. The man was hiding in a hole for a week—give him a break, will you? He'll come through when he's ready."

"We don't have *time* for that!" Dr. Kapoor bellowed. "The life of every last human is at stake."

"Enough!" roared Lewis.

"You two," snapped Gray, "get back to the lab and get to work. We want a report as soon as you have the formulas ready, with or without Dr. Mehta's help. As for the rest of you, keep us apprised of your progress and don't be afraid to ask for help. We're in this together." When no one immediately moved, he waved his hand in the air. "You're dismissed."

Miller waited in his chair as the room cleared. Lewis, having known him well enough to realize something was amiss, stayed behind. When only the three of them remained, Miller rose to his feet.

"All right," Lewis said. "Let's have it, son."

"Sir, I've got six Archaean Infected stashed on board in the Crow's Nest bar."

Gray's face turned scarlet. "Are you *out of your mind?*"

Lewis grabbed his temples and sighed. "By themselves?"

"With Cobalt, sir," Miller said. "Hsiung, du Trieux, and I have been guarding them on shifts since we've been back."

Lewis raked his scalp with his palms. "Why on earth would you bring them here?"

"These are the same Archacans who helped us take the compound back in Astoria. Without them, we never would have navigated those booby-traps or survived the assault at the research center. I couldn't leave them to the US troops back in Baltimore. We owe them."

Gray raised his eyebrows. "We owe them shit."

"We owe them a sample of the anti-fungal solution, sir, and safe passage back to land. I promised it to them. That was their commander's only price."

Lewis raised an eyebrow. "You're sure about that?"

"I know she's Infected, sir," Miller said. "But she's proven herself trustworthy twice now. I think giving her one sample won't kill us."

"No, but having them here on this ship might," Gray spat. "How do you know they're not pinning your team-mates down and spitting in their faces right now? The last thing we need is a parasite breakout aboard this ship. Jesus—if the RN found out, they'd blow us out of the water!"

"I understand, sir. I'm hoping the good doctors can get the formulas squared away ASAP so we can get them on their way."

Gray squinted at Miller. "And what if they don't?"

"We'll cross that bridge if we get to it," Miller said.

Gray sat back in his seat. "I don't like this. Just eject them. Turn them loose in a boat and get them off my ship."

"I made a promise, sir," Miller said. "It's the right thing to do."

Lewis snorted. "When has doing the right thing ever gotten us anywhere?"

As Miller approached the Crow's Nest bar, du Trieux yawned and rubbed her eyes.

"Go get some sleep," he said. "I'll take the next shift."

"Hsiung stashed the ammunition from inside the bar under that bench over there," she said, nodding across the deck. "I'll put it in my bunk until we need it."

"Anything happening inside?"

She shook her head. "Not that I can tell, but damn, they're ripe. Smells like death, even out here."

"I told Lewis and Gray about them."

She frowned. "How'd they take it?"

"About how you'd expect."

"Can't say I disagree with them," she added.

Miller set his jaw. "I hear you."

"The least we should do is get rid of them before we get too far out to sea. It'd be cruel to set them adrift on a boat in the middle of nowhere. Especially on these waters."

Miller pursed his lips. He wasn't sure what he'd expected du Trieux to say, but that hadn't been it.

"Any word on Morland and Doyle?" she asked.

"I ran into Hsiung in the infirmary before coming here. She was checking up on Doyle. He's out of surgery, got himself a brand new titanium knee. He'll be on bed rest for six to eight weeks, but I figure he's earned it. Morland has some bruising on his chest and a mild concussion, but he'll live."

"What about your hip?"

Miller scowled. "What about it?"

Du Trieux nodded, then looked away. "We got lucky."

"Hardly. Getting lucky would have been finding samples of the solution."

"You know what I mean, Miller," she said. "Did you hear what happened to the troops who engaged with the Army?"

"Yes."

"They walked straight into an ambush. Surrounded on all sides. We lost Clark."

"I liked her, too."

Du Trieux wrinkled her nose. "They knew we'd come. We should have known better. We should have been *smarter*."

"And done what? No choppers, no air support. Can you think of another way we could have gone in?"

"We never *should* have gone in, is what I'm saying," du Trieux said. "Humans are dying out. We should be finding a nice hole to hide in and building our numbers. Not knowingly walking civilians into a slaughter."

"You going to start with that same breeder shit Harris did?"

She reddened. "Forget it." Stepping away from the bar door, she walked to the crate of ammunition under the bench and pulled it out.

"Come on," Miller said. "Don't give up just yet. What do you want to do? Sail away into the sunset and accept our fate? What about the humans back on land? What about the rest of the world? Victory comes at a cost. You know that."

She hitched the crate onto her hip. "I'm tired of being the ones to pay it."

"I'd say Clark paid it this time."

"If you don't think we're next, you're fooling yourself," she said.

She was right, but for some reason he couldn't say it out loud.

"This is only the beginning," she continued. "If we get those formulas working, if we start distributing it—every Infected commune on the globe will be gunning for us. We're an easy target on this boat, RN gunship or not. This wasn't a step toward the end of the war."

She walked down the corridor and shot her last remark over her shoulder. "We started a bigger one."

GRAY PRESSED HIS fingertips into his temples.

Dr. Dalton, looking as if she hadn't slept in hours, sat beside him, her palms flat against the ping-pong table.

It'd been a full thirty-six hours since their last meeting. Exhausted, tired, and having only slept a few hours, Miller slumped in his chair and fought to concentrate. Given Dr. Dalton's expression, he didn't think the news would be good.

"Let's get this over with," he said. Lewis frowned.

"I'm sorry to report, gentlemen," said Dr. Dalton. "We've gone over and over the notes. We've interviewed this *doctor*"—she emphasized the word with thick contempt—"four times. Mehta's not giving us enough."

"Not enough for what?" Lewis asked.

"For a cure. I don't mean to be so downcast, but it's worthless information."

Miller sighed. The entire battle in Baltimore. Thousands dead, Clark lost, Doyle wounded. Six Infected on board. For *nothing?* "What do you mean? Mehta lied about the formulas?"

"Honestly," the doctor said, "I'm not even sure he *was* a researcher at Johns Hopkins. I think he was a technician—an intern at best. His notes on the formulas are elementary, and he's been no help in expanding on them. I thought if we gave him some time he'd step up, but apparently not."

Lewis cursed under his breath. "I don't get it. The broadcast said that they had it."

"And maybe they did—at one time," the doctor said.

Lewis scratched his thigh. "Suppose Kapoor was right? That they planted him?"

"More likely he wanted safe passage out of the building," Miller said.

Gray pounded his fist on the table. "What's missing in the research? There was a formula, wasn't there? A molecule?"

"To be more specific, it's not that we're missing something. It's just not going to work."

"Can you experiment with the formulas? Use them as a stepping-off point?"

Dr. Dalton shook her head. "The anti-parasitic you distributed from the air-bombs was a broad-spectrum anti-parasitic, which is used to treat a generalized variety of primitive protozoal, helminthic, and viral infections."

"Okay," Lewis said, uncertainly.

"Then you distributed the wasps, which was a dismal attempt at disrupting their reproductive cycle, but did nothing to stop them from spreading and created a sub-class of lesser Infected."

"Get to the point, doctor," Gray said, looking stern.

"My point is, in messing with the existing parasite you've created two separate strains, and thus we're going to need two separate cures. The one Mehta gave us is no more precise against either strain than the one you used in the air bombs. It's too broad. It's not tailor-designed for the Archaean parasite *or* its mutation. It'll be no more effective than the last two attempts."

Miller sighed. "What about the anti-fungal agent?"

"Again, it's a simple azole drug used to disrupt the growth of fungal membrane. It'll help a little, but azoles have been known to cause liver damage, affect estrogen levels in women *and* men, and cause severe allergic reactions in humans, including anaphylaxis and death."

"So what *have* we got, doctor?" Lewis asked.

"Nothing, gentlemen," she said. "We have nothing. We have an anti-parasitic that doesn't touch the Archaean parasite, and an anti-fungal agent which could kill millions."

Miller ran his hands through his hair and stretched his aching joints. He wished he were surprised.

"Is it enough for an ongoing cure?" Gray asked.

Dr. Dalton blinked. "I'm not sure I..."

"Is it fighting the parasite at all?" Gray expounded. "Can it slow things down?"

"It can't even break the sub-cellular membrane of the protozoa. The samples we have of the Archaean parasite aren't degrading at all."

"How old are these samples?"

"Since New York," she said. "We've had them in liquid nitrogen, so there's very little decomposition. Fresh samples might react differently, of course."

"And things have changed since New York," Miller said. "There's been further mutation within the Infected. I've seen it. Before, if they'd communed, they were literally unable to harm one another. Something to do with their shared over-developed sense of empathy, I think; who knows? But from what I saw in Baltimore, they have no problem with that now. They shot at the Infected Army without a moment's hesitation and the Army shot back. What if the solution isn't working because we're testing it on an old version of the parasite?"

Dr. Dalton nodded slowly. "We've had the same thought. But, how are we supposed to get a sample of the evolved parasite?"

Lewis, Gray and Miller shared a look.

"What if I got you a blood sample," Miller said. "Will that suffice?"

"Yes," she said, "but how...?"

Miller stood from the table. "You got a kit I can borrow? I'll be right back."

37

SAM PRISED THE plank from Binh's hands and fought the urge to slap him over the head with it.

"We've got to get out of here!" Binh cried, grabbing for it.

Sam held it out of reach. "You can't start a *fire* on a *ship!* Stop it!"

Behind her at the bar, three of her followers had broken off the end of the wooden countertop and tossed the pieces into a pile on the floor.

The last sat on the floor beside the shredded parachute, chewing small patches of fabric and spitting them into her palms. She'd told Samantha she planned to spitball the soldiers in the eye to infect them the moment they came back inside with food and water. Sam had tried to confiscate the nylon when Binh and the others had started tearing the place apart, presumably to burn their way out of the bar and to freedom—as if almost burning to death at the Johns Hopkins research facility wasn't proof enough of what a bad idea that was.

Samantha had lost control. For whatever reason, they no longer heeded her influence and were circling the room like a pack of wild dogs, waiting to pounce. She'd tried pulsing calm energy through Binh, had even attempted to start a chain—like the one back at the labor camp—but nothing seemed to reach them. They'd gone feral and turned against her.

In their defence, everything she'd told them wouldn't happen *had*. They *were* prisoners of the humans. They *were* trapped on the ship. Binh had shouted at her for nearly an hour how they never should have come on board in the first place, and she understood exactly why. A part of her even wondered if he were right.

Miller, who had made no promises, was true to his word. He'd brought food and water, but that was all. It'd been days since they'd snuck aboard, and yet he'd made no mention of the anti-parasitic or anti-fungal solutions, and neither had his cronies— no matter how many times Sam prodded them when they brought the food and water.

To add insult to injury, the food was awful. Watery, foul-smelling fish soup with lumps of biscuits as tough as rocks. Vegetable and grain stew with chunks of protein substitute. Even the water tasted funny.

Maybe it was the sick-smelling sea air. Perhaps the constant sway of the ship was driving them to distraction. Or the fact that neither of the bathrooms was fully functional, and the place had begun to smell. It could have been any number of things. Any way she looked at it, Samantha was screwed.

"You want to tell the whole *ship* we're here?" Sam yelled at Binh. "What do you think the captain of this ship will do when he finds out we're hiding in here?"

"He probably knows," Binh said, grabbing the plank from Sam's hands. "They're keeping us here to experiment on us. How else are they going to see if the formula works?"

"They're what?" cried one of the others at the bar.

"What are we going to do?" another one of them cried.

"We've got to get out of here!" Binh bellowed again.

"Stop!" Sam cried. "All of you, stop! Don't make this worse!"

Binh raised the plank over his head like a mallet. "How can it get any worse?"

There was a knock at the door.

Sam glanced at the window on the port side and saw the red tinge of sunset. Another round of horrid food was due. She hoped it was the Chinese woman this time; she was certain the other one would kill her at any moment.

To her surprise, it was Miller. He held no tray in his hands, however, and he was accompanied by the dark woman Sam didn't trust.

The Infected had quieted. Stunned into silence, they'd taken a moment from their destruction and eyed the open door behind the armed soldier—

fighting the temptation to run, no doubt. Given the woman's expression, they'd be a fool to try.

Sam supposed that was the point. "What do you want? We're going stir crazy in here. Do you have the solutions yet?"

Alex clenched his jaw and cast a wary eye across the Infected behind the bar. "Doing some redecorating?"

"They're anxious, Alex. We need to get out of here. Where's my solution? Why haven't you given it to me like you promised?"

"As soon as I can, I'll do just that. Believe me. But if you do something for me, I can speed up that process."

"Wasn't covering your ass at the research facility enough? I lost most of my commune. What else do you want from me?"

"Your blood," he said, swallowing thickly. "A blood sample from you, and one of the others."

"You see?" Binh cried. "I was right!"

Sam tried to keep her head. "Why?"

"For research on the formulas we recovered. We need fresh samples of the parasite."

Sam gritted her teeth and squinted at him. She couldn't tell if he was lying, but he sure as hell didn't look like he was telling her the truth, either. "You can't just come in here and change the parameters of our deal. This is bullshit."

"I'm sorry, Sam," he said. That, at least, sounded sincere. "But the moment we came aboard, I was no longer in command. It's out of my hands. I'm doing the best I can for you, but this is a sticky situation.

You never should have come back with us; I told you that."

"We had a deal," Sam said, her breath tight in her chest. "I want that solution." What she truly wanted was a moment away from her commune to talk to Alex in private, but if she left the room she wasn't sure what would become of them. They were still her responsibility, even if they didn't think they were.

"I know we had a deal," Alex said. "If you give me the blood samples, I promise I won't ask for anything else from you. I swear."

"Your promises mean shit, Alex."

He looked wounded at that, but it couldn't be helped. She was right and they both knew it. "What choice do you have?"

He had a point, the way things were going. Soon things would degrade into chaos and she'd have a decision to make: was she willing to sacrifice Binh and the others to gain her own freedom?

Originally, she'd have said no. In retrospect, she should have offered to come with Alex alone and left Binh and the others in Baltimore to fend for themselves. They would have been captured and recruited into the U.S. Army, and none of them would have been the worse for the wear. But instead she'd been selfish—something she didn't realize an Infected could be.

Sam grabbed hold of her sleeve and pulled it up over her elbow, extending her arm in Alex's direction. "Binh?" she called, nodding at him to approach. "You too."

Alex reached into the satchel slung over his shoulder and pulled out a pressure-release needle and collection kit. He pressed the circular plunger onto the crook of her arm, then pressed the trigger at the end.

She winced as the needle punctured her vein, but said nothing as they watched the vial fill.

"I appreciate this," he said.

Sam's breathing hastened, but she held her arm still. "Fuck you."

38

REPAIRS TO THE RN ship were nearly completed by the fourth day in the Chesapeake Bay.

Miller sat in Gray's office, anticipating the announcement that they would shortly be underway. This posed a great many problems, the first of which was what to do with the Infected still aboard.

"I want to thank you for coming tonight," Gray said. He nodded at Miller, looking off-color. "On such short notice."

Miller sat beside Lewis at the ping-pong table and tried to ignore the mounting pressure behind his eyes. He didn't like emergency meetings. He didn't trust them. If it wasn't about the repairs, it most likely involved some security breach on one of the smaller vessels in the S-Y fleet. Miller and Cobalt had been too wrapped up in keeping the Infected from burning a hole in the ship to know if there'd been an incident.

Gray stood and rubbed the heel of his palm into his left eye. "I realize it's late," he added, "but I have a proposition that I think would benefit not only the occupants of the *Tevatnoa* and the S-Y fleet, but the whole of the world."

"Okay," Miller said. "I'm all ears."

"I've spoken with Dr. Kapoor and Dr. Dalton— they've been working tirelessly on the incomplete formulas and now believe, with a bit of trial and error, they can construct an anti-parasitic formula that will attack both strains of the Archaean parasite. Using the research you obtained in Baltimore in combination with the medical research Bob Harris acquired in Astoria, they think it can be accomplished in less than a year."

Miller's stomach lurched. "You mean the research Harris got by experimenting on an entire Infected population in Astoria? *That* research?"

"Dr. Kapoor feels there is a vast amount of useful information, particularly with regards to the way the parasite affects the host's immune system."

Miller face had gone hot. "Why would you use that?"

"It's very helpful..."

"He tortured people," Miller said. He was on his feet, despite not knowing when he'd stood. "*Alive.*"

Gray licked his lips, then bit down on the corner of his mouth. "I realize the conditions weren't optimal..."

Lewis leaned onto the back legs of his folding chair and crossed his arms. "What's your proposition, Gray? Because it sounds to me like there's more to this meeting than using old research, am I right?"

Gray pursed his lips. "I propose we use the six Infected aboard as test subjects, so Dr. Kapoor can further Harris's research."

Lewis sighed heavily. "There it is."

Miller's skin prickled, and his fingers felt numb. "You've gone mad," he said, glaring at Gray.

Gray balled his hands into fists, his face unyielding. "I'm not asking permission..."

"I blew up New York City," Miller said, seeing red. "I slaughtered millions of people—*millions*, you understand? All in the name of humanity. I strapped a nuclear bomb to Bob Harris's lap in order to stop him from furthering that research. To stop him from making things worse—which he had. Repeatedly. And you agreed." He pointed his finger at Gray, fighting the urge to sock the asshole across the chin right then and there. "And now you want to pick up where he left off?"

He shook his head. "No, Gray. No way in hell. We have not sunk that far. Use Harris's research, fine— that damage can't be undone—but to continue it? Are you *high*? Have we sunk so low that we are right back where we started?"

Gray said nothing. Miller glowered, and Gray stood like a statue of resignation, emotionless and unfeeling. Miller wondered if the man's humanity hadn't died with his son.

Lewis raised his hand. "Now, hold on, Miller. Let's think this through."

"Hold on?" Miller spat. "You hold the fuck on. You can't be on board with this."

"I didn't say that, but..."

"But nothing, sir," Miller raged. "Those people are my responsibility. I promised them safe passage. You'll touch them over my dead body."

"Son..." Lewis said, his tone warning.

"I'm not your fucking son," Miller said. Turning from them both, he barged from the room and headed across deck, straight toward the stairwell down to the residential compartments. Tapping his ear, he opened a com channel. "Cobalt. We have an emergency. All hands on deck."

Doyle's slurred words drawled over the airwaves. "*Wassup, boss?*"

"Hsiung, get your ass to the railgun turret and disable it."

"*You want me to what?*"

"Do it now!"

"*Yes, sir.*"

"Morland, ready a mega-lifeboat for immediate departure."

"*Are we going someplace, sir?*"

"Quit chattering and just listen!" Miller shouted. "Du Trieux, are you at the Crow's Nest?"

"*Yes, sir?*"

"Ready the occupants for travel."

"*With pleasure, sir.*"

"And du Trieux, what's the passcode for your residential compartment? I need that crate."

Morland answered. "*It's 6-3-6-4.*"

Doyle's cackling laughter sounded over the com. "*I knew it!*"

"Doyle, hobble your ass up to the communications antennas and take out the short-range array, including the radar. No messages get to the RN ship. None. Take them all down if you have to."

"*Sounds like fun.*"

"You have two minutes, Cobalt," Miller snapped over the line. "Meet resistance with non-lethal but necessary force."

"*Yes, sir,*" they answered, one after the other.

Miller pounded down the stairwell and hooked a left, passing through the residential courtyard mid-deck and skirting a group of civilians holding some sort of memorial service.

Du Trieux's cabin was on the far end of a hallway, tucked between a disabled elevator and a maid's closet. After tapping in the code, Miller found the crate stashed on the side of her bed and wedged close to the wall.

Grabbing it, he heaved the crate onto his shoulder, closed the door behind him and made his way back to the stairwell.

"*Sir,*" Morland spoke over the com. "*I had to incapacitate a couple of patrols on the second deck. I'm not sure how long they'll be out.*"

"Deactivate their radios, zip tie them together, take their weapons, and stash them someplace they can't be heard."

"*Working on that now, sir.*"

Miller reached the second floor and ventured to the perimeter walkway. The mega-lifeboats sat covered and silent to his right. He hooked across the deck to the starboard side, since the RN Bay Class ship sat to their port. "Trix? How's it going?"

"*I'm being met with a little resistance,*" she said. "*But we're on our way.*"

"I'm on starboard. Get rough if you have to."

"*Already there,*" she replied.

Miller set the crate down on the floor and picked a lifeboat at random. He had the cover off and the launch sequence ready to go by the time Morland came back.

Hsiung's voice sounded over the com. "*Power's off to the railgun turret and I've disabled the controls at the source.*"

"Copy that," Miller replied. "Doyle?"

A series of grunting and groans was heard over the com. "*This is going to set my rehab back a few weeks. And why send the cripple to do the climbing job?*"

"You're least likely to be found up there and have to engage. Is it done?"

"*Nearly,*" was his strained reply.

Miller heard footsteps approaching from behind and turned. Du Trieux and Samantha led the group of confused, angry-looking Infected straight toward him.

"Alex, what's going on?"

"No time to explain. Get aboard."

She stepped over the mega-lifeboat threshold, but stopped just inside. "Where are my formulas?"

"Sam, you've got to go. Now."

"I'm not leaving here until I have those formulas." Her eyes filled with tears. "Alex, please."

"You're not safe here," Miller said. He picked up the crate of ammunition and lugged it past her into the lifeboat. "Can anybody here operate a boat?"

The Korean kid standing back in the corridor raised his hand.

"Controls are up top. Go."

The kid nodded and brushed past Samantha, who stood frozen at the hatch. One by one the others spilled aboard, passing her. She looked horrified, numb.

As the kid climbed the stairs to the second level, Miller popped open the crate and pulled out his old .45 Glock sidearm. He handed it to Samantha, then rummaged through the box for a magazine and a box of ammunition.

"We're only a few nautical miles from shore," Miller said, slipping bullets into the cartridge with his thumb. "Sail northeast. Get to land as quickly as possible. Go ahead and moor the boat on shore. There are predators in this water that will snap you in two if you try and swim it. *Sam*, are you listening to me?" He handed her the gun and she took it with a shaking hand.

She was crying. It was so uncharacteristic of her Miller almost reached out to comfort her, but there was no time for tears, and no way he could touch her with an active Archaean parasite still within her. "But, Alex," she cried, "I don't want to go."

"You don't have a choice. They want to experiment on you. I'm doing you a favor. Do you understand? You *have* to go."

"Alex..."

Du Trieux's voice came over Miller's com. "*I've got incoming on the second floor landing. Cut them loose, Miller. Now.*"

Miller jumped from the boat back onto the deck and activated the davit system. "Tell the kid to go full throttle the moment you hit the water!" he shouted.

As the boat descended, Miller caught movement out the corner of his eye. On his left, du Trieux had knocked two guards off their feet. On his right, Morland had done the same.

Hsiung's panicked voice sounded over the com. "*I've had to lock myself inside the railgun turret to keep from being taken into custody. It's covered in fungus in here. Why are we doing this, exactly?*"

"We're facilitating the escape of fugitives," Miller answered.

"*Splendid.*"

"*The antennas are down, but I've been found,*" Doyle said. "*Ow! Easy, you great lump—can't you see I'm injured?*"

Miller watched the lifeboat hit the water, and went to the control panel to detach it. The ship zipped to full throttle and cut across the water of the Chesapeake Bay like a razor.

Miller frowned. If it was the right thing to do, why did he feel like hell?

"*Miller!*" Hsiung shouted over the com. "*They've broken inside. What do I do?*"

He watched the lifeboat fly across the water and out of range. "Go ahead and let them in. It's done."

* * *

"I SUPPOSE YOU'RE proud of yourself, are you?" Gray asked.

Miller scratched the stubble on his chin and squinted in the light. Three days in a storage closet was a small price to pay. He knew he and his team were too valuable for Gray to get rid of, even if they had disobeyed direct orders and set back the vaccine research by years. In his mind, it was worth it. "Maybe," he answered. "Where's my team?"

"Getting out of their brig closets," Lewis said with a hint of sarcasm. "Same as you."

"Sit down, Miller," Gray said. "I want you to understand what you've done."

"I know exactly what I did," he said. "I saved six souls from a life of torture and degradation."

Gray raised an eyebrow. "Is that what you think?" There was a knock at the office door. He leaned forward in his chair and shouted, "Come in, doctors."

Dr. Kapoor and Dr. Dalton entered the room, holding thick three-ring binders under their arms. Neither of them made eye contact with Miller. They dropped the folders onto the ping pong table and took their seats.

"Explain to Miller, if you would, what you told me this morning."

Dr. Dalton looked sick to her stomach. If Miller didn't know any better, he'd have sworn she was about to vomit. Dr. Kapoor opened the binder, flipped a few pages of paper and then cleared his throat.

"Blood sample B demonstrated active mutated Archaean parasite," he said. "Similar to samples obtained from test subjects at the S-Y complex one year ago." Licking his fingers, he turned a page. "Sample A demonstrated no active Archaean parasite, but possessed a naturally occurring antibody which had neutralized the infection."

Miller blinked for a moment, unsure if he'd understood what he'd just heard.

Gray looked livid. "Did you catch that, Miller?"

"I did, but I'm not sure I fully understand. Where did you get Sample A?"

"You tell me," Dr. Kapoor said. "The DNA in the blood sample suggests a woman. Somehow, she shows signs of having previously held an active mutated Archaean parasite in her system, but it's mutated—again. A somatic mutation over time, or environmental factors—ultraviolet radiation from the sun, replication error during cell division—who knows? But it happened in her immune system. She developed a natural antibody which not only neutralized the Archaean parasite, but will prevent her from becoming re-infected."

"Wait," Miller said, holding up his hand; it shook. For a brief moment, he felt light-headed. "Samantha? She's immune to the Archaean parasite?"

"It would seem so," Dr. Kapoor said.

Gray seethed. "Everything clear to you, Miller?" He spread his hands onto the table in front of him and dug his fingernails into the particle board. "We had the cure. We had it on this *very ship*, right under our noses. And you helped it *escape!*"

"How is that possible?" Miller gasped. "Did she know? *Could* she have known she's immune?"

"There's no way to know that without asking her, is there?" Dr. Dalton said.

"Where did you tell her to go, Miller?" Lewis said, leaning forward in his chair. "Where can we find her?"

Miller's mind was a blur. There were so many things that could have gone wrong crossing the bay. They could have been attacked by tusk-fiends. They could have capsized. They could have drowned. Not to mention everything that could go wrong once she reached land.

What the hell had he done?

Miller slumped in his chair and ran his hands through his hair. He had been in the right, he knew. He'd acted quickly and decisively, and he'd saved six Infected souls from lives as lab rats. What kind of life was that? It was inhumane. And he had saved a woman who, at one point in his life, he had loved.

But in saving her, he had damned the world.

ABOUT THE
AUTHOR

Extinction Biome is the creation of jungle warrior, revolutionary, counter-revolutionary and outdoorsperson **Addison Gunn**. But who is Addison Gunn? Addison's too damn busy to answer that. Instead Gunn's wrangled some of the best new talents in the genre to pen this exciting new series...

Recovering TV writer **Anne Tibbets** is the author of *Shut Up*, the *The Line* series— *Carrier* and *Walled*—and also *Extinction Biome: Invasion* and *Dispersal*, as Addison Gunn.

Anne lives in the Los Angeles area and divides her time between writing, her family, and several furry creatures she secretly believes are plotting her assassination.

To discover more about Anne, visit:
www.AnneTibbets.com

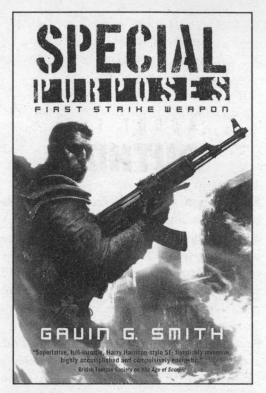

SPECIAL PURPOSES
FIRST STRIKE WEAPON

GAVIN G. SMITH

"Superlative, full-throttle, Harry Harrison-style SF: fiendishly inventive, highly accomplished and compulsively energetic."
British Fantasy Society on *The Age of Scorpio*

1987, THE HEIGHT OF THE COLD WAR. For Captain Vadim Scorlenski and the rest of the 15th Spetsnaz Brigade, being scrambled to unfamiliar territory at no notice, without a brief or proper equipment, is more or less expected; but even by his standards, their mission to one of the United States' busiest cities stinks...

World War III was over in a matter of hours, and Vadim and most of his squad are dead, but not done. What's happened to them, and to millions of civilians around the world, goes beyond any war crime; and Vadim and his team -- Skull, Mongol, Farm Boy, Princess, Gulag, the Fräulein and New Boy — won't rest until they've seen justice done.

987-1-78108-521-9 • UK £9.99 • US $16 • CAN $22

31901061049104